To Clare and Dave

Love Karen
xxx

the whitest woman on the beach

K.I.H. Barratt

Bloomington, IN Milton Keynes, UK

authorHOUSE

AuthorHouse™
1663 Liberty Drive, Suite 200
Bloomington, IN 47403
www.authorhouse.com
Phone: 1-800-839-8640

AuthorHouse™ UK Ltd.
500 Avebury Boulevard
Central Milton Keynes, MK9 2BE
www.authorhouse.co.uk
Phone: 08001974150

First published by AuthorHouse 6/6/2006

ISBN: 1-4259-3258-4 (sc)

Printed in the United States of America
Bloomington, Indiana

This book is printed on acid-free paper.

The English are so bad at funerals. Everybody tries to keep the noise down. The very next of kin allow themselves a quiet shudder during the service, a grey walk to the car, a squeezed arm. Nothing gets purged.

They'd held the cremation a couple of days before, strictly a family affair. Perhaps there's something about a young death that makes families want privacy, the more so when it's been quick and sudden. For the wider circle, all the eighteen-year-olds the family had never had a chance to meet – quick and sudden – they'd arranged a memorial service in the college chapel.

I wasn't invited to the memorial service. It would have been pretty bizarre if I had been, I suppose: but I felt so tied up in the whole business by that stage that I half imagined I might be. Stupid.

I'm not saying I wanted to go, you understand. I'm saying I'd underestimated – my god, by how much – the terrible drag I'd feel, the self-destructive urge to twitch those curtains so I could see the family, such as it was, gathering in the lane outside the window, and the friends: a forlorn clutch of ill-fitting types desultorily commenting on the probability of another shower, waiting to go on to the chapel together. Such a sad little group clustered in the lane beyond my window that sodden day when I was young. Another sodding sodden day.

Ten to ten and they moved off. I gave it fifteen minutes then followed.

By an oddity of architecture a window gave onto the interior of the chapel from inside the library at first floor level. I don't suppose it had been installed as a spying tool, but it worked as one; quite an ostentatious one, six feet of colour-by-numbers stained glass, some saint or other. I hunched against the frame and knew that I was invisible to the pews down below, though I could see the slice of congregation not blocked by the Jacobean oak screen.

I tried to think of the whole thing as a t.v. programme, *nothing to do with me really*. I could make all those drained faces green or red or purple at will, by just a sway of my head and by choosing a different segment of glass to watch them through. I could hear them singing *Abide With Me* even through the thick glass and I thought of the Titanic. Of course I wished time could run backwards so that events could be reshuffled into a better outcome; of course. I wasn't a complete bastard. That kind of arrogant martyrdom the young are so good at trapped me in the idea that the whole terrible show down there was my show, that without me it couldn't have happened: and wasn't that a feeling cold as hell. Because if I've learnt anything it's that there are different ways of damaging other people. There's damage that is meant. Then there's damage that comes from bungling. Finally there's damage that is caused simply by standing to one side. The last is almost as bad as the first.

It's obvious that there are some things for which you cannot atone.

This is the first scene that comes to me, but it's not where I should begin.

The first time I saw Ginny I was intensely lonely and intensely drunk. Two weeks into my first term away from home and I'd gained a pretty clear idea of my vast ignorance and vast naivety. Just to learn how to use the washing-machines down in the basement laundry of the college – in its archaic, overheated and cloistering gloom not unpleasant, somehow a little reminiscent of home – I'd had to loiter for ten minutes, surreptitiously viewing the procedure over someone's shoulder. Money was a nightmare. With some odd idea of denying the obvious consequences I'd used my brand new cashcard like a toy, and was quite unreasonably outraged when my daily limit was reached and the machine refused me. As for the academic side of things, I'd strolled with self-conscious cool round the History Faculty Library twice, and finally decided that the filing system was ridiculously overcomplicated and impossible for an Arts student to master. I wouldn't use it. In fact I wouldn't use the library.

The first time I saw Ginny was as a beautiful blur looming suddenly up against a backdrop of crushed bodies, through a mash of conversations and incredibly loud laughter. I'd tagged along with several others from the corridor of my residential block. People were friendly to begin with, good like that; later on their efforts died in the face of my oblivious self-absorption. Friday night: pub or party night. Pub that night; no parties. And as we walked disjointedly through the street or two to the pub, and as it became clear to me that I *could not* compete with the deft rhythms of the speech these *buddies* threw out, threw over their shoulders like empty wrappers, that maybe I would never be able to bark out semi-obscenities into the freezing air with that enviable ease, it was as if the whole world turned colder yet. The brand new drainpipe jeans I'd imagined would buy me status were a failed ploy. I understood that I would always be a little to the east of Eden, close enough to shimmy up the wall and get a good look, but forever excluded. That Autumn was unusually cold, and made more so by our underdressing.

I was too young. Gerry Purvis was a twenty-one year old South African who'd had to delay college while he served out conscription in his country's army. Dave Shannon was only eighteen, but he'd come fresh from Eton and had the self-assurance of a successful twenty-four year old, a merchant banker perhaps, just launching on a long and lucrative career. Jules Fitch was also eighteen, and probably just as gauche as I, if I'd had the wit to notice; but I lumped him with the others, and felt suitably washed away.

I was too young. The cold reminded *me* of Bonfire Night, of the Village Rec. back home with its Nissen hut scout hut and its dog dirt: it reminded me of the Vicar's cheesy welcome address to all of us huddled as near to the bonfire as the safety rope would allow, a familiar spiel that would be peppered with admonitions to 'let the little ones down to the front' and 'make it a cracker of a Guy Fawkes': it brought to me the neurosis of my grandmother, who lived with us and kept us in a perpetual state of anxiety, a kind of hilarious hysteria, my grandmother who would be tucking my ears under the abominable woolly hat she'd knitted me and which in the bitter love of my tie to her I would not be able to throw upon the bonfire with joy. It reminded me of the intense claustrophobia of my grandmother's weight on my right arm, my mother's on the left in the dark, our backs chilled, our fronts scorched; and it led me to the terror of walking now through these ancient lanes with no drag, with arms swinging or with hands pushing back my mass of uncombed hair. I imagined that the cold reminded the others – Gerry, Dave, Jules, or rather Purvis, Shannon, Fitch, as the boys'-school ethos dictated – of quite other events, places; events decisive and charged, places stirring and mysterious – Alaska? Iceland? If they noticed it at all.

I decided to get very drunk. This at least I could do with skill. I could hold my drink. It had been an important aspect of life in the sixth form and I'd bullied my system into compliance. I never threw up, I never fell downstairs or off my bike, I never revealed my love for strangers, or cried, or lost a contact lens. I never had to be helped home. I did grow silent and sometimes surly; but I was almost monosyllabic in those days before Ginny, anyway, and the silence muffled up the surliness and kept it hidden from public view. At sixth form level, in my rather tatty grammar school at least, taciturnity tended to establish you as intelligent. I didn't think the ploy would work now, with Gerry Purvis the South African who'd seen action during his conscription, action as in *blam* (what had he done? in our narrowness we never asked: or maybe we were scared to hear he'd toured the townships) or Dave Shannon who'd dropped into conversation how he'd joined in debate with the Home Secretary, as well as on another occasion a famous defector from the U.S.S.R., when he was a member of his school's debating society. Yet I had no other resource but reservation, silence. You wouldn't recognise me as the same individual now. I even tell jokes. People think I'm quite a card. Then, the language of general conversation was a foreign language, different vowel sounds and weird vocabulary. I couldn't get my tongue round it.

The pub was not particularly full, though it seemed so because it was really just two or three nooky-holes, as if we'd walked into somebody's front room by mistake. Ceilings were low enough for Shannon and myself to have to duck, and there didn't look to be a true right-angle in the place.

All the customers, every one, belonged to the university. The Christchurch lot wore suits, which, reflexively, gave me the urge to stare at the cluster of them round the bar. It seemed perverse. I was entirely locked into the idea that suits were an abomination your mother occasionally forced on you. *I'd* only worn one at my auntie's wedding two years before, and that had been hired from Burtons. On our estate we'd been considered *posh*. Now I had a daily battle not to feel common as muck.

We installed ourselves in a corner on church pews that might really have been very old. Gerry bought the first round – pints of Shepherd Neame; he didn't even have to ask. Talk was laddish, which I didn't usually mind too much, but it was laddish sport talk, which I did. I had a kind of pact with myself not to be interested in sport of any description. These days I even find myself watching the rugby, but then, *then*... **The past is a foreign country: they do things differently there**. That one's from L.P.Hartley. **They don't sell tickets to the past**. Alexander Solzhenitsyn. **Thank god it's now.** Me. I entertained myself instead with timing the conversation to see how long they'd keep it up, and smoking. I was good at smoking, too. Pretty clever to have kept the habit entirely from my grandmother's knowledge for four years, though admittedly aided by my mother's addiction – the curtains all over the house were deeply impregnated with the smell of smoke already.

"Did you happen to see," Shannon said, "That big hit I made on Talbot?"

Purvis obliged, in his undiluted South African accent: "Yis, he went down like a sick of potatoes."

"Sack of shit. He's such a piss-artist, Talbot."

And so on.

It was much later and half way through my eighth pint that her face was suddenly there, out of focus yet distinct against the muddled backdrop that the rest of the packed room had increasingly become. Perhaps she'd been there for some time, but that's the start of my history of the whole *thang*. She always said later that she knew one of the others – Gerry? – and that's how she came to join our little party and, although that could easily have been the case, since in those first few weeks we tripped over opportunities to expand our social circles, I never quite believed it. Though hardly what you'd call an intuitive animal, I had nevertheless a kind of instinct about that.

It was a face I immediately *liked*. Her hair, framing her face rather as children's crayoning fuzzily frames the 'U' face they've just drawn, was extremely short and red. Her eyes were quick, witty, clever eyes: dilute blue. She wore an earring on one side; something small and discreet I can't retrieve from memory. And her face was rather like that child's 'U', pleasing and rounded to just the right degree. Her mouth was wide, with a distinct outline and slightly full lips. It seems I must have shamelessly, drunkenly stared at it to have such a clear impression still. Yet I thought she was staring at me. Sometimes girls did that to me. I could use false modesty now, and cloud the issue, but I said I'd try for absolute honesty. I knew I had something that drew them, for what it was worth. I was attractive. A kind of power, but the power of a ten year old at the wheel of a lorry.

The face seemed nearer, further away. Then a body, tallish and thin with medium sized breasts, followed the face and Ginny was sitting beside me where (I thought) Dave Shannon's fleshy bulk had been. On the other side of me, where (I thought) Jules should still be sitting with that slightly vague look on his face, I noticed with hazy surprise a complete stranger, and beyond him the turned backs of a different group and conversation and evening altogether. I wasn't too drunk to feel pleased at the change, but drunk enough to take credit for the workings of chance and feel smug that I'd manoeuvred it all so well. And Ginny's face was near enough now for me to know I'd landed a god-given chance, a one-off chance of the kind that only semi-conscious fantasy usually gives, and I experienced a lurching, panicky, out of control urgency to act, *to say the right thing*. If I couldn't say the right thing now I'd never be able to say the right thing, but if I could, then maybe I'd have company on my patch of the plain east of Eden, maybe I wouldn't give a monkey's how tall and splendid the tree of life grew beyond the wall.

I was immensely glad to be so drunk; so drunk I could stare straight into Ginny's eyes. I was so drunk that I could almost have brought to life the fantasy that was rapidly unfolding in my imagination, the fantasy where a space cleared right here, right here in front of the table entirely covered with empty, half-full, nearly-full glasses and Ginny and I sank down onto the flagstones of the floor and took off just enough of each other's clothes to make love, right here in the smoke-filled atmosphere so heavy with the fumes of alcohol you'd not be surprised if it ignited at the strike of the next match, right here under the noses of the young, male punters who almost uniformly comprised the pub's clientele, right here, so that

I'd know, now, *immediately*, whether I could have Ginny and what her beautiful body looked like, felt like.

"Hello," said Ginny eventually. Her voice was very slightly hoarse and always a fraction slow, as if, lawyer-like, she were examining everything she said before she said it. Which she was.

I nodded, smiled, shifted with what would have been restless excitement if the eight pints hadn't weighted it down into a swaying lurch. It really was as if all the surrounding noise drained back away from us in a receding wave. Yet we had to lean incredibly, superbly close to hear each other.

"Can you speak?" she said quizzically, a little nervous – I imagine, not that I would have noticed then – but trying to disguise it with an arch *moue* of the lips that I wanted, *wanted* to reach out and touch.

"Yeah," I managed, "I can speak." I remembered what you did then, and offered her a cigarette: my last one.

"I don't smoke," she said, "Anyway it's your last one. I couldn't deprive you of it. You have it."

"Naaa." I shook my head. Lighting a cigarette seemed far too elaborate a procedure in my present state. Anyway, for once I didn't need it. I had to concentrate on the percentage of my right side that pressed against Ginny's hip. Perhaps a concentration of energy would dissolve the four layers of material between us. Then would the skin be warm or cold? How white? She had the tanless, untannable skin that goes with red hair. I reached out carefully for my glass, then drained it quickly and told myself to open my mouth and say the right thing, quickly, before the pointer on my gauge of inebriation began to slip back towards sobriety, towards control and tomorrow, towards my own tedious inability to catch even a shadow of the unusual, vaguely Americanised, deeply incisive young man I wanted to be.

"Have you ever listened to The White Album?" was what actually emerged. Instantly I wanted to smash myself into oblivion. Even through all the muffling layers of inebriation I still knew this was tantamount to committing social and sexual suicide. *The White Album? You mean The Beatles? You still listen to The Beatles? Where have you been for the last five years?* I almost groaned. The intoxicating

8

thread of my floor-fantasy had led me into this, and now I hadn't the speed of thought to change direction. Yet she seemed unfazed:

"A couple of times," she nodded, knitting her brows. I watched the small furrow appearing just above her eyes as carefully and with as much interest as I might have watched Creation; and those eyes: truth-drug eyes, making me tell the truth for once; the pale exquisite eyes of the sexy Russian spy who's just slipped the truth-draft into James Bond's champagne.

I let it come. "The best track has to be 'Why don't we do it in the road'." I held her eye. I had a superstitious dread that if she looked away now, the whole opportunity would be lost. I must have looked like our old dog used to look, begging at table. "Do you know the one I mean? It's this guy and he wants this woman so badly he just wants, wants to..."

"I get the gist of it." Supercilious? Charitable?

"It's an amazing track. It just says it all.."

"Oh."

I still held her eyes but her face seemed to have receded.

"I just know, or it's just the idea—" I talked as quickly as the drink would allow, scrambling for the words that would keep her with me, "The idea of…" but by then I'd forgotten what The White Album was supposed to prove and I could sense the moment slipping, slipping like all the other moments. The appalling whiteness of an isolation that always threatened to claim me entirely was washing away all the colours, bleaching the sudden vividness, the possibility of vividness I saw just within my grasp. And I can still feel chilled by the probability that, if I'd dried up at that moment, Ginny would have shrugged off whatever phantasmagoric version of myself she thought was calling to her and stood up bored and baffled and left and I would have stayed the empty boy I was, maybe for ever. I would have slapped layer upon layer of unabsorbed, unlearnt-from experience over the blank space at the centre. Despite all that happened because I didn't dry up and shut up, *all that happened* saved me. Sinking and slipping, I made one last lunge:

"You're just the most incredible person I've ever met."

At this point, fictional fashion would dictate that we hurried back to my room to make pumping confident love among the rumpled sheets, uttering cinematic groans and exclamations as we energetically rode to climax together. I'd be on top, or, just possibly, if we're talking *now*, she'd be sitting on top of me, heaving herself up and down, eyes to the heavens. If the fiction were a comedy, no doubt the bed-head would humorously bang a waterpipe or the bed joints would creak loudly so that neighbours could cast disapproving or prurient glances at one another as the rhythm quickened. If it took itself more seriously, there'd be some sinister suggestion of the violence underlying sexual attraction; we'd throw each other around like Jeremy Irons and Juliette Binoche in *Damage*, or I'd shake her by the shoulders a bit, or she'd scratch me with her fingernails, or maybe somebody would slap somebody. Of course, the reality was quite different.

Roughly half way back to my room I threw up. Tall stone walls embedded with the occasional narrow window loomed above us on all sides as Ginny held the volume of my hair back from my face and I leant – quite neatly for one so far gone – well away from us both, over and into an ancient corner. I felt a great deal better afterwards, better enough to have a proper sense of the deep unsexiness of the image I'd just presented.

"I never throw up," I said again.

"It doesn't matter," said Ginny.

"I mean, *never.*"

"It's happened to everyone," she said.

"Have you ever puked up because you've..?"

"No," she admitted.

I remember it that nobody was about and I remember how the steep grey walls that used so to impress me and oppress me with their age and their history, as if they had absorbed over the centuries all the brilliance and the arrogance, all the elitism that kept most people out but, once it had let them in, accepted almost anything they did, all the quirkiness and snobbery and liberalism and eccentricity of the people they'd sheltered and elevated – those walls for once seemed kind. Ginny and I walked as if in a huge grey cavern, the starless sky a ceiling lost to sight. After she'd held my hair back I found I could touch her, which before I'd not been able to do. I put my arm around her back and she put her arm around my waist. There was not such a big difference in our heights. We did not kiss. I was far too aware of the acrid taste in my mouth, sobering up by the minute and regaining common sense. Besides which there was an expanding sense of limitless time, limitless opportunity to come. It was a marvellous moment. I think back now to it, leaning back in my chair in the middle of writing some tedious little report or drifting into sleep beside the occasional click and murmur of the baby-alarm, and I conjure up the cold and the deep grey of pavement, wall and sky and the irregular rub of my shirt and her jacket as we tried to align our steps and I cry out for the gift of a Virtual World in which we could walk for ever seventeen and eighteen through cavernous chambers effortlessly generating themselves before us, jumping the cracks of paving-slabs unfolding like the steps of an elevator.

When we reached my room, I scrubbed my teeth until the gum bled into the basin built in by the built-in wardrobe, then I made coffee for us both. The milk in the carton balanced behind the taps had gone off, as it invariably did in the heat, so we had it milkless. Ginny thumbed through the record collection leaning against the built-in window seat and, when we'd settled ourselves on the floor with our backs against the bed (you have to imagine the smallness of the room), she asked, "Where's your record-player?"

"I haven't got one."

"Just the records."

"I'm going to buy one."

"Have you got The White Album in among that lot?"

I was too pompous in those days to enjoy being teased. I nodded. I put my arm round her. We put down our mugs, lay down on the prickly cord carpet squares and kissed. We lay there, kissing, fully clothed. She had a neat and compact mouth that I imagined I could learn like a map. Outside and right next to the window the ragged voices of a group of homecomers discussing 'Criminal Law' and 'Tort' in large tones briefly intruded, then sank away. There had been no need for me to draw the curtains since I'd not bothered to open them that morning, and somehow the strident voices behind them added to our privacy rather than intruding. She was solid and real, warm as a radiator. Her smell seemed familiar and I kept nearly remembering, *nearly* remembering some significant other time, some long ago moment set in the glowing colours of – oh, I don't know: boiled sweets. There was a sense of coming home. Eventually and at an uncharted moment we fell asleep. Some time later still, we woke stiff and a little too cool even in spite of the room's warmth.

"I'm going to have to pee," Ginny said.

We crept from the room – she was after all an Unregistered Guest – and down to the end of the corridor, where we took turns in the tiny white cubicle. Then back, shivering, thankfully back into our cube of heat and back, thankfully, to the turned key in the lock. We lay on the bed, and shuffled by degrees into what was to become my favourite position, curled sideways together, my body's backward 'C' cupping hers, my arm enfolding her, my hand resting lightly somewhere beneath her chin. Before we fell back into the cloying sleep of hangover, Ginny suddenly laughed.

"What?" I asked.

"What did you say your name was?"

"Oh. I didn't. Simon."

"Simon," she echoed.

There was a brief pause. "Well?" I said.

"Well?"

"What's yours?"

"What do you think it is?"

"I don't know. Jane. Caroline. Sarah."

"Virginia." said Ginny.

That's how easily she handed herself over to me. If you'd told me then that I'd bring her harm I'd have counted you as mad; and bad. It almost makes me want to be the apparition, appear at her shoulder as she settles down to sleep in that bed such a long time ago and warn her off, tell her about the three kinds of damage: the damage that is meant, the damage that comes from bungling, and the kind of damage that is caused simply by standing to one side. It makes me want to tell her to pull her clothes on and run: almost.

That morning after we'd met, Ginny and I hurried nothing. In the morning, late morning, I woke up to find her propped up on her elbows looking at me. I should have felt this a creepy intrusion. I didn't. Being with Ginny in those first weeks was not so different from being on my own. I moved around the room, yawned, blew my nose as if this were the case. I smoked without feeling the need to cup the cigarette with tip pointing to palm in the manner of sixth-form affectation as if this were the case; and the contrast between how I felt with Ginny and how I'd felt with the two or three – two, if I'm honest – girls I'd gone with, been with, *done* things with surprised me and delighted me. Ginny's eyes on me. Her eyes on me in the green half-light of the green curtains in our goldfish-bowl room. The locked door. There was no need to hurry. Every moment that morning was a stretched-out touch. Every moment was expanded by an almost masochistic wallow in the fact that if we wanted to, if we *wanted to*, we could touch in reality.

Touch we did. While I filled the kettle at the basin, she clung around my waist. While we drank the tea – black – I ran my hand lightly over her hair and over her shoulder, claiming her inch by inch. I was almost lightheaded with desire for her, but with the green light of day and the return of the full and horrible knowledge of the connections of mind and soul with body – zips, moles, inelegance – the fantasy of instant sex had walked away down the road a little and stood looking at me uncertainly. I never wanted Ginny's body to remind me of the other naked, or if I'm honest nearly naked, bodies I had approached and desired sure enough, but with a kind of make-do distaste, a kind of shut-your-eyes and drink-too-much self-deceit.

I see I'm already rescripting what really happened. *Own up, Simon.* All right: I had never been that fastidious. I never had to shut my eyes and the drinking too much had nothing to do with sentiment. Equally there wasn't a snowball's chance in hell of Ginny reminding me of the others. I knew she was different. Girls were drawn to me: yes, some. But nothing had always tended to come of nothing. I might have been a demagnetising machine for all the good my sharp jawline did me. As for the girls in question: iron-filings, all of them; and as for the two: iron-filings with tits and smiles.

That's how most of us boys were then. That's how we talked. The girls had all been fed on *Jackie* and *Diana* and starry dreams of dependency, while us boys learnt what we knew of sexual politics from Biggles and Superman and *Shoot!* – i.e. nothing – and nobody ever disabused us of the notion that women were there to put up with things – not even the women, then. The girls worked hard to drag romance out of the most unpromising material. I always think about that when I read about yet another incarcerated murderer to receive marriage proposals through the post, from women who believe *all he needs is love.* I bet they don't get many of those in Holloway.

Ginny was unprecedented. Her fascination with me had the smile of a sphinx and the trackability of a yeti. We didn't *go all the way* because it's only in films that those moments are easy. We were very young.

Ginny stood behind me on the end of the bed while I washed my face, and, as I straightened up, she drew the hair back from my face. A fleeting reminder, that, of the night before. By the rather ghoulish light of the shaving strip over the basin I could see her pale face hovering above mine. I answered its smile.

"Have you ever seen Zefferelli's *Romeo and Juliet*?" she asked, then coloured in case she was revealing too much sentiment, in case I thought she was being slushy, in case...in case. We were all so trapped by our own coolness in those days, dead scared to commit the faux pas of a gushing reaction or the indiscretion of an uncool word: *uncool* was an uncool word, while we're at it.

"No," I said reluctantly. I was to get used to this particular format of exchange. *Have you ever seen...?* No. *Have you read....?* No.

Her embarrassment was interesting but I was slightly worried about what she might come out with as she went on, "Oh well then, you won't know what I mean. It's hardly worth saying, it's just that you remind me of – I mean, when I saw you in the pub I noticed straight away you looked just like – your face I mean, not so much your hair, that's not quite dark enough but you really have got a look of –"

"Romeo?" I adopted our tone of safe and skimming sarcasm.

"God, no. I couldn't have fallen for *him* across a crowded room."
A glimmer of alarm in those eyes I could see in the mirror, a quick
self-edit and censor, then, "God, no. No: Mercutio."

"Mercutio?"

"Definitely."

"Well. What's he like, then?"

"Oh, dark. A little wicked. Loyal but volatile. Incredibly
attractive. He's the angry young man."

"So...which bits can I have?"

She smirked and smouldered with very obvious theatricality
– we were both securely back on flippant track now – but didn't say
anything: raised an eyebrow at me. Angry, dark, wicked and attractive,
I hoped my shadow of a smile translated as erotic challenge. Years
later, when I finally got to see Zefferelli's film, it really did seem to
me you'd need a pretty vivid imagination to spot any similarity at
all between old Mercutio and me at seventeen; or twenty, twenty-
five... Still. *Then*, if Ginny looked at me and saw Mercutio, all well
and good; and, even if I'd guessed the disappointing truth that
she'd taken a leap of faith to do so, it wouldn't have been me who'd
disabused her of her mistake. And anyway, you *could* say that if
Ginny had been able to find enough raw material in me to mould
into the shape she wanted, then from one angle at least that's exactly
who I was: Mercutio.

"The actor who plays Mercutio," she said matter-of-factly, "has
very tight black curls."

"Oh," I said, feeling ungenerous towards him.

"What do you think you'd look like with dead short hair?" she
said.

I shrugged.

"Well..." she mused, "I think you'd look good. A little bit hard,
maybe".

The compliment balanced out her daring in broaching the subject
at all. The hair, my hair. *Nobody* had long hair that year, or the year
before, or the year after. Long hair was unfashionable on women and
deeply unfashionable on men. Heavy metal freaks grew their hair
long and wild and strode with their special kind of shy aggression
through the shopping centre, but that was about it. I had decided

in this respect to be deeply unfashionable. Through the barrage of derisive comments and tedious jokes in the sixth form common room I had stuck to this perverse decision.

"Well," Ginny said, as her hands slid more closely around my face, hiding the hairline and distracting me with the light precision of the touch, with the leaping knowledge of the possibility of her fingers on other parts, on every and all other parts of my body, *soon, soon*: "You've got a very strong sort of a face, you know? The hair kind of *blurs* it. I could cut your hair if you want. I cut my own."

Absolutely nobody else would have been allowed to suggest this and keep my respect. Ginny was my instant darling and allowed almost anything. The idea that I might allow myself to be cropped was so preposterous, though, as to be less than the shadow of a reflection of a possibility. I turned and buried my face against her shoulder, conscious with a thrilling precision of the mass of her breasts against *my* shoulders.

"I always cut my own hair," she continued, lacing her arms around me, "I really hate *salons* and *parlours* and all that complete crap about mousse and gel and hi-lights. Anyway I really enjoy cutting my own. You've got to stay in control of your own body."

I thought about the irregular teddy-bear fuzz on Ginny's head and smiled invisibly into the material of her T-shirt. We kissed.

We kissed and held each other, clung on like drowning slaves thrown overboard. We kissed and I drowned, dissolving in green.

"Ginny," I came out with, finally, in a whispering moan that expressed as nearly as I could the painful ache of my love, lust and desire, of what I would now give its proper name: need.

"Virginia," she corrected breathlessly. She edged her hands beneath my shirt and laid them flat against the small of my back. She closed her eyes.

That's how the morning passed, a peculiar kind of time out, an episode grabbed from beneath the nose of causality, an hour or two during which it was impossible to believe we had aged. At moments I thought I'd have to explode; or at least that I might reveal my inexperience by ejaculating into my underpants. But I didn't. Eventually the edge of sensation in my stomach transformed itself into a different kind of hunger. I realised we'd eaten nothing, and I was starving.

We went shopping. Stepping out into the Autumn air was like surfacing into a foreign country, so transformed had we been by the green and airless element from which we'd emerged. We could have been the aliens that various eccentrics believe have infiltrated earth populations. We bought bread in the baker's in the Covered Market, a small and seductively soft batch that we pulled apart and ate as we meandered along, creating an obstruction on the pavement because we had to walk touching – hands, arms, better still hips. We went shopping, venturing into the modern precinct that usually seemed utterly irrelevant to me. It was the kind of place you can find in any and every English town – Curry's, M & S, Woolworth's, Wimpy – the kind of place I now know intimately. *Now* there's no glamour to be found in it, as I glaze over behind the push-chair, in search of some astonishingly banal object: trainers, batteries, drying-rack. *That* day it was brushed with a trail of colour. For once I knew myself to be at the pivot, not stuck in irrelevant orbit around the people who *really* counted, who *really* did things.

In Curry's I self-consciously produced my brand new cheque-book and signed away £59.99 for a record-player in futuristic smoky black: flash. In Woolworth's Ginny chose three L.P.s: *London Calling*, The Clash; *The Scream*, Siouxsie and the Banshees; *Specials*, by the band of the same name. It took her about three minutes, flicking through the stacks with those long, careful fingers – pianist's fingers; though so far as I knew she couldn't even manage the first notes on a recorder. Her speed was awe-inspiring.

No way could I have chosen like Ginny. I dithered and prevaricated, yet she was patient as a refugee when it came to waiting. She waited now, leaning against my back while I chose, and while I chose I was weighing my desire to move forwards and impress Ginny against my need to stay with the known. Ginny's choice had been rigorously up-to-the-minute, whereas my impulse was to fill in the one or two Pink Floyds I hadn't managed to collect. I was also very partial to early Bowie. In the event I made a tentative step into the future and opted for *One Step Beyond* – Madness, of course.

We ended up in a cafe in the Covered Market, which was a square arcade of an affair, thirty or so businesses under one roof and locked behind tight iron gates at night. The cafe, all spider plants and wobbly tables, a kind of solidification of the homespun, was itself a low-ceilinged room within the enclosure of the market, its windows overlooking an interior of stalls. Sitting at our wooden table, drinking coffee from our great thick-lipped mugs, the box holding the record-player taking up its own place as if it were our preternaturally quiet child, we were effectively dug in twice over.

"Why are you only seventeen?" asked Ginny, "You should be at least eighteen to be here at all."

"I skipped a year of school."

"Clever boy." She helped herself to most of the cheese from the top of our shared baked potato. Then non-sequentially, "Do you dream? Do you remember your dreams?" It seemed my Ginny was Queen of the Non Sequitur.

"Sometimes." The *girlyness* of her question couldn't help but be a little disappointing.

She waited, while I managed to secure the last mouthful of cheese. "Not often," I added.

"You were dreaming last night."

"Was I?" I wasn't too keen on this. Had I cried out, moaned, shouted in my sleep? It sounded akin to incontinence. What private thoughts might not have leaked out of me?

"What do you dream about?"

"I don't know," I lied. I remembered my dreams very seldom, but when I did it was invariably because I had woken in distress, the images terrifyingly clear. The dreams I remembered were nightmares.

"I bet you can tell me at least one dream. I just can't believe you never remember." There were those Russian spy eyes again, clear as water.

So I told her. Hesitantly I told her of the stairways, of the rooms stacked on each other, of the rapid pursuits up and up through trapdoors, chimneys, wall-cavities, of the clammy things I found behind the doors that opened as I rat-ran my spiralling ascent, descent, of the sheer weight of the miles of bricks above me, of the never-never of anything beyond. I couldn't convey the horror of a building so vast it made up the whole universe. *No fresh air.* For a half-second the cafe took on the claustrophobia of a cupboard.

Neither could I bring to mind the last time I'd launched on such a monologue. I shut up suddenly.

"Weird," she said, and "The Tower of Babel." She raised her eyebrow theatrically.

"What?" I said.

"Sounds like the Tower of Babel."

"What?" I said.

"You know." She was obviously trying to dredge something up. "God was angry. It reached to the sky." She frowned with concentration, and I was a little distracted by my hungry need to mark and catalogue another expression I'd not seen before – god knows I could have swallowed her whole. Finally she shrugged. "Well, anyway, it's Biblical." She gave me a wry smile. I traced it with my forefinger.

We ate a chocolate caramel fudge shortcake together, then carried the record-player back to my room, locked the door behind us and played our new records loud and in strict rotation while we, yes, kissed.

That was the first day.

On the third day we decided to try to get a grip on our slipping work schedules by spending two hours apart at our respective faculty libraries. Actually it was Ginny's idea and actually I reneged immediately on my side of the agreement and wandered instead over to the minute ancient library of my own college, a walk of perhaps one hundred and fifty yards. There I shuffled myself up to the end of an ancient carrel where I could at least see out of the window over the college quadrangle, giving a passing thought to the variety and quantity of bottoms that must have polished the oak (ash? cherry? god knows) as mine did. Ceremoniously I laid open my pad of A4, pulled my Parker pen from the side pocket of my jacket and wrote the title of that week's essay across the top line of the page. With a quick glance over my shoulder to make sure I was quite alone, I drew a leather-bound volume from the shelf a foot behind me and used it as a ruler to underline the clear black ink of the title. I paused. Then I added, on the line beneath: *notes*. From another pocket I fished a reading list, which I stared at bleakly for a few minutes.

The essay was already a no-hoper. Half the books on the list should have been tracked down, rummaged through, written up by now. I let the reading list float to the narrow desk, the one on which innumerable monkish fingers had slid, tapped, rested. I'd worked my arse off for two whole years to get here, to put it where far more venerable backsides had spread – I was ignorant then of the university's chequered career, of eighteenth century profligates who whiled away their time betting on horses and picking up venereal disease – and now I found to my extreme unease that the subject of study that had given some kind of coherence to my late adolescence struck me as – couldn't deny it – *boring*. I didn't give a monkey's elbow about the essay I was supposed to be writing. At that moment I didn't recognise myself. Wasn't I the one who'd fired up in defence of Henry VII's parsimony in Mr. Callaghan's Upper Sixth history lessons? The one who'd always claimed the History Prize book token?

Bound up and gagged, I was, by the confines of Ginny's body: tied by touch. She was spread thinly over everything my eyes fell on, every surface my fingers brushed. The sky was a white rib-cage and the earth a mildly curving spine. So much I'd been able to construct of her through the T-shirt and the cords. There was a little more length than average in every part; shoulder to elbow, neck to base of spine, hip to knee, ankle to toe. The dip at the base of her spine was quite concave and each vertebra waiting close to the skin. The inside of her elbow was marbled with blue veins so delicate they were only just visible. Faint freckles scattered themselves randomly over her upper arms. Above her shoulder blade was one minute mole that she herself had probably never noticed. I rewrote my prejudice against moles for her. Can you hear that, Ginny, over the years? I wish I'd told you then.

There is a ridiculous 'sixties film called *Fantastic Voyage* for which I've got a lot of affection. One of those Top Scientists so popular in the 'sixties imagination – you know, the kind who hold the key to preventing world catastrophe – gets shot and the only way to save his life involves the shrinking of a medical team and their vessel and its injection into his blood stream. That's the part I love; that they can't sort out the scientist's blood clot but they are able to shrink several complete individuals. *Anyway,* this little submarine careers around inside arteries getting attacked by anti-bodies, whooshes along like a raft full of tourists trying out the white water, blasts through the thrombosis or embolism or whatever and eventually just in time, *just in time,* JUST IN TIME slips out of a corner of the scientist's eye in a tear drop. In a tear drop. The poetry of that tear drop!

Anyway, anyway; *that's* how I wanted to know Ginny's body. I wanted to start with an Ordnance Survey of the outside. I wanted to see every square inch, then kiss every square inch. I wanted to know it so well that under torture I'd be able to spill every single bean. If I graffitied it on a railway bridge I wanted it to come out looking like a Michelangelo. Then I wanted to encroach. I wanted to explore every orifice but, oh, so tentatively, so delicately. Then even that would not be enough. I wanted to know her as well as if I'd created her. I wanted to understand how the flexing of a tendon caused her fingers to circle. I wanted to sit in that silly little submarine and catapult through her capillaries, to look up at the walls above as they rushed by and learn the colours, learn the minute flaws in them, be startled by the silver-flecked cliffs of underground caves, even lean out and make the rapid imprint of my prehistoric palm on their streaming surfaces. And I wanted to have all this as mine for ever.

I slid out of the carrel, mooched about the library for a little pretending interest in rows of books brittle with age, but remarking to myself really how every item of Ginny's clothing I'd seen so far had been black, including bra strap and knicker edge, wondering why touching the tip of another tongue with your tongue should give the same sensation as licking a battery, how I'd ever been able to tolerate the fishy flesh and deadening conversation of Alison Rampton and Annie Bamber – embarrassment, *embarrassment* just in the memory of their names, never mind the rest – and finding myself by and by in the theology section; at which point a thought struck me.

The bibles were on the bottom shelf, an astonishing collection of versions, translations, sizes and shapes. I was spoilt for choice. Deciding on one of the King James' on the basis of its navy blue,

I pulled a volume from the shelf and walked it back to the carrel, where I laid it open with the gingery hesitation of the superstitious non-believer. There was, of course, no convenient index in its final pages, so I decided, stubborn bastard that I was, to read through until I found what I was looking for. It was fortunate that it lay within Genesis. Creation, Fall, Brother-Murder, Procreation, Noah, Further Procreation and then – "Ah," I said.

> *And the whole earth was of one language, and of one speech.*
> *And it came to pass, as they journeyed from the east, that they found a plain in the land of Shinar; and they dwelt there.*
> *And they said to one another, Go to, let us make brick, and burn them throughly. And they had brick for stone, and slime had they for morter.*
> *And they said, Go to, let us build us a city and a tower, whose top may reach unto heaven; and let us make us a name, lest we be scattered abroad upon the face of the whole earth.*
> *And the Lord came down to see the city and the tower, which the children of men builded.*
> *And the Lord said, Behold, the people is one, and they all have one language; and this they begin to do: and now nothing will be restrained from them, which they have imagined to do.*
> *Go to, let us go down, and there confound their language, that they may not understand one another's speech.*
> *So the Lord scattered them abroad from thence upon the face of all the earth: and they left off to build the city.*
> *Therefore is the name of it called Babel; because the Lord did there confound the language of all the earth: and from thence did the Lord scatter them abroad upon the face of all the earth.*

That was it. That was it? Well, so what? I'd expected a bit of detail: fire and brimstone and raining hail, maybe, a proper exploration of the wrath of the godhead: at least a tower that reminded me however hazily of my own tight dreams. When Ginny mentioned the Tower in the cafe she must have added bits from her own imagination. And I wish – going off at a tangent – that I could say I picked out the navy blue Bible and spent time that should have been spent reading *The Puritan Revolution* on the verses of Genesis because I did Ginny the service of hanging on her every word, of wanting to find out how her imagination worked and what her history was, but I can't. I was curious to find out what the Tower of Babel was and meant because in my conceit I imagined every reference to any aspect of myself, conscious, semi-conscious, sub-conscious, god knows probably unconscious, to be of rivetting importance. I expected all paths to lead back to the homestead that was my substance: no scenic detours, thankyou very much. But Ginny got her own back, if you like; for though her flippant comment bounced to one side of the target, the target shifted and altered to catch it. The next dream that I had seized upon my new knowledge and triumphantly accommodated a sharper sense of crime and punishment, a queasy permeation of desert landscapes shimmering under the hot eye of a spiteful god, a sense of the fabulous.

I returned the book to its proper place.

I found I was no longer alone in the old wing of the library. Reluctantly I acknowledged Jules Fitch, hunched over a dreadful scrawled mass of illegible writing. Fleetingly I wished it were legible and I had the speed-reading and extra-super photographic memory of a superman, for Jules Fitch was reading the same subject as myself, shared a weekly tutorial with me, and the volumes of scribble under his nose no doubt contained the rough-worked substance of the essay I hadn't even begun. I'd have tried to get away with just a brief nod, but he put his biro behind his ear as I passed and collared me with unnerving eagerness.

"Donaghue!" Which was my surname, of course, and had earned me the nickname of 'Donny' at school. Donny as in Donny Osmond. Fortunately most people at the college seemed to have grown up in a world free of the Osmonds and the name had not resurfaced. Fitch, for no reason I could see, appeared to be jittery. "How's the essay going? Seems quite straightforward on the whole, don't you think? Did you get hold of the Wilkins?"

"Not yet."

Actually I had a slight prejudice against Fitch. One lunchtime in the pre-Ginny days of those first two weeks I'd endured an entire meal's-length conversation about his endless merits. I'd overheard, you understand, sitting with my plate of cod and chips in the crowded hall of the college. Three of my contemporaries, girls all taking English, had parked themselves opposite me on the long trestle and treated me to a long-winded analysis of Fitch's good points: his hazel eyes, his blonde hair, his high cheek-bones, his peach-shaped bum, his broad shoulders; and also his intelligence, respect for women, sense of humour blah blah etc etc. I took it personally. Here's the honesty: I couldn't admit that I liked Jules; I was jealous. In a way that it's troubling to remember now, I made it something of a hobby to make note of his weak points.

"W-what did you think to that last tute?" stuttered Fitch. *Tute* as in *tutorial*. " Frank can be quite a tartar, can't he? I mean, he doesn't let you off the hook, does he?"

Wasn't he the chatty one today? I was used to the Fitch who showed himself in tutorials – over-polite, disconcertingly sharp – or the one who cropped up in pubs – a touch reserved – but this Fitch was a new one on me. He laughed conspiratorially and I meanly smiled in weak response. "Actually I've just finished with the F.W. Knotsworth," he rushed on, "– if you, I mean if you need it. But you've probably read it already, have you? Have you, ah, already read it?" His eyes darted towards mine and I briefly met them. They were a rather stunning Autumn brown, damn him. I decided there was something creepy about him, a kind of horrible crawling apology, a sucking-up that put you off him; but I wanted the Knotsworth, quite badly. I struggled with the difficulty of making myself beholden, decided I was desperate enough. My decision to boycott the History library had been making my life difficult.

"I could do with another look at it," I answered coolly, not meeting his eyes; and though *I* was the one asking the favour, it was *I*, oddly enough, who experienced the mildly sadistic pleasure of the dog-owner teasing his over-enthusiastic dog; dangling the lead, perhaps.

"Well, well take it," Fitch said too quickly, "Absolutely. No problem at all. I've done with it." He handed it over. I watched his large, smooth hand on its cover and noticed the slightest of tremors. A hangover, I judged, not giving it more than a passing thought. "If you could just put it in my pigeon-hole, I mean there's no hurry, but, when you've finished... You know what the fines are like. Or you could just drop it into my room." He flicked his pen off the desk with his elbow clumsily, didn't pick it up. His voice speeded up. "Yes, just drop it round. Any time. You know where I am? I'm on the Terrace. You're in the New Block, aren't you?"

I had no doubt he was smiling at me in that doggy, over-intense way. I took the book. "Thanks," I managed, and would have escaped had not I noticed over his shoulder and through the window a familiar flash, a Ginny shape. Fitch had squashed himself into a seat overlooking the college garden and it was across the lawn of this place that I thought I saw her. Involuntarily I leaned over him to see, forcing him to swivel in the same direction. I'd hardly been away from Ginny in the few days I'd known her, but then, as later, the absence would throw up images of her. I'd always be thinking I could see her, moulding her out of the most unpromising material. The figure disappeared round the corner of our building.

"Oh that's, um, god, can't remember her name. Begins with 'M'," said Fitch, "I've never met anybody so completely screwed up. She was at a party in St. Catz I went to. 'M'. Something."

So it had not been Virginia, my Ginny.

I turned and left Fitch with a flicker of a smile and a half-salute. Gathering up my small collection of belongings from the desk I headed for the more conducive squalor of my room, where I actually achieved some work. The Knotsworth might have the furry green cover of a book that had lost its dust-jacket a decade before, but it held a hidden treasure. Fitch had jotted notes in its margins. Neither were they the notes you usually came across, enigmatic short-hand – *See G.N.J. para. 3* – or funny ha-has – *Charles completely lost his head, didn't he?* – or indignant weedy riposte – *He is wrong, wrong, wrong!* – or childishness – *I am so bored*. They were marvellous juicy notes in almost complete sentences, ideas and references and glosses and even – bless him – a couple of lengthy quotations clearly ascribed and connected by a winding arrow to the point in the text they illuminated. These became the skeleton of my final essay. Not surprisingly, it was a starving man of an essay, bones jutting up in great ridges through its thin flesh, since the Knotsworth represented only one side of an argument, and I didn't have the advantage of the other five books Jules had no doubt pored over, or the notes I'd seen on his desk in the library, but at least it had a skeleton, wasn't just jelly. The tutorial in which I presented it was excruciating. There were just the two of us, Jules and I, in that tutorial 'group' and we took it in turns to read out our week's work. It was my turn to read, Jules' turn to hand his work in. I have no doubt that Frank (first names all round) spotted the remarkable similarity between the efforts of the two of us when he came to read Jules' later on, and read in it the rounded versions of the very same arguments he'd heard dropped from my lips so recently. I expect Fitch was implicated in the scam. I know the next week Frank gave the both of us an extremely hard time. Yet Jules never broached the subject. It's patent that I should have felt cheap at my shoddy behaviour, but at the time I'm afraid the episode gave me a nasty kind of pleasure.

It was almost as if I were punishing Jules for some hidden crime.

Later, it goes without saying, I felt quite differently about the link between myself and Jules Fitch, for link there was, though I was ignorant of the fact until too late. It's the way it works, isn't it? All that happened later changed the shape and substance of all that had happened before.

The Tower of Babel. There is a painting by Bruegel. Apparently he painted at least three of the same subject; but the one which draws me to it hangs in Rotterdam. The scale of the thing; the scale of the painting dwarfs the efforts of most of us. Bruegel's Tower is not so much a tower as a colossal hump. It sits slap in the centre of the canvas and rising out of its pretty, pleasant, tame Netherlands landscape like a gross tumescence. Anyone who's seen even a postcard of the Coliseum will spot the similarity immediately. The Coliseum has three layers of lolly-shaped arches and a fourth layer without arches. It has the appearance of a cake, but a stodgy one, flat and very solid. Something with bran added, maybe. Bruegel adds layers, irregularity, excess, serves up a wedding cake to carry you through not merely the first christening but through those of a whole houseful of children. Breugel's tower is zanier than a coliseum. Its construction follows a vast dogmatic spiral whose centripetal movement will one day finish in a point: if the tiny builders ever get that far. For work is in progress.

The edifice rises to – what? – only half of its final height. Now if Bruegel had painted the finished structure, *that* would have been blasphemy indeed. *That* would have been to reverse the direction of the punishment and visit it upon the Punisher. *That* would have been to erase God. A godless universe, and the children of men sitting at last up in the clouds, chatting.

Where were you in 1966 when the first pictures of the moon were beamed from Luna 9 back to earth? We were all sandwiched together on my grandmother's settee like different fillings, parked in front of her television rather than our own because she'd splashed out on one of the very first colour sets. Not that you got a lot of colour out of those first grainy moon shots; bluey-greys and greeny-greys, perhaps a hint of peach. It must have been that my dad had set the alarm because it was weirdly early for a school day, all wrong in that unnerving, thrilling, transgressive way. They hadn't even got me dressed; I'd been bundled into the car like an abductee, driven the half a mile to my nan's bungalow and carried up the garden path between the wintery stumps of her rose-bushes.

We all got terribly excited all the way back in 1966 because Luna 9 sent back images of the other side of the moon, and, believe me, there were plenty of people – and not just me, five years old and sitting with my cup of Ribena on my mother's lap, wrapped up in a quilt – plenty of people who expected to see wonderful figures lurking behind the scattered rocks of the lunar landscape. There were more than one or two who expected a kind of freakish version of the New York skyline, complete with oxygen domes and sky-roads and flying saucers zipping between mile-high sky-scrapers, dipping over the square heads of armies of worker robots, the whole given spookily garish colours by illumination positively Conran in its modernity. We held our breath.

We saw rock. We saw an absence of life so irrefutable that even I had trouble being cheered up by my mum's suggestion that *anything* could be hidden behind that bumpy bit on the horizon. The rock we saw was chill and nondescript, though this is not to suggest that we were unimpressed. We were awe-inspired, sure enough, by the very fact of seeing what had never been seen before – *never* – and bolstered by the fact that this gave us an instant superiority over all those millions who'd just happened by sheer misfortune to have been born too early. Elizabeth I hadn't seen this, had she? Neither had Dr. Livingstone, Charles Dickens, Lawrence of Arabia. Even Churchill had just missed his chance. We were oddly moved by the loneliness of that cold place that seemed made of dust. Yet even I, though incapable of expressing a hundredth of it then or a tenth of it now, felt the first tremor of a unique loss. My grandfather had always said that he hoped he died before we conquered the moon (his phrase), before we established whether life existed there, before we stamped on its poetry; and he managed it. And that's the point: the rocks pockmarking the moon's other side might just as well have been building-site debris, and the ruckled surfaces we saw on my grandmother's colour t.v. might just as well have been the roof-garden of the tallest tower ever built. We'd erased God. We'd all be sitting up there soon, chatting above the clouds; and we could all hope to god we'd find more to chat about than how boring it all looked from up there.

There's a cloud drifting in on the right of Bruegel's version of Babel, a nice plump thing, though rain-laden by the look of its colour. It obscures a small section of the tower, the summit of which, jagged and unfinished, bristles with scaffolding, rises up with the architecture of a mad cathedral. People, dozens and dozens of them, mere specks at the tip of a fine brush, can be picked out if you look carefully enough. What's more there's a highly organised look to all the human activity that buzzes at microscopic level. It is obvious that the painter wants the viewer to feel the tower is a possibility, a proper possibility that only needs scaffolds, pulleys, cranks and cranes, and of course a few centuries of human effort, in order to exist.

But what Bruegel doesn't show, can't show is its interior. The Bible talks of a city and a tower. Bruegel has put the city in the tower. This bothers me. What kind of a city would it have to be? A honeycomb city, as complicated as the insides of a 'thirties wireless: rooms upon rooms upon rooms, but leading where? The outer chambers with their fifty foot archways must be flooded with light. Those behind might have their own internal windows, openings in the sheer walls to let in secondhand light; but then what about the third, the fourth, the *fifth* chamber? And what is there to find at the very core of the place? What could the necessity be for rooms so buried that without artificial light they would have none at all, so that if you were plunged into darkness in one of them your eyes would strain to adjust, strain to receive the most minute residual light, and find none? Pitch black that us moderns hardly ever experience, plenty of us anyway, sleeping in the glow of streetlamps, driving behind headlamps, missing the stars in skies reddened by the big city just over the horizon. This black would be darker than even the darkest night. Think of the complete disorientation reliant on no-comparison-to-be-made: the loss of direction, gravity. Every person has their own particular – how should I put it? *Foible* is far too weak, *terror* too strong (unless it be in the extremity of nightmare) – *queasiness, uneasiness, fear.* Loss of footing could bring it crawling out, or loss of air, loss of freedom of movement, loss of confinement, loss of control. Every person has that moment of recognition that threatens to embarrass ('If you'd just like to follow me up the spiral stair – yes, eleventh century; rather a squeeze, isn't it? Watch the handrope, it tends to swing out – two hundred and fifty-three steps up to the battlements...') and mine was cemented into those pointless dungeons.

That Autumn, saturated through and through with Ginny, triggered a series of dreams to remember. This was the case even before things started to fall apart, even in those first two weeks. Initially I'd guess I had the optimism to feel I'd come home, that I felt safe enough with Ginny to dig up a few worms from the murky soil of my subconscious. Later uneasiness became a fact of existence and the dreams sprouted effortlessly out of that. Men seldom remember their dreams, or so the Women's Magazines say, the one I saw at the dentist's at least, while women frequently chew them over together. I wouldn't know. But I do blame Ginny for the growing acuteness of my recall. She asked most mornings what I had dreamt, and more and more what would have stayed a nasty taste in the mouth, nothing more, easily swilled out with morning coffee, defined itself into clear and detailed sequences. What is more, images would reverberate faintly throughout the day, like the imagined calling of your name that your mind makes out of the shouts of children playing in next door's garden or the sound of a radio play drifting up from the kitchen. *Now* I'm lucky if I remember my dreams for more than a few seconds. The radio alarm comes on at seven and the news washes them all away; and that's how I like it.

On the afternoon of the morning I had been thoroughly humiliated by Frank for my feeble essay (oh, the look on Jules' face, a kind of caving in as it slowly dawned on him that the progress of my argument seemed mighty familiar; and *why the hell* wasn't he angry? I had seen fist fights over less), I lay on my bed fanning my face slowly with the new reading list Frank had handed to us at the end of our hour with him. Ginny, whose subject was English Literature and Language, who had been sitting eighteen inches away from me at the desk and reading a great fat Dickens with seeming absorption for an entire hour, took off her N.H.S. spectacles and turned to me.

"Do you know you had a nightmare last night?"

"Did I?" I replied ingenuously, letting my gaze follow the specs as they waved gently to and fro with the emphasis of Ginny's hand. I was already fond of these specs. They suited Ginny, gave her a John Lennon gravity.

"Mm. You almost shouted out. I had to wake you up. Don't you remember?"

"No." Escalators. Chambers white and clinical as Boots the Chemist. Up and up the escalators pursued by? Pursued by? No exits. Incredible speed of movement.

"Well, anyway; you did. And I smoothed your brow for you, like a good Victorian wife."

"A good Victorian wife? In my bed at two in the morning?" I was getting better at these little shots at repartee. "Why don't you come and show me how you did it?"

She smiled ironically but indulgently, laid the glasses beside the paperback; and then there was a brief but unmistakeable knock at the door. The first knock, if accuracy's important, for at least a week.

"Oh god," I groaned, and shifted so my incipient state of arousal was hidden by the booklist.

"Come in," said Ginny.

Jules Fitch opened the door as carefully as if there'd been a sleeping child behind it. My heart sank. That's exactly what it felt like; the slow and leaden descent of something vital in my chest. I sat up and waited for him to swear at me.

"Hello," said Ginny.

"Oh." Jules looked surprised, paused just inside the door then asked her, "Don't I know you? We've met? At a party?"

"No," shrugged Ginny, giving him one of the smiles I particularly liked, "I don't think so, but you never know. My name's Virginia. Does that help?"

"I thought.... well – hi. Jules." It hadn't been first names when I met him. I expect I was lowering as he turned to me. I was certainly irritated that he looked, damn him, *depressed*. I told myself that if he'd been angry with me I'd have apologised, that such wimpish behaviour deserved none of my respect, that it was not such an awful thing I'd done, that I could have come up with all the same arguments for the essay, no problem.

"I was wondering about the book," he said, turning to me with a kind of Eeyore expression in those eyes that, like a sailor, all the nice girls loved.

"I've taken it back. Already. Late Wednesday, I think. The library had shut but I dropped it off at the book drop." The lie just slipped out, as the image of the oversized letterbox just to the left of the entrance of our hometown public library slid helpfully into my imagination. I could feel Ginny's eyes on me. She had the habit of flicking through any book she came across, giving it a quick thumbs up or down, dropping it back where she'd found it or, with a shade of pretentiousness, carrying it off to a corner. The F. W. Knotsworth had the day before received the thumbs down from her, so she knew, as I did, that it lay submerged under items of yesterday's clothing I'd balanced on the corner of the desk by the bedhead.

"Oh, that's great." Jules sounded relieved, even *looked* relieved. At the Faculty Library an overdue book was like God's black mark, so they said. It was difficult to persuade the librarian at the checkout to lend you any more, and the fines rose steeply after the first week. I wouldn't know, since I'd stopped going. The work side of my life had subsided into a spongy kind of guilt, one that could dry out or swell up depending on how much work I could see Ginny doing. Then here was Jules, Mr. I'm-going-to-get-a-First Fitch, hassling

31

poor lazy little me. Pretty weird to be so hot under the collar about a library book, as far as I could see. I imagined that his concern was with the inconvenience not the cash for the fine. I still slotted him into the top drawer with Dave Shannon. In this, as in so many of my assumptions, it turned out that I was wrong.

It occurred to me that Jules was lingering expectantly. His eyes meandered gently over the room, over bed, desk, armchair. Perhaps he was playing a 'spot the clear inch of surface' game. If so, he was bound to lose. Every surface held or repelled clothes, books, cups, biros, tissues, cutlery, milk-bottles, record-sleeves, loose change, screwed-up receipts. It was how I liked it. I thought I was being original. Every morning since Ginny came I'd pinned a note for the cleaning lady on the door: 'Please do not disturb'. The 'please' had been Ginny's suggestion. Now as I noted Jules' rather adult dress sense I mentally reconstructed my idea of his room: identical to mine, minus the above list. I'd forgotten his room was not in the New Block, as was mine, but in a slightly crumbling row of eighteenth century houses everybody called 'The Terrace' at spitting distance from it.

It occurred to me that Jules was hoping I'd offer him a cup of coffee. I couldn't fathom why he'd *want* a cup of my coffee. Strictly Co-op own brand it was, while he, I imagined, only drank filter. In fact he could see the jar; it was twelve inches from his shoe, in the middle of the floor. For quite other reasons, anyway, you'd have thought it would have choked him. I willed Ginny not to leap in to compensate for my lack of neighbourliness. It was very probably the book burning beneath the dirty shirt on the desk that kept her smiling sweetly but silently.

Eventually he had no choice but to go. This he did with a last glance at me that I did not understand, except that threaded into it was some kind of plea.

As the door closed, Ginny's smile faded. She put her specs on and looked at me. I had to say something.

"I am going to take the book back. There was no point worrying him."

"Wouldn't it have been easier just to give it to him?"

"I don't know why he's so bothered about it, anyway."

"Why is he so bothered about it?" she asked with a kind of blankness I hadn't yet identified as dangerous.

I shrugged, and she dropped the subject. In retrospect, it wouldn't surprise me if she hadn't been protecting that enhanced image of me she'd rather have kept intact. The Mercutio effect. Through those John Lennon specs she could see a Simon Donaghue with rainbow edges. There must, god knows, have been some explanation for her love for me. I look back at that boy on the bed and I see lean, hungry, *handsome*, yes, but *loveable*? not so sure.

Later on when it had got dark in that creeping autumnal way I left Ginny ploughing through her interminable Dickens, telling her I'd drop off the book, **the book**, at the Faculty Library and buy us some chips on the way back. Since Ginny came, I'd not eaten in the college hall. Most of our nights now chips featured at some point. *There's* something to add to the list of surface-covering objects in my room: old chip-papers. Even *now*, walking past the fish and chip shop on the corner of our road, mid-afternoon when they've closed after the lunch-time rush, I get a whiff of that room in the stale smell of the spilt fat of a hundred fryings past.

And it could have been that I walked the ten minutes or so to the History Faculty Library and found the book-drop and slipped Jules' book out of my pocket and through its welcoming flap. It could have been that it landed safely inside with a dull, echoing thud. I try to imagine another Virtual Reality walk through streets thick with rush-hour traffic – such a problem with traffic, Oxford – along pavements where I brush shoulders with hail-fellow-well-met types whose breath frosts up in the air and where I have to keep one eye over my shoulder to avoid being mown down by cyclists trailing college scarves whose only thought is to get out of the cold. When I reach the library I look up at its rococo frontage and think how bleak public buildings look when they're empty and I take the book from my pocket and make a silent apology to Jules along with a resolution to admit to him that I lied, for the book is already overdue. But I have trouble with the late 'seventies feel and can't remember, quite, how the cars were less streamlined and the clothes less casual. The Virtual version goes wonky, cars slamming into walls and passers-by growing twelve inch noses and the Faculty Library curling over like a soggy stage-set, the pillars supporting its portico rubberising into two bendy tubes and the mullions between all the fiddly panes of window glass bellying out to give each window a beer gut and the twirls and swirls of stone crests and spirals under every frame flying off to bounce along the pavement. So I try to comfort myself with the perhaps-truth that one book made no difference, that events would have run along the same channels regardless.

I went nowhere near the library, except insofar as everywhere in a medium-sized town is pretty near everything else, but lingered along the High Street towards Magdalen Bridge, rewinding the odd comments Ginny had thrown into the conversation after Jules had left the room. 'Have you noticed what an incredible brown his eyes are?' had been my least favourite. Magdalen College itself crouched behind scaffolding – I never saw the place without it – and the scaffolding gave the bell tower more of the appearance of one of the Apollos waiting for lift-off even than it would have had anyway. Undergoing extensive renovation, its stone was being buffed back to its original soft pinkish-orange and its dissolving gargoyles saved from oblivion, protected from traffic fumes for another few decades. A large skip sat squarely in the gutter before the college's facade, half full of rubble and the binbags that materialise wherever a skip is parked, and it was into this that I lobbed the book.

I am sorry, Jules.

With a grubby self-satisfaction I made my way back up the High to the chip shop.

"All done?" asked Ginny as I walked through the door carrying bags of chips in one hand and a wrapped bottle of the cheapest red Oddbins had to offer under the other arm. I looked at her in her John Lennon specs and ached for her. "All done," I said.

* * *

I reckon I've stumbled across the cathedral, which I know is somewhere pretty close to the centre of the airless city, underneath a jumble of concrete corridors and set on solid rock. Thousands of people have been here before us, but they're long gone, leaving just a sense of themselves and what they expected from us. The cathedral is narrow and elongated as the interior of a submarine, yet the walls rear up sheer as the sides of a quarry. Stained glass windows stretch upwards like pieces of spun toffee. Though beyond them, I know, are only acres of rooms, light of a deep residual kind glows in red through the patterns on the glass, patterns that are just like the scribble you make with a biro that won't work. The whole place is stuffed full of office furniture. So far so good. I have a small, rather unattractive little boy at the end of my arm, whom it's imperative I don't lose. 'This is The House Of God,' I tell the boy solemnly, to try and scare him into good behaviour; but anyway the grip I have on his hand keeps dissolving into air and there's a growing sense of inevitable failure as I can't keep him away from the walls, which suddenly are unsafe. Right down the other end of the cathedral Ginny's in a phone booth engrossed in a long, hilarious conversation with I don't know whom; but it's somebody she gets on with really well and she's throwing her head back and I know everything she says is just what you should say if you want to be loved by the in-crowd and she looks just like Debbie Harry (lashes-lips-hair-bust-hips-heels) and it's obvious that she won't be interested in *me* any more, not after this. If it weren't for the ugly child I might be able to try running over and beating on the glass of the booth, but now he's dragging on my arm with a dead weight and I notice he's actually subnormal in some way, with sullen eyes and a distorted head. Within the wall just beyond us the first faint stirrings of a malignant intelligence rustle, then rapidly, exponentially grow into a shifting, buckling, bulging of the plaster out into the room. It's a possession by a massively powerful evil spirit whose miasmic substance can infect in any and every direction with inhuman speed. The bulging wall palpates with just the tense softness of the skin on a blister. I have an absolute horror that it will crack and seep the mysterious clear liquid that blisters give up if you rupture them. By now the entire structure squeezing us from either side and soaring far above our heads has soaked up the contamination and the only place for it to go is *into* us. 'Put your hands on your ears' I scream to the boy, 'Keep your mouth shut. Don't –'

"Simon."

"*Chri-*"

"Simon. You're in your room. It's fine. It's all right. Simon."

"*Jesus Christ.*"

"What was it?"

"Oh God."

"Look. Safe in the squalor of your room."

"We went on a submarine once. At Portsmouth. I remember..."

"Is that what you dreamt about?"

"I don't know. No...a cathedral."

"Was I there?"

"No. It's all going. Christ."

"You're soaking."

"Yes."

"What was scary? What was happening just before you woke up, well, before I woke you up?"

"Oh God, I don't know. Some kind of...evil."

"Why are your dreams so, oh, *Gothic*? Funny, isn't it?"

"They don't feel funny. God, it must be nearly dawn. Thank God it's nearly dawn. I think I'll just avoid sleep from now on."

"*You?* Avoid sleep?"

"I hope you're not laughing at me."

"Would I?"

"Highly likely."

"How you misjudge me."

"Not I."

I looked at the corner of my desk and the rubbish piled on it with a great affection. The more boring the real world the better, for now. Even better, the solidity of Ginny's shoulder cutting off my view of the rest of the room. The seam of her T-shirt had given and an irregular triangle of skin revealed itself just at that lovely curve where the upper arm began. I was crammed up against the wall (slight shiver of a reminder), while Ginny had wriggled round to face me, presumably when she shook me awake.

"I'm glad you're here to wake me up."

"I'm glad I have a use."

"You have a few more uses than that."

"Good. What?"

Wouldn't it have saved a lot of anguish if we could have made love then? The terror of my nightmare was simmering nicely down into a spicy-edged lust. I could have come up with some smooth, suggestive comment and we could have stripped off those last few items of clothing. Naked, at last, and nothing to hide. I could have insinuated my arm beneath her neck and across her back; then she could have wound her arm and her leg around me and that could have been it, effortlessly, easily: all out of the way. I could have done it, untroubled by the idea of Ginny getting pregnant. Girls sorted themselves out in that department, didn't they? The first time might not have been too good, sure enough, but we could have improved upon it, day by day, night by night.

The truth of it was that we couldn't.

Never before or since have I lived in a state of such fine-tuned sexual expectation. It informed everything. Speculatively I unclothed the teenagers in the bread-shop, bored my gaze through the brick walls of halls of residence to guess at the tricks beyond, doodled ink swirls on the margins of my lazy note-taking and watched them turn into the Y and W of an exaggerated female form. I allowed myself to ignore the resistance, the kind of electrical feedback that was gathering between myself and Ginny. I imagined I was giving her time. I could use that notion drifting around my head that when you were *serious* about a girl you waited longer before you pounced. I could tell myself that I held the initiative, that the right moment would arrive spontaneously. And meanwhile touching her was almost too exciting, a kind of torment.

I find that I have no desire to go back, that I have never been back to Oxford, save to give it a cursory wave as we drive up the M40 towards Birmingham on our way to the Lakes with tents piled on our roof-rack (god, how I hate camping, but it's cheap) and the back window obscured by tennis racquets and orange juice cartons and anoraks and, now, once again, bumper packs of nappies. Yet it would be true to say and impossible to say to anyone that the fortnight after I met Ginny was the best, that although now I have a kind of peace it is the peace of compromise, a middle-aged cup of cocoa peace. That fortnight held as much and was as highly charged as a year of the present.

We celebrated our first week together by taking a day off work. There would have been no sin in this had we been working consistently the rest of the time, but of course our days on had been few. We buried the knowledge of work piling up – like junk mail filling the freezing hall of an empty house – and wandered around the Ashmolean museum looking not at ancient Chinese ceramics but at our entwined reflection in the immaculate glass of the display cases. We bought more black things for Ginny in a charity shop, more records – *Pretenders*, *The Jam*, more *Clash* – and books from upstairs in Blackwells; a stack of secondhand novels tangentially relevant to Ginny's course, to appease her conscience. At around four, as the day closed rapidly in and traffic grew heavy, we lunched. Since we were so out of synchronisation with the rest of the world, we had the pizzeria nearly to ourselves. It was one of those places with check table cloths and dangling wine bottles in baskets and framed photographs of Venice and improbable stuccoed archways that appeal *because* of the tackiness of decoration. I suppose I'd better admit that at seventeen, with feet that had never edged across the shiny white of any airport departure hall, let alone across the flagstones of St. Mark's, it was I that was naive. By omission I suggested to Ginny that I'd swanned into any number of restaurants, rather than just the mock-tudor Berni Inn to which my mother occasionally treated my grandmother, calling the pizzeria 'not a bad little place'. I offered to pay, *big man*, strangling the rapid-rising image of cheque-stubs accumulating in the increasingly thumbed cheque-book shoved into the bum pocket of my cords.

Loud music played: the repertoire of an Italian cousin of Frank Sinatra, by the sound of it. The waiter tucked us behind a couple of pillars, no doubt after a shrewd assessment of our Oxfam style, where we managed to get through a couple of bottles of Valpolicella as we ate and talked: as Ginny talked.

"Why don't you like Jules?" she asked.

I shrugged. "He's a slimeball."

A short silence.

"How do you mean?" She lay down her fork and pulled my fingers away from my wineglass so she could stroke them. "I mean, as a description that's a little brief."

I made an effort: "There's something about him.."

"He seems O.K. to me." Her index finger traced a spiral in my palm, outward in, then slowly, slowly inward out. Every nerve ending in my body seemed to fizz with the trail of that finger. The pool of electrical charge flowed down and settled in my groin.

"Where does he come from?" she went on.

"I don't know."

"How old do you think he is?"

I shrugged, shifted in my seat.

"He's the kind of person you can imagine being incredibly successful, don't you think? He's got a sort of T.V. Presenter look."

I *wanted* to say, *you only saw him for sixty seconds, damn it, damn him; damn his Bambi eyes.* When I said nothing, she changed tack.

"Don't you ever wish," she said, "that you had no past? That you'd sprung complete into the world? That you owed nothing to anybody?"

She was talking to the wrong person here. 'Stuck in the past' hardly served to describe me. I *was* the past. The present I tolerated, now that I had Ginny. The future was a terrifying confusion of images from adverts, men in suits talking big money, families eating chicken dishes together, people taking out insurance and buying houses and doing any number of actions that I could never imagine myself capable of performing. Life a dreadful pressure to take on *responsibilities*, that word the over-the-hill people tried to trip you up with. But I did want to let her know that I knew I owed her something already; and if we had been on the last glass of the second bottle rather than the last glass of the first, I would have been able to find the words. I thought she'd be able to pick up on my body's ridiculously easy response to her, though *how* I thought she'd do this is unclear, since I sat as blank and enigmatic as a standing stone: osmosis, I expect.

"I mean, I know the past makes you what you are, etc. etc., but don't you just think it drags you down? Two steps forwards, one step back?"

Something was clearly expected of me here, but I couldn't have told you what.

She waited, then went on more tentatively, "I wish this last week had been the first week of my life. I wish there'd been nothing before it. I hate the past. I hate everything in it." She laughed shyly. "I love you, Simon. I want to be with you for ever."

And although with the last sentences she'd only put into words the distillation of my own feelings, I experienced a chill of fear. 'For ever' meant an endless suffocating stream of the advert. images, did not mean the airless safety of Ginny and me on the bed in my green room, meant mortgages, car servicing, painting and decorating, babies. Then the fear receded and I saw Ginny given to me on a plate, Ginny jumping out of a cake for me in a spangly blue swimsuit, Ginny all for me, not Jules Fitch or Dave Shannon: me. I leaned forward and kissed her on the mouth. A kiss spiced with salami and mushroom and Italian plum tomatoes.

Looking back across the years to these little scenes, it's not so much a matter of watching them recede out the back window as whipping out a magnifying glass, picking out details I hardly registered at the time, blowing the whole lot up a hundred times. Though I imagined Ginny's naked body a thousand times during those first two weeks, I had to rely on an archeological reconstruction, for I never saw all the bits together, and some bits not at all. And this just seemed a means to an end, and the end was the imminent, *imminent*, I hoped to god, time when I'd see the whole lot in glorious vivid technicolor: wide screen. *Now* I whip out my magnifying glass and scrutinise those scenes which, god knows, the older I get seem more and more scenes played out between children. And obvious to me now is the massive detail which I missed entirely at the time, that the most vivid colours were to be found then, that I had what I was waiting for.

"Fancy a game of cards?" she asked, as if casually.

"I haven't got any."

"No, but I have." She took a chewed up old pack out of her jacket pocket, sat down on the floor and started to shuffle.

"Do you take those with you everywhere?" I asked, making an attempt to hide the dismay in my voice.

"I'd feel naked without them," she said.

She was always surprising me like this. Girls – sorry, all you post-feminists out there: that's what it was like in the bad old days – girls didn't play cards, did they? They might join in to be obliging, or so they could hang around the boys, but otherwise? Cards to me meant the Upper Sixth common room, definitely Boy's Own: betting with matchsticks, illicit fags, obscene jokes, ink-stained shirts, shredded ties...

"What shall we play, then?" She sat cross-legged, leant back against the blanket spilling off the side of the bed. "Rummy? Poker? What can you play with two?" she asked herself.

"I don't mind." Actually I'd only joined in the cards games in the sixth form out of a stunning boredom. Cards were only *boring*, not *stunningly* boring. "What about Snap?" I suggested. We'd only just got out of bed and I was brushing my teeth. Neither of us were properly dressed; just those damn T-shirts and underpants. The room was vaguely malodorous. If we played Snap rather than Black-Maria-Double-Rummy-Whatever I wouldn't have to give even half a mind to the game.

"Snap?" she said, "*Snap?*"

"Yeah," I replied indistinctly. I spat into the basin. "Why not? Good game, Snap." I wiped my mouth on a towel that held the smell of many days past, then dropped it back where I'd found it. "Exciting game. Fastpaced."

"Are you being serious?"

I realised she really couldn't tell if I was being facetious or not. I began to enjoy the attention. "My favourite. It's always been my favourite."

"Really?" she said cautiously, "What do you like about it?" eyeing me, wary of being taken for a ride.

"Well," I said slowly, realising that being centre stage was, surprisingly, pleasant. I could get used to this, couldn't I? With Ginny, anyway. "Well, you know, it's a question of...how can I put it?...it's probably the...the," I paused, rubbing my chest thoughtfully, "It's the *skill* involved, you know?"

She threw the pillow at me; and I felt I'd finally made it into the sitcom world of romantic comedy, where every exchange leads to a frolic.

One of my recent modest little home-grown theories is to do with cards. Recent as in *now*. I can hardly bring myself to own up to it, but we've begun to play Bridge with friends. And I've noticed how, try as they might, people *cannot* help revealing things they'd rather not reveal about themselves as soon as they've got that hand spread out in front of them; and if you want to speed up the process, oil it with a couple of generous gin and tonics, socialise it out of them with the unwise night-cap whiskey. You've got the sly and secretive ones who nurse the cards to their heart. You've got the sloppy, enthusiastic ones who quite like success but then feel mean. Then there are those who just can't drum up the ambition to try for more than ten minutes, because *it's all too much effort and, anyway, what's the point?* counterpoised with those who come alive with the competition, who really get excited, who just want to win, must must must win, *what's the point of playing if you don't want to win?*

Well: I was an *it's all too much and what's the point...* My competitiveness centred around Commandment Number Whatever, the one that deals with coveting. It wasn't the useful sort of competitiveness that gets you up off your backside, more the kind that has you bemoaning the fact that you weren't born with it all. But Ginny, my god, was a *just want to must must must.*

I did quite well, because it was Ginny's long fingers dealing the cards and Ginny's long legs crossed so close to my forehead as I lay stretched on the carpet that I could see the oh-so-fair hairs on her shin stirring when I breathed out; I did quite well, making a tolerable effort for at least fifteen minutes. Then I gave up.

"Snap," said Ginny.

Two Queens.

"Snap."

Two fives.

"Snap." Ginny looked down at me rather than the pile of cards – first time for fifteen minutes. "Simon Donaghue," she said, "You're not trying."

"Yes, I am. You're just quicker than me. I expect I'll get the next one." I yawned. "Let's get on with it."

"Snap," she said, after another six seconds. "You're just not trying."

"I am."

"You're not looking at the cards. You're just putting them down."

"I'm doing my best."

"You didn't look at that one."

"Which one?"

"You wouldn't know which one, because you didn't look at it."

"I don't know how you can say something like that about me."

"You're losing on purpose."

"How can you be so cruel?"

"You're losing on purpose to get the game over." She stopped with her card half way to the floor. "How can you *bear* to do that? How can you not want to win?"

"It's only *Snap*. I can live with myself after not winning a game of Snap."

"But it's the principle. It's the instinct. It's the kick."

"You can't really care, can you? I mean…"

"How can you just give up? Anyway, it's a kind of cheating. Makes the whole thing a waste of time, doesn't it?" She was cross, nonplussed.

"Yeah, but it's all just time-wasting, isn't it?"

"What?"

"What what?"

"What do you mean, 'all'?"

"Games."

"All games?"

"Yeah."

"But they're practice, aren't they?"

"Practice for what?"

She didn't exactly answer: "Well, look, there's no point doing anything unless you put all of yourself into it, is there? Is there? Simon?"

That shut me up. I pulled her down onto the floor with me, jumbling up the cards, made her laugh with the unexpectedness of it, kissed her, but, damn it, she'd reminded me about myself. How jealous I was of her doggedness. She really wanted to win that stupid little game, any stupid little game, because she really wanted to *win*. Why couldn't I care about anything that much? What the hell was I going to do with myself? Thank God I had Ginny. *I* could pick out those vowel sounds that told me *she'd* not grown up on cheap squash and spam sandwiches. Maybe if I just hung onto her heel there, she'd drag me up and away with her.

Well, we swum through those two weeks. Perhaps that's how long you can ignore the rest of the world, a fortnight. I'd done almost no work, Ginny maybe a little more. In our next tutorial, Frank raised his eyebrow as he took in my essay, giving it a dangerous flick of the forefinger to emphasise that he'd spotted that it consisted of a mere two sheets. There would be trouble to come; yet I managed to forget Frank as soon as I had walked out through his rather tall and elegant doorway – the Regency wing, you know. As Jules read out his essay and Frank made the occasional interruption; while Jules cleared his throat and Frank excitedly took him up on a point: – I fixed my eyes on the cream-washed panelling of the wall and divined the constituents of the smell of Ginny's skin with the accuracy of a perfumer.

We swum through the days, tied by touch, my dread for the future and Ginny's anger at the past drowned out by the sound of *The Clash* and diluted by the Oddbins bottles that we drank every evening. And if I struggled up out of nightmare I could use Ginny to steady me, superimpose images of her face, hands, breasts over those other rapidly-dispersing images of suffocation and impotence. We ate together, shunned the company of others together, played cards together, walked like Siamese twins together and slept together, non-euphemistically, in that semi-chaste, semi-clothed way we had evolved together. Yet when we phoned home, as we both did two or three times, we did it as surreptitiously as if we had been masturbating.

* * *

44

The beginning of the end coincided with one of my rare altruistic moments. Come to that it could well have been my first altruistic moment. I wanted to mark the celebration of our second week together. How long we could have gone on celebrating our little packages of time together I don't know. Seems embarrassing now, improbable that I could have been so, well, *soppy*. But, then, I'm not so enamoured of the past these days. I've come round, halfway at least, to agreeing with Ginny, that the dust of the past dulls the colours of the present.

We'd met on a Friday. On the Friday coinciding with our two-week anniversary there was to be a special dinner in college hall. These occurred every now and then, apparently, though this was the first I'd come across, and that's what they were called, because a little more effort was put into them: Special Dinners. This one was a freebie and bound to be popular, so booking was necessary. I forget whether there was some special occasion that the dinner marked, but I remember that it was with an enormous sense of achievement that I slipped to the Porter's Lodge and signed up for two places: Simon Donaghue and Guest. Doesn't seem a lot now, does it, but *then* I felt as if I'd taken some stunning initiative. This was what having a *girl* was all about. Suddenly it seemed a good idea to show Ginny off and, with something like a Special Dinner, that's just what I could do: wave her under admiring noses then whisk her back under wraps again. I hoped Fitch, Shannon, Purvis would be there at a little distance: close enough to see how good Ginny looked, far enough to avoid anything but a brief greeting. It could be our coming-out, our presentation at court. I kept it as a surprise, a trump-card I'd whip from up my sleeve on Friday evening as Ginny's thoughts began to turn to the chip shop on the High.

On the Thursday evening we decided to go to the late film at the P.P.P., the Penultimate Picture Palace, the arthouse cinema. Pleasingly makeshift, this place had toilets marked *Pearl* and *Dean*. During popular films it had people sitting in the aisles – though I ought to mention that the whole place was only middle-sized barn size. We're all a little more cosmopolitan now, more accustomed to cunningly packaged groceries, cosmetics, t.v. programmes, events, countries, even *people*, god knows. But then, how laughably easy to impress I was. The lack of popcorn seemed bohemian, the real coffee served in plastic cups and the chocolate cake you could buy with your ticket tantalising mouthfuls of a more adult world, but one in which (exultation) your mother would have felt ill at ease. Long gone. Shut down.

You can probably imagine our walk through a foggy night, our detour through the bar of The King's Arms, the queue outside the cinema in which anyone over twenty-five – and there were a brave few – would have felt marooned and crumbling. I would need to tell you, though, how Ginny was uncharacteristically quiet and preoccupied. We walked mostly in silence; but as we queued Ginny wormed her way under my donkey-jacket to hold me more tightly than usual, and I wasn't worried.

The place was packed out. It would have been regardless of the title of the film on offer, which happened to be *Death in Venice*. There still lingered the grab-life-by-the-balls philosophy of the first weeks of term, and we are talking of the days before clubland when after eleven at night nothing stirred. The late night film began at eleven, more or less, and scooped up the dozens who didn't want to go back to institutional rooms to drink instant coffee or warm beer from the window-ledge.

As luck would have it – not mine, but that of some malicious fate hopping in the wings – Ginny and I found seats in the middle of a row near the back and directly in front of Dave Shannon, who was lolling low in his seat with his muscular rugby-player's arm draped around a girl with the most extraordinary blonde hair. If I'd noticed him sooner I might have managed to manoeuvre us into different seats. Now that I had Ginny, I wasn't interested in Shannon any more, with his rather brutal intelligence and his bulldozing self-confidence. Still, I was surprised to see him in the P.P.P.. I always did have a tendency to pigeon-hole and in my book film-goers were different types altogether from rugby-players. What's more, my thunder had been stolen. *I'd* wanted to orchestrate the moment of public display when I'd show Ginny to the world, unveil her to the public gaze like the new statue in the town square. I'd been glad to forget that Jules had managed a preview. Up to that point we'd operated a little like spies, sliding out of my room at odd times and cultivating an offbeat timetable.

There was some satisfaction to be had, however, in deploring Shannon's predictability in loading himself with a girl who so neatly fitted the cliché of desirability, which didn't stop me from taking in as much of her as one exploratory glance would allow. Ginny was a little behind me, too occupied with stepping over a pile of dufflecoats to catch Shannon's opening broadside. Leaning forward towards me as I lowered myself into the seat, but not so near that his immediate neighbours could miss what he said and how he said it, he greeted me with, "Hallo, Fairy-cake. Got yourself a tart, have you?"

I understood immediately that this constituted a declaration of war. It might have been banter; but there was no playful punch, none of the provocative smiles – he could do several – that I'd grown familiar with during the first two weeks of term, when I'd been tagging along to the pub with him most nights. Instead there was that set-concrete look I'd seen him turn on the boring or the foolish. Shannon did not suffer fools gladly. It took me a few seconds longer to work out how I'd offended the godhead, what had managed to destabilise our *entente cordiale* of yesterday. Then I had it. Shannon was pretty thick with Jules. The F.W. Knotsworth disintegrating beneath damp binbags in the skip outside Magdalen was the root cause of this attack.

It was not that I was overly surprised by Shannon's antagonism. I'd heard him demolishing the characters of various individuals and known somewhere that he might one day make me into a target. And I'd been called far worse than Fairy-cake – the long hair, of course. I was very surprised, though, that someone I thought of as so thick-skinned should rise up with such wrathful alacrity in the defence of a friend he'd only had for a few weeks. I had a lot to learn about friendships, about loyalty. Much of it I never did learn: I can't say I have any close friends, not men at least. There are men with whom I share pints; or nowadays chilled bottles of French lager.

I scowled at him, but said nothing. Afterwards I thought I might have retaliated along the lines of, 'At least *she* doesn't look like one' which would have been unfair on the blonde-haired girl, or 'More than *you* could manage, bollock-features', but even these sorry attempts took me five minutes of glowering in the dark, staring unseeing at the screen. Meanwhile Ginny had negotiated the dufflecoats and the necking couple to arrive at my side.

"Introduce me," demanded Shannon. For all that he'd called Ginny a tart, he seemed remarkably interested in her. No doubt he was using the term generically. The blonde-haired girl stirred herself to smile vaguely in our direction, perhaps trying to speed things along so she could have her Dave all to herself again, perhaps aware of his sudden alertness, his sniffing into the air. I couldn't bear even Shannon's eyes on Ginny for very long. It would have been necessary to prise open my lips to get me to utter a word at that moment, and if I had, it wouldn't have been an introduction.

"Virginia," said Ginny, who, after all, had no idea of the fleeting scene playing itself out at subconversational level. I knew the way Shannon's sense of humour operated and how he'd be working out some wordplay on the name. 'And are you?' he'd have said, another time. Why do women like men like Shannon? Bloody Heathcliff-Rochesters, testosterone running out their earholes.

"Dave Shannon," he said, and shook Ginny's hand. He shook her hand. He shook her hand, if that's possible, suggestively. Not only did I despise him for mimicking the adult world with its uncool etiquette, but I hated him proportionately more with each second he kept hold of it, Ginny's hand, my Ginny's hand. It took longer than it should have done. Even Dave's girl, Miss Passive, stirred restlessly. I'd have liked to smack him on the chops. I scowled more deeply, but Shannon was a big man.

"Well, have you seen the film before?" he asked her.

"No," said Ginny, "but it sounds intriguing."

"It's what you might call different. Dirk Bogarde lusting after little boys. Or boy."

Ginny looked faintly shocked despite herself. "Wow," she said. Remember we hadn't been through the 'eighties. *Gayness* was *in* among liberals, but it was over there not over here, *them* not *one of us.* To be gay was to be an exotic, a lion with a zebra's head, a lily fruiting strawberries. Gays were supposed to behave like Julian Clary. Anyway most people conflated homosexuality with paedophilia. Then just think: back to the time when a brand of surgical appliances on sale in Boots called itself *Aids*, and none of us noticed the pun. Thinking of a time before Aids is like trying to look at a word and not to read it, to see it as lines and curves. How far we've come. Back *then*, 'child abuse' would have been telling a kid to shut up. What Dirk might have been contemplating was 'interference'. Another country.

"Wow," said Ginny.

"Absolutely fantastic shots, though. Definitely worth seeing." He gave a knowing nod or two.

"You're into film, are you?" Ginny livened up, shook off whatever was worrying her.

"Absolutely. The love of my life."

"Brill."

"A woman after my own heart. Excellent."

"Have you seen any *film noir*?"

"I'll tell you my absolute favourite: *Criss Cross*."

"Is that a Hitchcock?"

"Yes."

"Haven't seen that one. What about The Third Man? Do you think that counts as *film noir*?"

"Must do. Think of all those light and dark contrasts."

"That amazing bit on the, oh, what's it called? The Big Wheel in Vienna.. ... the Prater; or is that the name of the park?" Pedantry coming from Ginny was new on me, not to mention her intimacy with foreign cities. On she ran, "And isn't all the footage of the bomb sites amazing? And what about when Harry Lime runs through the sewers?"

"Yah, the subterranean shots. That really is a superb film, isn't it? Orson Welles looking like a ten year old."

Ginny laughed.

"Fucking marvellous," he added. That was more like the Shannon I was familiar with. For the rest; I was baffled by his change of style. One Shannon for the boys, another for the girls. And I wasn't particularly keen on the way he pushed his fringe away from his forehead, though I couldn't pinpoint why. As for *film noir*, what the *hell* was *film noir*? Black film. Something out of Harlem? And who the hell was Harry Lime?

"Are you a member of the film club, uh, Virginia?" I didn't like that *uh, Virginia*. People do that now, assume first name terms after the first minute, but they didn't then. It's an American import, a spin-off from the wonderful world of counselling: *now. Then* it was an intimacy.

"Is there one? A film club sounds great."

"Where have you *been*, girl?" Playful tones. Was *Shannon* really being puppyish?

"Busy. I'm a busy woman." Kittenish?

"Seriously, though, uh, Virginia, it's not bad. They show some good stuff. Quality's not so brilliant – the odd pause between reel changes, hair on the film – but for an amateur outfit... Always plenty of alcohol. Actually the guy who runs it's a good friend of mine. Practically an alcoholic, but a bloody good old boy. I'll tell him to give you a reduction on the membership. Well, it's peanuts, anyway: I'll tell him not to charge you at all. The next showing's a Bunuel. We had a, let's see, a...we had *If*, then, uh, *Jules et Jim*.... You should go. Join." *I'll be there.*

Miss Passive took the chunk of chocolate cake from Shannon, the cake he'd forgotten about and was holding in his other hand, the one that hadn't touched Ginny, and with a couple of big bites finished it off for him, wiping the crumbs from her lips with red-painted fingernails. I felt a sudden flash of sympathy for her. The desired effect was achieved. Shannon turned his animated gaze away from Ginny and looked at her.

"Hey. I was looking forward to that."

Miss Passive smiled at him obliquely. The lights went down rather suddenly. With a terrific crackling the film began.

All I retain of *Death in Venice* is a hazy recollection of Dirk Bogarde looking extraordinarily handsome and stricken and moving slowly about Venice in a white suit. I don't even know who died, although I suppose it was poor old Dirk, since I only saw fifteen minutes of the film anyway.

I was glazed with rage. Superimposed on the screen were images of my hands and feet wreaking violence on Shannon's body. I couldn't even hold Ginny as I had anticipated, with Shannon's sharp eyes on my back and his sarcasm positively taking material shape and emanating through the close air towards me. I could see Ginny darting glances sideways at me questioningly, but I kept on staring at Venice and the white suit, and drawing murderous images upon them.

Finally I leant towards her. "Let's go," I hissed. She frowned, then had no choice but to follow me as I pushed by the whole row of irritated spectators, who half rose and tutted and fell back in a wave. Comments followed us as I took her hand in the aisle and waded through the bodies huddled on its steps.

Outside Ginny stopped before the ticket-office and folded her arms. I was conscious of the suave figure of the ticket-seller loitering beside the exit door in a tight, tight pair of trousers which showed off – as if it were anything to show off – the smallest, tightest backside in the county. He was, presumably, listening; probably *through* that same tight little backside. I paced in the damp air, avoiding the question that her entire body wrote with its rigidity.

"Well?" she said finally.

"I don't like him."

"You don't like him."

"No."

"Who?"

"Dave Bloody Shannon. I don't like him. He's a wanker."

"That's it?" She waited. "That's why we've missed the end of the film we just paid *two pounds* to see?"

I stared at the silent pub next door to the cinema. In the fog it looked as if it were the last building for miles: *last pitstop before the desert, folks*!

"*Simon.*"

I couldn't bear to tell her I thought he'd been flirting with her in case the saying of it made it into the truth, in case she agreed. In case she'd enjoyed it.

"Simon. You're being outrageous."

"He's a complete wanker."

"That's so outrageous it's...it's outrageous."

"I don't like him."

"You don't like him. So who do you like? You don't like anybody." I'd never heard Ginny raise her voice, let alone shout. I'd never seen her angry, so hadn't known until that moment that this was how it always happened: a steely calm, then.....*shazzam*. Her words rang out, only partially deadened by the mist which wrapped itself around us.

She started to walk in jagged, furious scissor-steps, back along the Cowley Road. Casting one glance back at the ticket-collector, who was fairly successfully assuming insouciance – the yawn, the reading of the poster – , I frogmarched after her. There were few people about to witness our farcical transit.

That was about how far you could see, ten paces. Though I could have caught up at any point, I was cautious of this different Ginny. We must have marched along like this for a good few hundred yards. Occasionally somebody would leap out of the fog at us – a drunk, say, or a snogging couple, fate's pointed comment – and disappear just as quickly. Then Ginny had to stop to let a car pull out of a side-road. I drew alongside of her. We both watched the car sliding timorously out into the traffic, which was itself crawling.

"I like you," I said, "It's not true that I don't like anybody. I like you." I love you. *I love you so much it terrifies me.*

She had been poised to charge across the road away from me. Instead she turned and reached towards me and buried herself against my chest. Enormously relieved, I wrapped her up inside my jacket and lay my cheek against the soft fuzzy hair at the side of her head.

We walked on together.

"Look, Simon," she said heavily, and for one gaping second I believed she would say, 'Look, Simon, this isn't working and...', but she continued with, "I've got to go home this weekend. I might get away with just one night. It depends how it goes."

I knew nothing about what 'home' might contain or even where it was, for I'd never asked. She knew something of my family, having dragged details from me one by one. I was silent while the thought crept on me that her visit might be, after all, a Dear John kiss goodbye. Then I said, "How what goes?"

She sighed. "My family," she announced, as one might say, 'My prison sentence', "Can I tell you about it after the weekend?" Her sentences wandered around uncharacteristically for a while, then she added more decisively, "I'll tell you all of it then. I got a letter from my father this afternoon." Quick, sharp look. "Did I tell you I went back to check my pigeon-hole? Well, anyway, I did, and there was Dad's letter. Apparently he's been trying to ring me all week, but I wasn't there, of course; I was with you. I have to go home and help them...sort something out."

This all sounded suspiciously vague and improbable. One minute she was letting her degree fall apart to lie with me in my pigsty of a room, the next she was spinning thin tales of filial duty. For the first time I doubted her word.

"Okay," I said, chilled, confused by the apparent openness of her touch, her proprietorial embrace.

"Is it really okay?"

"Yeah, sure."

"I've got to. You can't get away, can you? They just won't let you."

"What?"

"I mean, the past just catches up with you, doesn't it? Drags you back. Oh, never mind." She seemed disproportionately upset. I felt proportionately disoriented. Wasn't Ginny the sensible stable one? Wasn't she the one who was supposed to pull me along in the sanity of her wake? What the hell would I do if Ginny wasn't the person I'd imagined?

"When are you going?" I asked.

"Oh, I hadn't thought it through. Tomorrow afternoon."

"But you'll come back with me tonight?"

"Well, yes." Then she added uncertainly, "If you want me to, I mean if that's okay." She drew away a fraction. I pulled her back.

"Yes," I said, with as much emphasis as I could manage.

"I'll go by train," Ginny said distractedly.

"Can you afford it?" I asked, with the idea of giving her the money.

"What? Yes, I've got the money. Dad sent me the money."

"Good." Then I shut up. This strange, inattentive mood of Ginny's unnerved me. We walked back the rest of the way in silence, but for once it was not a particularly companionable silence. Ginny was somewhere else altogether.

And in the morning she actually got up at nine and was gone by ten. I should have walked with her to the station, but I couldn't see beyond my resentment at her leaving me at all. It was too early for the scout – the poncey word for cleaner here – too early for her to have finished cleaning the corridor, so Ginny left by the window to avoid discovery. This was easy enough since the window swung open from the bottom and along its entire length, but somehow my uneasiness was underlined by the out of kilter action. I found myself searching the room for signs of her, as if I might discover the whole fortnight had been a romantic fabrication born out of my isolation and lust.

There were very few signs of her. Over the back of the armchair lay a T-shirt of mine she'd borrowed. Did that count? I buried my face in it. It smelt more of me than of her. The toothbrush beside mine on the basin was reassuring, but prosaic. She could buy another toothbrush. The belief that she'd never come back, once admitted, was difficult to kill. The whole day to fill and no-one to fill it with. I dressed, confusedly gathered together notepad, pens, reading-list, wallet, cheque-book, packet of cigarettes, a bottle of whiskey I'd leant on in the first week at college but forgotten, half-full in the wardrobe, once I'd moved onto wine with Ginny, and shoved them unceremoniously in a plastic carrier, then left as quickly as I could.

Where could I go that would be guaranteed to contain nobody I'd have to talk to, nobody from my tiny, overblown universe? I could have strode through Christchurch meadows if I'd wanted to be soothed by nature's harmony, had I not suspected that nature's harmony in the meadows would include Dave Shannon and Gerry Purvis jogging to strengthen their calf muscles or the English lot – Beverley McKenzie, Caroline Funnell, Stephanie Zielinski – back from rowing practice. You see I'd lost track of average timetabling: ten on a Friday morning was too late for early morning practice. I'd temporarily mislaid the sense of other people's lives, the lectures they attended that I skipped, the regularity of their weeks. Gerry Purvis was launched on physiological sciences, a degree that almost invariably led to a medical qualification. He was more likely to be dissecting a formaldehyded corpse in the lab. than exercising.

I took my carrier bag down Bear Lane and Blue Boar Street and ended up climbing the few steps that led up through the chunky late Victorian doorway of the local museum. Nothing to do with the University: town not gown. That was the whole idea. The kind of place you might be taken on a Junior School outing, where you'd be handed an activity sheet: *draw a prehistoric tool in the space below.* As I'd hoped, it was deserted, save for the homely woman behind the postcard desk: somebody's mum. Artefacts dug up in local fields, maps of the area in the Iron Age, you know the sort of thing: *The Story of Oxford.*

The museum was in the basement of the Town Hall; you were led down into it and chronologically through a series of object-filled rooms. I shuffled my way through several thousand years before I reached what I thought might be the furthest point from the entrance, which happened to fall during the Tudor Period.

In a room of perhaps seven by seven, heavy-duty cardboard had been used to construct facsimile walls. The objects on display, replicas of silver and gold college plate, were positioned behind glass in the arched facsimile windows in the centre of the facsimile walls. Standing in this room, you'd wandered into the notional corner of some college quadrangle, by the chapel maybe, or in the cloisters; but it was a disorienting experience. You were neither indoors nor outdoors. Carpet was underfoot, yet the cardboard walls were papered with huge photographic images of old stonework that were so true to the original you could see blemishes and cracks, and track the path worn into the stone by a few hundred years of dripping water. You could see where there might once have been a down-pipe, spot the point in the looping decoration around the window-arch that had not stood the test of time, where the pendant had been knocked off. I stationed myself with my eyes on a silver salt-cellar so ornate it defied description and allowed myself the luxury of misery, to sink all the way down that long steady spiral.

There was a sense of peace in the background hum of a dying strip light; the only sound save for the occasional shuffle of feet moving across the ceilings above. I leaned my forehead on the glass and let my breath steam it. It seemed to me that I would never make it through three years of university, that I was simply not capable of the effort. The excitement I'd envisaged it would deliver, sit-ins and demos and all-night parties and *drugs, man*, had shown itself to be mere mirage, an after-glow from the 'sixties. It came to me that I'd dragged all my fatal flaws along behind me when I left home, though I'd thought they'd stay on the village rec. and in the sixth form common room. It seemed to me that Ginny could have held me together but was leaving me to fall apart. I imagined Ginny with a Dave Shannon, how skinny she'd look pressed against his broad torso, how white her fingers would look against his brown arm, how he'd match her vivacity comment for comment, how they'd talk *film noir* talk as they lay post-coitally in his breezy room. I watched the minutely swaying reflection of my body in the plate glass of the case and thought what a waste my health was. My tall, spare, apparently attractive body should have belonged to somebody else, somebody who'd value it. It was so uselessly resilient, pulling itself together after nine pints, ten pints with no problem, recharging itself so that I could soak it again. Me, I wanted to dissolve it in acid. I could have dispensed with it altogether.

The spiral had a familiar shape and feel. It was an old friend. I'd been down its first few curves often, further infrequently, all the way down only once or twice. Down the bottom there's lethargy and indecision. At the bottom of the spiral there's no right place, only a permanent nullifying dispossession, a restless paralysis. It's the ocean bed, with so many tons of water weighing you down that you can't flex your little finger. It's the cellars of an antique city buried under a thousand years' worth of sand. It's coma, anaesthesia. It's six feet under already.

I stayed there for an hour or more, I think. Nobody approached me or challenged me, no visitors passed. I wouldn't have noticed if they had done. Perhaps they did. Then I walked back to the college. I checked my pigeon-hole in the impossible belief that Ginny would have sent something for me (how? by pigeon?) and found a curt note from Frank: 'Come and see me to discuss your last essay. 5.30.' This was unheard of and ominous. Tutors generally found undergraduate teaching a chore and certainly didn't call them for extra chats unless it was a euphemistic chat. But in my present mood I couldn't feel alarmed. I put the note into my pocket and forgot it. I walked back to my room.

As I opened the door I almost had a moment's animation. The room was unrecognisable. It had been rigorously cleaned and tidied, the curtains drawn back to let in what light Autumn had to offer, the cushions of the window-seat reinstated, the desk regimented, the floor cleared so it was possible to walk straight across it, the sink scrubbed. It still didn't look as I had imagined Jules' room to look, but it was the room of someone else, someone who was putting in more than the odd hour's work, someone who rowed or had joined the Drama Society, someone whose parents visited and were taken out to tea. I had been colonised. On the desk was a message written on a piece of paper torn from a jotting-pad: 'Sorry to intrude but could not let you live in this mess any more. Your mother would be shocked. Best wishes, Sheila.'

It was the first time I'd considered the existence of master keys.

I decided to do nothing, or rather I made no decision, but fixed upon Ginny's return as the moment I'd make one. Ginny never returning could not be borne so would not be thought of. I locked the door, drew the curtains, tipped out the contents of the carrier bag onto the carpet and took the bottle to bed with me. Fitfully I slept, and dreamt rather nastily of chasing my father down through the cavity walls and bare rooms of an ancient sprawling mass of masonry. I never caught up with him, but knew, each time I edged from another narrow passage into another room, that he'd just left, that I'd just missed the chance to explain myself to him.

* * *

Fathers: now there's a topic. I like to think that though I may have been an also-ran husband, I've been a good father, so far at least. Here I am, boarding the train to Victoria at Brighton's pretty, poorly-modernised railway station, which still echoes ever so faintly with the pretensions of Victorian trippers. As I fumble with my railcard and yawn into the still brisk air, my daughter's always one step and one thought ahead of me. *My daughter*, Alex: there's a miracle and a half. She's in Year 10, and so much more brisk and organised and, I suspect, *mature* than her father was at the same point in the tedious trek across the teenage years – though perhaps it's just the glasses perched on the end of her nose. Just creeping now into her tone is the deepening knowledge of her poor old dad's fallibility, which she tries to suppress – tone and knowledge both – so she can stave off independence just a little longer. Only on the *boys* front is she a late developer, stuck in the past just like her father, and, three years after her contemporaries started serious flirting (god knows what they get up to now), she can still sometimes indulge herself with an '*erghh, boys: disgusting*'. Here we go, off up to London on a spare Saturday to the Science Museum so that daughter can research her Science Topic on Electricity. Terribly interested in Science is daughter: Father left a little breathless by it; but anyway, today is *quality* time, just the two of them, baby left at home with mother to pursue more fundamental scientific investigation shredding paper. Daughter has unmistakable Antipodean stress to speech from steady, guilty absorption of *Neighbours* at other people's houses, father being curmudgeonly concerning C.C.V. – Completely Crap Viewing. As a consequence daughter's statements have a tendency to sound like questions. With a fraction more emphasis they're used as questions. In fact, under this system the syntax of interrogation could be dispensed with altogether and a great deal of trouble saved.

"There's a new theory(?)." Daughter drops her jazzy rucksack onto the upholstered seat, arranges the music magazine she's bought in the station W.H.Smiths on the table so that it is easily visible from the aisle, and settles herself opposite Father. "I can't remember where it was, right, but somewhere they're doing reee-search into magnetic forces(?), electromagnetic forces(?). There's a woman, a scientist, right, who thinks that some people actually have, actually kind of *have* their own force(?). Every time they go near something electrical, you know, a washing machine or, um, could even be just light switches, they all just *break down*; they all stop working."

"Do you mean the fuses go?"

"Yes. There was this Danish woman, right, and her friends always knew she was coming because all their electrical equipment fused as she was walking up the garden path(?). They'd say, 'Uh-oh, must be Lisa' or whatever she was called; Mona, I think. Hey, *Mona Lisa!*"

"Ho ho."

"'Uh-oh, must be Mona.' Then she'd knock. She lost her job and everything."

"What did she do?"

"Dunno. Sat around I suppose."

"No, what was her job?"

"She was a computer programmer(?)."

"Tricky."

Train lurches into movement.

"Do you think that could be true, Dad?"

"You mean the whole story?"

"Do you think you could get, you know, human batteries?"

"Hum. Who can say?..."

"You're going to say that thing again, aren't you? Groan. *Don't* say that quote again, Dad."

"What? What am I going to say?"

"'There are more things in the world, Horatio, than are dreamed of-'"

"Get it right, smartie-pants. If you're going to be squashing you've got to get it right. 'More things in Heaven and Earth.'"

"Why do you keep on quoting things, anyway, Dad?"

"Why do you keep on trying to squash your poor old pa?"

"Oh, sorry Dad-dy." Theatrical but affectionate kiss for Father. Father mollified but with another lock chopped off: dear old harmless Samson.

Next shot: here I am, on the beach with small son. It has its own grisly charm, the beach at Brighton. To one side of the Palace Pier is a modest patch of stones small enough to pass for gravelly sand. Elsewhere pebbles stretch like the foundation of a wide carriageway never constructed, pebbles grey and regular. It is winter, but relatively mild thanks to the Gulf Stream flowing past out to sea. Plenty of idlers share the beach with Father and Son. Son finds it almost impossible to balance on the pebbles and pivots round on the end of Father's arm like a pair of compasses.

"Henry. Hen-er-ee. Can you see that boat? Look. Over there. On the sea. On the Briny-O." Father feels smug and old-handish as he squats to guide son's arm into a point. All those other toddler-bound dads look bleak and amateurish by comparison. All they've got to go through, all they don't know, gives them an exhausted air; and their clothing looks permanently crumpled. Not so Father. *He's* together enough to have had a haircut within the last week (nice and short, suits the early middle-aged) and his denim jacket (dear old denim, resurrected yet again) says *this year*. He knows that whatever happens time passes. It's his strongest weapon, the passage of time, and his worst enemy.

"No, you'll hurt your teeth. See the pebble, it's hard. Ouch! Did you see Daddy hurt his teeth? The pebbles like being on the beach. Or we could throw them. Do you want to throw one?" Despite Son's running nose, which Father wipes, Son glows in Father's eyes. Son is a little prince of exquisite talents. Son is a colossal well-kept secret, a reservoir from which faith can be drawn, a compensation.

Much can be written on the subject of fathers. How about a few choice quotations? My little Alex, so enjoying her irritation at this peccadillo of mine: these are for her. The macabre: **But the father answered never a word/A frozen corpse was he,** Longfellow's 'The Wreck of the Hesperus'; or maybe the portentous: **Let us now praise famous men, and our fathers that begat us,** Ecclesiasticus 44; but never – I hope to God – never: Ezekial 18, **The fathers have eaten sour grapes, and the children's teeth are set on edge.**

* * *

Quick rewind, back through all those kaleidoscopic years.

It was at around six that I finally roused myself. I'd managed to rid myself of one day without Ginny, at least. Fragments of the dream of my father laced themselves in and out of the concrete and uncompromising ordinariness of the room and I had a sense of being watched, observed in a diffuse way from the ceiling, the walls, the curtain. I remembered the Special Dinner and the two places I'd booked, *Simon Donaghue and guest*, and it came into my mind that my father would have wanted me to go. A sentimental wash had been dribbled over everything.

I was at that stage of inebriation that thinks itself sober; more easy to achieve by a slow and steady intake of alcohol such as I had drunk during the long day. As I stared at the luminous hands of the alarm clock on the desk, which had been donated to me by my grandmother and had only, thanks to Sheila, just emerged from under the heap of clothing that had covered it for a week, the very heap, don't you know, that had hidden the F.W.Knotsworth, it came to me that I would keep the faith, that I would go to the dinner and celebrate two weeks of Ginny; and hope to God I wasn't attending the wake of my hopes.

I bathed in the bathroom on the first floor, which held the only bath I've ever come across with enough length to be really and truly comfortable, washing my hair impulsively on noticing that the previous user had left their shampoo on the basin. Hair still wet, and flicking drops of water like a dog just out the river, I walked to Oddbins to the irritating internalised nagging of my grandmother, *Do you want to catch pneumonia? Do you want to get meningitis?*, and bought a bottle, no, two bottles of Valpolicella all for me, all for me on my own-e-o. I chose Valpolicella because Ginny and I had drunk it during our last celebration. I was conjuring her, you see, dragging her back to me by any means possible, or rather by all means superstitious. I'd have thrown apple peel over my shoulder at midnight if I'd thought it would work. As it was I'd put on the T-shirt that she'd worn, as if I really could make her materialise by hokum, as if she'd step quietly from behind the shelves of German wines or attach herself to my arm as I rounded the corner of the lane. The feel of the cheap cotton was light but carried with it a clear picture of how differently it had hung on Ginny's body. On me, the T-shirt was just a covering; on Ginny it hid and revealed, swamped her half the time and then with the suddenness of the sun coming from behind a cloud showed me the distinct outline of, say, a shoulder-blade, or, marvellously, her breasts. When she wore it, a continuous random string of half-formed images flicked on and off in my head, erotic flashcards – like the promptings of subliminal advertising, only, instead of the split-second frame of the chilled bottle to get everybody spending in the over-heated cinema, there'd be a detailed milli-second of limbs, hers and mine, beautiful hers and mine closer than they had ever been in reality; and never a T-shirt in sight.

There was no picture in my mind of Ginny at home with her parents. I had no curiosity about Ginny anywhere else, only with me. She should have been with me. My body felt curiously abandoned without her, as if perpetual cold currents circulated over the skin, as if I were segregated from the rest of the world by a thin layer of vacuum.

With Special Dinners the idea was to book places on a large floor plan stuck on a certain notice-board a week before the event. This ensured that you sat near friends, or away from bores and undesirables, depending on how you looked at it. I'd not known this (it's amazing the plethora of detail you miss through the misanthropic avoidance of chitchat and company), so when I finally arrived I had to roam the already crowded hall homing in on the remaining unclaimed seats. Three forty-or-fifty-foot rows of tables, tables shuffled together so they gave the impression of barges or longboats, stretched away from the doorway along the hall, parallel but at right-angles to the High Table, where sat the substantial and animated figures of the fellows. I soon found out, by trying to claim the first place I came across, that typed name-cards had been propped against every wine glass. I knew how it would be, as I scanned the unfilled gaps. I knew that, sod's law, I'd have been put next to the English lot, beside whom there gaped just about the right-sized hole for *Simon Donaghue* and his *Guest* to fill. Better, I supposed, than rubbing shoulders with Dave Shannon. As it happened I was slap-bang next to Stephanie Zielinski and her pals, and diagonally opposite Shannon, Fitch and Purvis. I thought of it as malign fate, but of course it was no such thing. The Steward, who organised the seating for these dos, had probably picked me out as a recluse who needed a little encouragement. Very probably he'd made sure I was sitting with people he believed I liked: my friends. Ours was a tiny college. Of course my (lack of) progress was being viewed from odd corners with interest, concern, whatever, though it hardly occurred to me. I felt isolated. I believed I operated

62

in isolation. We were only just getting to know Maggie Thatcher in those days, and she wouldn't come up with her fatuous and sinister 'There is no such thing as society' for years; but there I already was, trying to live it. Now I can see the steward's manoeuvrings as a kindness. Then I would have been spooked to discover myself part of a community against my will.

The wearing of gowns was compulsory. I'd had to go back for mine, and then rummage for it at the bottom of the wardrobe. Since I'd picked it up second-hand, it had a shredded appearance at its best moments. Now it looked as if it had spent the weeks since Matriculation (i.e. Arriving Here) at the bottom of a wardrobe. Still: it had the kudos of being – yes, really – an Exhibitioner's gown, more fussy, more wings and pleats than a Commoner's gown. These titles, eh? *You're common as muck. Don't make an exhibition of yourself.* I'd been surprised to do so well in the Oxbridge exam. myself. What's more being an Exhibitioner meant extra cash for your trouble.

Shannon viewed the state of the thing with evident joy. Never had he commented, to me anyway, on the fact that I'd gained this accolade and I'd suspected all along that he was, simply, green-eyed. I'd take a bet that it was the one attribute of mine that he coveted. I swung my legs over the bench to take my double place: *Simon Donaghue* next to *Simon Donaghue: Guest*.

"Fairy-cake. What joy to see you. And what the hell's *that* you've got on your back?"

He did it cleverly: he wound me up with just enough implied good humour in his voice that anybody overhearing would think: *friends.* I could have let him work off his anger on me like a bull rubbing its itch off on a post, could have taken the required amount of punishment, expiated my meanness with the F.W.Knotsworth. Perhaps then he'd have let me off, ignored me even. I didn't.

"Fuck off, Shannon," I said, because I was drunk and because I wished I'd said it at the P.P.P. when he'd had his hands on Ginny, because I blamed him for her absence, because he was a public school boy, because he reduced me in my own eyes to his image of me, because his neck was too thick, his fingers too blunt, because I was sick at heart.

"No need to get narky, sweetheart," Shannon was gleeful, pleased to get a rise out of me.

"Just fuck off, Shannon." It's possible to say *fuck off* absentmindedly, casually, even affectionately. I said it with as much nastiness as could be injected at low volume. A ripple of embarrassment went round our immediate neighbours.

Shannon leaned his elbow on the table and eyed me speculatively, apparently unimpressed. Finally he decided to save me till later. With an obvious and very public swing of the shoulder he turned towards Gerry Purvis and started up a conversation I could half catch on the subject of the foibles of a string of individuals totally unknown to me.

To be truthful I was a little shaken, and could almost have been grateful for Stephanie Zielinski's interjection in the track of my tears, sorry, thoughts.

"Don't let him get to you," she said, twisting towards me so our conversation was near as dammit private, "He's just terribly immature."

Stephanie, mid-Atlantic and *sensible*, was one of the tiniest women I've ever come across. Whenever I saw her – on the other side of the street, tacking across the quad – she brought into my mind the principal boy of a pantomine, with 'his' teeny-pixie looks and flat chest and dainty feet and plucky, chirrupy good humour. Without fail, I could see her hopping across the stage, rallying the children in the audience, *Oh, yes, it is!* She was one of those girls who are eighteen going on thirty. Maybe I've caught up with her now, or maybe she's thirty-four going on fifty: bed by ten and pension provision all sorted out.

Grace, in Latin, for which we had to stand, interrupted her, but after we'd shuffled back into our previous positions, she went on, "It's probably not such a good idea, you know, to get on the wrong side of him."

I poured myself a glass of the Valpolicella, and gave her half my attention. She had rather dark eyes that lent themselves to earnestness and her hair was scraped severely off her face. I visualised spectral scissors snipping the hair-tie she used, so I could indulge my mild curiosity as to what she'd look like with hair wisping out from round her pert little face.

"Not that I'm saying he's *dangerous* or anything ridiculous like that, it's just that he's an extremely *forceful* character. You know he's becoming something of a voice in the J.C.R.? You know he's already something or other in the Union? He's in with the drama lot, the sports lot... I mean, he tends to influence a lot of people's opinions. And you tend not to be around a lot of the time..."

Soup was laid in front of us. Sheila, who obviously earnt extra money by filling in as a waitress, gave me mine with what my grandmother would have called a 'look'.

"Okay," went on Stephanie, resignedly, like the best pal on a soap-opera, "so you don't need my advice. But somebody needs to let you know what's going on."

I looked at her properly. The drunkenness wouldn't quite let me decide whether I should be worried by what she was saying. "What's going on?" I asked, refilling my glass, and then, recklessly, *Simon Donaghue: Guest*'s as well. I noticed Sheila had left a bowl of soup in Ginny's place, presumably assuming that my *Guest* was late.

"Your friend's been held up?" Stephanie offered, as her eyes followed the direction of mine.

"Looks like it."

"You should tell the staff, you know. If he doesn't turn up it's a waste of good food."

"Oh, she'll come," I said, just to be ornery. I started my soup: mulligatawny. That's what it had said on the menu in the Porter's Lodge.

Stephanie showed persistence that you might call admirable. "Have you noticed how dreadful Jules looks these days?" she asked. I suddenly got it. She liked *analysing* people. Of course. She *was* studying Eng. Lit.. She was seeing how long it took, she was seeing what it took to interest me. Please notice how honest I'm being with this account of myself. I could have fabricated any amount of old twaddle, put myself across as Mr. Charm. I ascribed to Stephanie, arch-Friendly Stephanie, the worst of motives, decided she was attempting to draw me out to furnish her with a few good anecdotes, a kind of scoop that she could broadcast on the bottom corridor's long-haired recluse. She wanted to write a meaty paragraph on me, as if I were Little Nell or Jude The Obscure. That being the case, I'd ham it up for her.

"He's such a *nice* person," she said, with a quick sidelong glance at Jules' *niceness*, "But, well, look at him – I mean, when you can without him.... Don't you just think he looks *grotty*? You know, we're worried about him." *We?* "Do you know he works himself silly?"

"Hum the first few bars and I'll see," I said quickly, and started on Ginny's soup as well.

"Sorry?" She thought she'd misheard.

"Why? What have you done?" And I laughed, because she was too earnest to understand the silliness, and looked uncertainly over her raised spoon.

"I kind of wondered if you ever saw him," she persevered, "to talk to."

"'The things which I have seen I now can see no more,'" I intoned with a graveyard face, which was Wordsworth and had been, for reasons obscure, a catchphrase in our Lower Sixth English 'A' Level group, one of those daft lines that act as a coded instruction to collapse into laughter. Friday afternoon behaviour.

"Obviously," she came out with drily, giving up on me. As the soup bowls were cleared she turned back to Caroline Funnell and Beverley McKenzie. I was a touch disappointed. The wine had given me a belief in my own wittiness and the desire to flaunt it. Furthermore I could feel Shannon on my forward flank sensing my exposure. I glanced towards his group, and quickly back again. Not only was I the object of his scrutiny, but there was its echo in Jules' bleak gaze. Stephanie Zielinski was right about Jules. He looked, as my grandmother would have put it, like The Wreck of the Hesperus. He looked screwed up and thrown away; but you wouldn't have noticed him at all without somebody pointing him out. The noise in Hall was terrific, that conversational waterfall middle tone that crowds always manage, broken by the sharper voices of colliding crockery and dropped forks. Everything was overlit; and all the extroverts were holding forth up and down the room. It was only when you made yourself notice that you wondered whether Jules had opened his mouth for anything but soup.

Shannon started a conversation at political rally volume for my benefit, though I couldn't at first work out from which angle he was stalking me, not till he broke cover.

"Purvis," he began, addressing him as an actor would his foil, making us all his audience, "You're the philosopher around here, aren't you?" Purvis had time only to register the comment with raised eyebrows before Davey-boy went on in an obviously phoney, cassock-and-shamrock Irish accent, "Well, we all know, don't we now, except for the Pope, bless him, that God," he raised his glass, "is dead?"

Stephanie Zielinski stiffened, then blinked several times. I wondered if she wore contact lenses.

Shannon dropped the accent. He wasn't *that* good at accents. "So we all accept that without God there can be no absolute morality?"

"Well-" said Purvis.

"So, actually, morality's relative, yah?"

I was young enough for all of this to be fresh, and against my will I found it dangerously interesting. I tried to fathom what relative morality might be, while my eye got stuck following the tip of the spoon Jules was trailing in circles over the tablecloth.

"So a definition of morality is reached by nothing more than mutual consent? Likewise any definition of criminality is just what we all fancy it should be? Obviously you all agree with me." The last was a joke, but one that he meant.

"Is that supposed to be a definition of your terms?" said Caroline Funnell, surprising everyone, "Define your terms."

"Can't be bothered," Shannon said, and various people laughed. "I haven't made my point yet."

"Get to the point, you arrogant bastard," said Purvis indulgently.

"Patience," said Shannon, "I'm getting there. Crime. Crime's just a word a group or, ah, a nation, agrees to give to certain actions. Otherwise every legal system across the globe would be identical. Say we're in our little tin-pot country and I'm your average little tin-pot general. If I say murder's allowable, I'm only wrong if the majority of you disagree with me."

"Rubbish-" began Stephanie, but it was only me who heard her.

"Morality-" began Beverley.

"Your argument's shooting off all over the place," said Caroline Funnell, "What-"

"Oh, Monstrous Regiment of Women: I'm being assailed!" And that was supposed to be a joke too, "Anyway; supposing you could get away with any crime, however gross or extreme. You could indulge whatever fantasy you wanted with ab-sol-ute-ly no comeback. Okay? You wouldn't have to face any punishment, you'd feel no guilt...."

"*You'd* feel no guilt anyway," said Purvis, "You're a bloody great big brick wall," and laughter followed.

It would have taken that insult times a hundred to have deterred Shannon. "What would your favourite crime be? What would be your own personal tailor-made crime?" he said. Then, "Right. What was the image that flashed into your mind when I asked you that? Honesty is obligatory. Purvis?"

"Armed robbery," he obliged.

"Yes, I can see that," said Shannon, "Shows that ambitious streak in you, eh, Purvis? And your bone-idleness, eh? You'd only want to put yourself out once. I expect you're thinking of a Great Train Robbery type haul, aren't you?"

"And why not?"

"Quite right," shrugged Shannon facetiously, "Fair enough. And what about you, uh, Beverley?"

"Fare-dodging," she quipped.

"I don't believe you," said Shannon quickly.

"Dog-snatching," she countered, "Like Cruella de Ville."

"Getting there, getting there. I can *almost* see you stuffing Dalmations in your pockets."

He was still scudding from bush to bush, camouflaging himself. "Caroline? *Ms* Funnell?" he said, moving on super-quickly before there was time to notice where he was hiding, "*Ms* College Feminist?" Some kind of in-joke this must have been, with me on the outside of it.

"Don't be boring, Shannon," snapped Caroline but with more tolerance than he deserved, then, "I'm not sure I want to play this particular little game."

"Caroline," said Shannon, all mock charm, "For me? Won't you do this thing for me?"

She laughed at him. "Oh, all right. You're a terrible man, Shannon. Well, what about...how about-" She looked at him provocatively. "Bigamy."

"You can't have bigamy. There's no such thing as a female bigamist."

"Why not? And how can you know?"

"Dictionary definition."

"When have you looked up the dictionary definition? Why would you be doing that? Why would you want to know that?"

"I was planning on it myself," he bantered, and she laughed; and he dodged to the next bit of cover.

"Fitch?" he said.

Fitch trailed his spoon round in those tight little circles, slowly covering the ground where his soup-bowl had sat. It was obvious he wasn't aware of any of us.

"Fitch?" he said, as everyone sobered up a shade; and he had the wit to move on rapidly, "Stephanie?"

"Yes?" she answered.

"Your perfect crime?"

"I think this is a ridiculous conversation," she said in convent tones, "And I don't intend to join in on it. I'm sure you'll all manage without my contribution."

Shannon contorted his face in a parody of horror, "Stephie," he said, "Steph-an-ie. We can't manage without you. What a kick in the teeth. That's Stephanie's crime: Grevious Bodily Harm."

Stephanie became as rattled as I ever saw her, but nevertheless gave a tight smile: *See? You can't make me angry. I can take a joke.* And, anyway, she was not Shannon's target and he wasn't that interested in her. The time had gone, the ground had been covered.

"Donaghue?" he said; a friendly enough 'Donaghue', as if we'd only had our little exchange earlier by mistake, as if I really shouldn't be churlish about it.

One to one was all right. One to two made me restless. Opening my mouth in groups was about do-able, but only to give simple-sentence replies, preferably just the one word or two. Giving opinions was not an option; holding the floor unrealisable, if not fantastic.

"I don't know," I said, surprised how clear the words sounded, considering the ranks of eyes watching them come out.

You could tell Shannon had expected this reply. "Let's make one up for Donaghue," he said immediately, and here he was, legging it across no-man's-land, nearly on top of me, double-barrelled zap-gun ready aimed, and "How about paedophilia?" Cries of 'tasteless!' "All right. Sodomy. Down the local lavatories-" Interruptions of 'This is a mealtime' and '*Shannon*'. "No. I've got it." he said. Nobody could fail to notice the shift, could they? No longer was he playing for laughs. He lounged along the table in my direction but I don't think for one minute that there was a relaxed muscle in his body. I couldn't take my eyes off him, as if by looking I might prevent the wrong words slipping out between his fleshy lips, catch them before anyone noticed. 'Plagiarist' I expected him to hiss; 'thief'. The questions that would follow, the answers he would be happy to give... The actual words he spoke threw me: "Donaghue's capable of the ultimate. Donaghue's the murderer among us. There's one in every crowd and it's always the least likely. The quiet one capable of anything and everything-"

"David," said Stephanie sharply, "David." He had to listen because she half stood and blocked his view of me. "What's yours?"

"What?" he said, surprised out of his usual long slow *sorry*?

"What would your crime be? Now it's only fair that you take your turn. And honesty is obligatory."

Dear Stephanie. I thought she'd saved me by chance. Now I see it was by design.

Shannon never treated the company to his answer. It was the roast pork which saved him, arriving under his nose at just the right moment, allowing him to smokescreen with the jokey comments he threw over his shoulder to the waiter on his side of the table.

"You won't be needing this dinner then, will you Simon?"

I twisted round to find Sheila planted behind me with two plates of meat.

"Have you been stood up?"

I rallied, "Oh, no, she's only gone out for a moment. You can leave her dinner for her." I met Sheila's dubious gaze. It was perfectly obvious she didn't believe me, but it's quite a leap from that to open

70

contradiction. She stood irresolutely, the steam from the pork slowly misting her glasses.

"She'll be back any second. She's just gone to the Ladies." I tried a glance at the entrance to the dining hall, an experimental bit of drama; but the long view shimmered gently, then swung. I tried an honest John look at Sheila. "She felt faint."

Sheila was in too much of a hurry to argue, since the servers had to shoot along like air-hostesses to get the food on all the tables still hot, but she pursed her lips when she said, "We'll have to hope she feels better soon, then, won't we?", and walloped the plates in front of me.

The English lot enjoyed this. I could tell from their attentive postures, the pause in the flow of chit-chat. And in a desperate way I was enjoying the performance. I topped up my glass, then very deliberately Ginny's glass. I wondered how I might elaborate on the act. Catching Caroline's eye, I gained a heavy satisfaction from her flicker of panic, the kind of flicker that you can feel in yourself as you pass the ranting stranger in the shopping precinct, the person singing too loudly on the railway platform. I ate my dinner. Then I ate the other dinner. I realised how hungry I must have been. I looked forward to my two puddings and my two *desserts* of fruit.

There's a definite moment, when you put down your wine glass and miss the spot you've been aiming at by an inch, clinking it and nearly breaking it against your plate, or when you reach for the salt and knock your neighbour's glass completely over, that you know you've drunk too much; and by the time you've reached it, you've drunk *far* too much. I reached this point as the syllabub arrived. I couldn't bring to mind who was sitting where unless they were in my direct line of vision. I was blithely unaware that I was dangling my hair in Stephanie's dessert until she pointed it out to me. I can't remember if I ever got my second portion of syllabub. I played games with the noise levels in the hall, covering up my ears then suddenly uncovering them. I finished off a glass in one swig only to realise that it had contained white wine: somebody else's.

With a shocking break in normal causality the hall fell quiet and stretched emptily around me. One moment I was laughing uproariously at a joke I'd overheard the Third Year on my left tell his friend, something about a rabbit, the next I was staring along a row of empty coffee cups, marvelling at the symmetry of their arrangement. The last two or three diners, up at the other end of the row of tables, discussed Economics energetically in splendid isolation; but my isolation was more splendid. Sheila tapped me on the shoulder. "Come on love, now, there's a good lad. Off with you. Come on now, it's 'Time Gentlemen Please'. Take yourself off. Tuck yourself up."

I walked oh-so-deliberately to the doors, congratulating myself on disguising my wretched state so cleverly, and rounded the jamb with only the slightest stumble. Familiar voices were talking:

"That *awful* boy. Next time *you* can sit next to him." Laughing.

"Where are all the real men?" Laughing.

"I couldn't bring myself to finish my syllabub." Laughing.

"Not after you'd got the three foot hair out of it, eh?"

"Complete pig."

"Vile."

"Why *are* attractive men always such bastards?"

All laughing, and all gone before I saw them, before I managed to negotiate the short corridor into the quad.

"It's damn chilly," I proclaimed to the night, and meandered to the steps of the sundial that sat centrally in the quadrangle. It was a biggish construction, a few hundred years old and, by daylight, a beautiful soft sandy colour, suffused with a pink tinge. Now it presented itself as a grey heap of stone, but welcoming nonetheless; a landmark, an anchor. I parked myself on its lowest step, and stretched myself out.

"I'm going to stay here until morning," I said.

It can't have been that the quad was deserted, not on a Friday night at nine or ten, but it seemed so to me. I lay and stared up at the sky, obligingly clear and star-flecked, and allowed my romantic impractical soul out of its kennel.

"I'm going to live under this sky. Nothing else is worth dying for. Beauty is truth. God that is so true."

And: "Why doesn't anything in life ever, ever, I mean EVER, live up to expectations?" The last word caused me trouble. I'd become conscious of my tongue. "Hmm?"

And after another while, time as slippery as oil, "Like that song. That song. God, who's it by?" I sang, "'Is that *all* there is?'" Then, "One of my mother's damn records...'Is *that* all there is? Is that all?'"

A few silver clouds drifting over: "I could just live in that sky. That's the Plough...that's the Hunter...that's somebody or other's belt.. major, minor..." I bullshitted, "Asterix...ha."

When I looked down again I was mildly surprised to see Jules stretched out beside me. "Hallo," I said, "Where did you come from? Did you come from the sky?"

"Hallo, Simon," he said, in the voice of a sad old man.

"I'm probably imagining you. My mind has conjured you up." I looked back up at the stars. "Being young is useless really, isn't it? You're too...*stupid* to appreciate the freedom. When you're old you appreciate the freedom but your body's just crumbling away." I rambled on gently, sliding down the spiral, inviting back the mood of the morning, and doubtless pre-empting that of the following morning. "It *is* a spiral, you know, Jules my friend. You just slide down it. Wheeeeeee. Down at the bottom we is." I giggled.

"I think of it," murmured Jules, more sober than I but not sober, "I think of it as a pit. Pitch black. The most terrible loneliness: such a terrible loneliness. Nothing else. Like being buried alive." His words seemed to strike instantly at the heart of what I was trying to say. He seemed to know exactly what I was talking about. But he wasn't making a joke of it.

"Jules," I said, "you're the only person who's ever understood me. And I really mean that." I didn't think even Ginny would have understood my spiral, which was almost a real place. You could feel the walls as you went down, trail your fingers over every tiny fissure, try and get a grip to slow yourself down, drag yourself back up, inch by inch: or sometimes the walls would be smooth as ice, free-fall, no-hand-hold smooth, and down you'd go, fast as swimmers on a chute. "Do you see what I'm saying?" I spun along into the dreadful confidentiality of drink, incapable of even pausing to wonder what had happened to the inscrutable silence I usually maintained when totally pissed, "We're the same, aren't we?"

It was too dark to see much of Jules. He took a swig from something.

"What have you got there? Give us some."

Without a word he handed me a small hip flask: cold metal top, leathery sides.

"This is nice," I said, "something you might take, you might take across the desert." I didn't recognise the liquid in it, except that I could tell it was alcohol. "If you were in the Foreign Legion, you know, or something..."

"It was my father's," he told me carefully.

"Where's the pit?" I asked, thinking: *it's at the centre, isn't it Jules? Buried under a million chambers and a thousand tunnels, right down there in the dark.*

"Where I am now," said Jules.

Then Jules was weeping and from out of nowhere Gerry Purvis was hauling him to his feet and talking to him as you might to a horse that needed coaxing into a box and leading him away across the flagstones of the quad and, despite the quantity I'd drunk, I was embarrassed.

"Weird," I told the sundial, "Wee-erd."

After some time – could have been ten minutes or an hour – I found myself on my feet halfway to the Porter's Lodge and the main gateway. Perhaps an hour had passed, since the quad now was plainly deserted, though I thought there were voices coming from somewhere hidden.

"You can all stop talking about me," I told the invisible voices, "I'm in an altered state." It seemed an incredibly clever objection to make. I congratulated myself on losing none of my acute judgement, on having the nous to stay coherent. I could hold my drink, couldn't I?

It was a cold night, though I was oblivious to the fact. Breath condensed in the air. In the complete stillness of the night the quadrangle took from its modest size an intimacy, became the hall of a cold and lonely castle. The effect was completed by the staircases that at regular intervals led off and up. They were doorless and

74

could easily be translated by the mind from entrances into warmth and company to exits out into a colder world yet. Cloud must have covered the stars I'd stared at earlier, the sky I'd thought I owned and when I looked up, as I did now, unsteadily, it was to see flat mud black, a daub ceiling. At that second a terrible bogey-man loneliness crawled out of the stones to get me. Images of desolation and the irretrievable: Superman orphaned as his home planet explodes, Ruth in tears amid the alien corn; Hiroshima; concentration camps and the loss soaking into the very bricks of them; the children of Vietnam running napalmed down the road. So unfashionable then as now to admit to any consciousness of spirituality. Mine was a negative spirituality, an awareness of not being connected to any saving grace, the spirituality of a lost boy, melodramatic with his loss.

And then there she was a few simple paces away turning out of the lodge, my saving grace, my golden girl, treading so silently down the couple of steps you doubted she'd ever add her weight to the human tons that had worn down the stones into foot-shaped grooves. Her face timid and challenging and excited, whiter than white beneath the wall light by the lodge and against the dark glasses she had on.

"Ginny." I breathed the word out in a puff of condensation and stepped forward into the final scene from an epic of early cinema – here he is, returning safe from the trenches to his English Rose with only a superficial arm wound (nothing disfiguring), though the hero in these is never out of his head – and swayed towards her.

"Simon Donaghue?" she queried, although she must have been able to see that it was me – the hair, of course. "Simon?"

"You came back," I said needlessly, staggered the last yards and clung on to her. For a few seconds I thought she was going to stay rigid in my arms – leap of fear – then she settled against me. "I'm totally pissed," I added, equally needlessly. "You came back. You *said* you'd come back." I felt I'd been let in out of the snow by the back door; grabbed the last rung of the ladder, caught the last 'copter out of Saigon, been pulled off the singing railway track, lost my ticket for the Titanic. "You came back."

Too soon for me, she disengaged herself and led me by the hand out past the Porter's Lodge, under the high arched porch and through the college gateway, helping me duck through the dwarf-sized door set into the twelve foot wooden gates. By contrast with the deliberation I had to use to balance, she darted left and right with strobe-like rapidity; or so it seemed. Her face and figure loomed close, then far; a constant disorientation.

"Why are you going so fast?" I asked, "What's the big hurry? I was enjoying that." I ground to a halt and leaned back against the timber of the gate, yanking her back towards me. She was wearing clothes I didn't recognise, clothes I wouldn't have imagined Ginny in: a fitted black dress that kept you conscious of her shape, tights, shoes with a heel, a big black hug-me coat. Dark glasses were *in*. A new Ginny; a new overwhelmingly desirable one. Her lips were more distinct in the night than they should have been. "You're wearing make-up," I said with a mild surprise the alcohol translated into frank amazement, "You look like Debbie Harry in those glasses."

"Well," she said, looking away from me, "I sort of came to a decision."

Another leap of fear. I held her hand more tightly, enclosed her arm with mine so she was drawn against me. I wanted to take her under a streetlight so I could scrutinise the expression on her face, but I wanted to keep her close and still more, so made do with the strange shadowy smile I could make out in the half-light thrown by the lamp fifty yards away. I had the stupid idea that if I held her tight so she couldn't move she'd throw away any ideas of leaving me.

"I decided I want you," she muttered into her collar.

"You've got me," I said with relief.

"No, I mean, I *want* you. Now."

"What?"

"I want you, you stupid man." She pulled away from me and to keep my balance I had to let her go. "Oh, *come on*," she said, almost aggressively, "Quickly."

"Why quickly?" Confusion was uppermost, but my body was responding with its own anarchic logic. Rousing itself to a colossal *yes*, focussing itself to a point of simple wanting. Far rather *quickly* than *not yet*. Rather without understanding this odd mood of Ginny's than *never*. I felt I'd slid through the oily wine into one of my own fantasies, the kind that in their intricate tantalisation had

76

accompanied me through the sixth form along school corridors, under bus shelters, had sat with me in the homey dullness of my bedroom, making the mundane reality of timetabled days and television nights worse by contrast but keeping hope alive. The stranger who throws herself at you; the stranger you throw yourself at. Why don't we do it in the road? Pull down the blinds on the moving railway carriage. It must be now. I want you. Now or never. O.K. then, if you insist: now.

"Let's go to my room," I managed.

She shook her head, came back and linked her arm impatiently in mine, and we wandered off down the lane, on and off the pavement in turns. The neighbouring college lay only a few yards along, larger and grander, Windsor Castle to our Gatehouse. Effortlessly we walked under its elegant arched gateway. This was its back gate but taller than the front gate of my own college. There were people about, but not a great many. We were trespassers, but our disguise was foolproof: we were undergraduates among undergraduates. We walked through stone cloisters, crannies, passageways, past noticeboards noting the achievements of the lives of strangers, into smaller then larger quadrangles until we knew we were lost. Crazy pinnacles perforated the skyline, ran above us like an undoing zip. We let ourselves get lost, then walked randomly until Ginny grabbed my arm and, suddenly laughing wildly, dragged me through the nearest stone archway out of the night air into the building itself and the silence of a wide flagged corridor intermittently lit by a neon strip that had just decided to give up the ghost. In the flickering light we stopped. I tried to kiss Ginny but she turned her face sideways.

"O.K., I dare you," she threw at me, breathlessly, "We choose alternate doors, and we have to go through them. No matter what." She buried her face in my arm, threw her arms round my neck; moved too quickly for me to enfold her, catch her; was off, sweeping me up the vast Cinderella stairway unrolling Disney-like before us, pulling us both through the massive set of double doors that were suddenly there for the opening. A dark hush, a moment's complete blindness, the smell of stewed meat, then after a second's adjustment we could see that we were in the Dining Hall of the college. Three times bigger than my college's hall. In the darkness tables and their benches only visible in the dull light from high windows, long lines of portraits: disapproving dignitaries. That was all I had time to see before:

"Your go," she half whispered, and dragged me back through the doors the way we'd come.

"Ginny," I remonstrated. I hated to be coerced, even when smashed. Yet I couldn't feel proper irritation, not when I knew that tonight something would happen, not when I was beside myself with a consciousness of her body here, there, a little in front, to the side, near to me, farther from me. Hadn't she promised? I *want* you.

"Your go," she insisted.

"All right." I said, "My go."

"Shhh."

"What do you mean, shh?"

"You're practically shouting."

"I'm not shouting."

"You'll get us thrown out, naughty boy."

"I wasn't shouting. See?"

"Not now, but you were."

"Anyway, you've got to go through the one *I* choose now." A devil seized me. I took her hand and half ran her back out into the quadrangle. "Simon," she cried, yet had no choice but to come with me, to *run* clicking on her heels over the flagstones then across the perfect lawn in an uncoordinated diagonal, leaving an uncoordinated diagonal trail of small round holes. "Up we go," I whooped, and dived through an open door and up a flight of stairs. "That didn't count. That door didn't count. It was already open. This one's mine." I threw open the first door we came to on the first floor. Common room. Fug of old smoke. Deep leather armchairs like something out of a Gentlemen's Club. Newspapers lying about. Green curtains. Alarmed-looking girl with square specs swinging round, arrested in the motion of pinning a notice to a green baize board. "Whoops. Sorry. Wrong door." Then ridiculous panic, intentionally blown out of proportion: "Quick, quick, get away. She'll get us thrown out."

Laughing like eleven year olds, we rolled clumsily along the corridor past white-washed door after white-washed door. This corridor was so narrow and low we could have been on board an ocean liner, with cabins off to either side, and actually my compromised co-ordination gave the passage the roll of a choppy sea. Sound was muffled into a backstage scuffle and mumble; could have been stewards running with champagne to men with middle partings and dinner jackets and women with drop-waist dresses and cigarettes in holders.

"Where *are* we?" demanded Ginny.

"How should I know?" I answered indignantly.

"Don't you know this place?"

"Never been here before in my life."

"Thought you might have *chums* here or something."

"Chums? In *this* college? Me?" I focussed in on the idea, as if from a great distance.

"All right; you might have had a, a *lecture* here or something."

"How many lectures have you seen me skip off to, Ginny-Ginny?" For some reason I couldn't let this drop, "I mean, this college, how on earth would I know it? You *know* I don't know it." I winked facetiously; or, at least, so I thought.

She changed the subject. "You've got to choose soon."

"All right. Down here." I plunged us down a precipitous stairway narrow as the corridor had been. "Along this way." Caramel coloured passageway, then dead end: locked door. "Back this way." Snorts of hilarity while I tripped over her. "Right. No, I've changed my mind: left." Corridor looking just like the last, only with noticeboards with pinned sheets that flapped out as we ran by. "All the bloody same these corridors. Up here." Wider flight of stairs. Nice bit of red carpet; brass runners; shiny chestnut banisters. *Money, money, money* sang the walls, like Abba. "Oh, God. I know, I know – this way." Ginny flushed and wide-eyed ducking and diving after me. Our hands tight-held, sweaty. Keeping quiet along a smart red-carpeted corridor, polished wooden doors with name-plates. Too fast to see names on them. Suppressing laughter; holding breath. "Right turn." Ditto. "Down." More wide polished stairs. Both nearly arse over tit on fourth stair. Loose runner? *Here?*

I swung to a halt outside an impressively tall door with a brass knob bulbous as a nose. "This is it!" I announced with a flourish,

79

"Knew where I was going all the time. Right. O.K. What's behind this door?"

Ginny, catching her breath, shrugged. "It's my go."

"Rubbish," I said, "What's behind this door? Go on."

She shrugged again.

"No idea? Well, I've got no idea, either."

"Let's not do this any more."

"Why? You started it. You haven't let me have my go yet," I demanded inaccurately. She wavered, so I tightened my hold on her hand and turned the brass knob. The door gave with a tell-tale, fairy-tale screech onto furry darkness. I stepped through, pulled against Ginny's resistance and got her through after me, then closed the door behind us. It closed with the same tortured screech, only in reverse, the note falling rather than rising.

We stood close together, listening to our laboured breathing, wondering where the hell we were. Images released by drink and excitement – anticipation – rushed up and rapidly dispersed: we were on the edge of a sheer drop, the ledge in a shaft; we were inches from all four walls in an impossibly small room; we were in the midnight ward of a military hospital, mutilations stretching away on either side in invisible ranks of metal-framed beds (wait for the groans- 'Nurse, Nurse, oh God help me!'); we were stranded in a desert, a moonscape, a vacuum. As our eyes accustomed themselves, involuntarily searching for what little light there was, I saw at my elbow a padded seat with a severe back and beyond it a row of the same, arranged along the sturdy decency of what was obviously High Table. Then there they were again, the row of small-paned windows set high in the wall, the row of robed dignitaries set for ever in oils and gilt frames – no, not dignitaries but Kings, Queens, Prime Ministers, the former benefactors, the latter, my god, *old boys* – the rows of plainer tables, impossibly elongated things, stretching away from High Table at right angles into shadows that could not be deciphered. At the end of the indecipherable dark I knew there would be a massive pair of double doors. I gave a short laugh of surprise.

"What?" whispered Ginny.

"Well, look. Can't you see? Look where we are. We're back in the bloody dining hall. Oh, Ginny, it's your shades." It all struck me as terribly funny, that my wild circuit had led us back to where we started, that we'd found the door reserved for the privileged few, those who deserved the elevation of High Table, that Ginny still had her dark glasses on and was blind as a bat. "Take them off," I said.

"I don't want to," she said, and there was something in her voice that told me *now* had finally come. Two weeks I had waited. She drew me to her, I drew her to me; who knows?

It was hardly the zipless fuck. Ginny was working in total darkness, I in dusk; mole and bat. Ginny might have been sober, I was nothing of the kind. I was hampered by the weight of expectation, by the accumulation of the images that I had been conjuring up and elaborating on for a fortnight as I lay pressed to Ginny night after night; by the embellishments my mind had worked on every inch of her skin. The zip on her dress snagged and I had to concentrate in an agony of impatience while I unsnagged it. She had trouble with the metal stud that fastened my trousers at the waist, and more trouble with the zip beneath, so taut was the material. The shoulder she revealed, the slice of midriff, thigh, shone its white in the dark like phosphorescence. We took off just enough. As it had happened in my fantasy of the first night I laid eyes on her, we took off just enough to make love.

I could pretend that we made love on the table. That would be a nice touch and a more iconoclastic image, a kind of a Peter Greenaway conflation of the appetites, Coq au vin, but *that* would have been quite beyond us. All we could manage was a slip-slide to the floor, and that is where, finally, she guided me inside herself and I shortly, sharply, painfully rapidly came.

Now I would ask myself, the excitement over, if she had come with me. *Then*, if pushed, you might even have got me to admit to the belief that a woman gained pleasure through her man's pleasure; and that's the fault of Biology lessons in the third form, *Lady Chatterley's Lover*, Paul Skinner, the boy I sat next to in General Studies in the fifth form, *Forum*, something I overheard in a pub, and my mother- for not giving me anything to go on. Misinformation, half information, veiled comments: don't be too hard on me. **Even God cannot change the past**- and if you're interested in ascription: look it up.

Anti-climax is probably just about the right word for what followed. "You made a lot of noise," said Ginny with what was probably sulkiness, but which I gave a more favourable interpretation.

"Did I?"

"Yes." With emphasis. "Thank God I'm on the pill." She shifted me off her and half sat up so she could lean against the table. Briskly she sorted herself out. It turned out she was quite capable of manipulating the difficult zip on her dress herself. I rolled on my back and shuddered with exhaustion, satiation. "We'd better get out of here," she added, and pushed my arm.

"Oh, let them find us." I had a picture forming in my head of the kitchen staff clustering round us in the morning, the dwarves discovering Snow White sleeping nude. I giggled, but weakly. "I don't care."

"Come on," she said sharply, "Get up."

"No," I crooned, "I'm going to stay here and just drift off...they'll find me...they'll find me just lying here... they'll think I've died... *if I should die, think only this of me...Calais.* I think it's 'Calais written on my heart'. No, it's not, Simon, it's something like 'written in my heart'."

"Get dressed," she hissed urgently.

"You're always in such a hurry. I know what it is. Listen, Ginny: 'When I am dead and opened, you shall find 'Calais' lying in my heart.'"

"Look: you do your trousers, I'll do these buttons. Think you can manage?" Sarcastic.

"Don't be mean to me, Ginny. Oh, all right, I'll do it. I'll bet *you* know who said that."

"What?"

"The bit about Calais. Awful place now. We went on a day trip."

"I don't know and I don't care. Up you get. Come on."

"Mary Tudor. Up I get."

I don't remember how we got out of the place or walking back to my room. By this time my body was finally sinking under the influence of alcohol and events. If Ginny hadn't got me to my feet when she did, I truly think I'd have lain under that table in a deep and delicious stupor until the morning. There's a vague memory I can retrieve of Ginny fumbling in my pockets for my door key and another of her body icy beside mine in my narrow bed, a third of waking in the light of early morning with a sense of a new space beside me, but that's about it.

The first true memory of the day comes still with a wince of self-disgust. I was still drunk in that room-swinging sort of way. The poisons in my body were having a field day, romping through the chambers of operation like vandals through a palace, casually wrecking. That's what I felt: wrecked. I wish I could say it was the last time I ever felt like that, that from that day I never abused my body again.

I wouldn't have woken then unless Ginny had opened the door rather noisily, juggling two carriers through it. I was slowly acclimatising to the real world and stupidly deciding that Ginny couldn't be stepping through the doorway because she was in bed with me. Wherever she was, she was as good as a long drink of cold water – which was precisely what I longed for at that second. I rolled over onto my side so I could half-smile a welcome and I thought, *she really did come back*. I must have resembled a resurrected corpse and the smile can have been nothing short of ghastly; still Ginny treated me to a smile back. It was not exactly a smile. Better than a smile, a bright suffusion of interest and connection. She looked round as if getting her bearings, let the carriers half drop to the floor, breathed out with the relief of somebody coming home. I've replayed it all so much I can see her now: step, step, smile, drop, sigh. With slow movements she pulled off her jacket and dropped it on the chair, straightened the waistband of her trousers, then, as if bringing something to mind, reached quickly into the top of one of the bags and pulled out a couple of envelopes. "I had a look in your pigeon-hole for you," she said, giving me a sympathetic grimace, "I hope these bear good tidings of great joy, but I've got a feeling this one doesn't." She walked over and dropped one of the envelopes on my stomach. "Something about that handwriting looks donnish. A decent pen; see? And that's a middle-aged hand, don't you think? And it's just got your name on it – there's no address." I brought to mind the note from Frank I'd stuffed into my pocket the day before – *the day before?* seemed a year ago – knew without a doubt this represented his next attempt to call me to account for my tepid attempts at written work, and groaned.

"The other one," she went on, dropping the second envelope rather flirtatiously close to my groin, "Fortunately looks like a real letter. From home, I would guess." I sighed, but let the letters lie where she'd left them. "Thanks," I mumbled in the thick voice of morning-after. She bent down and kissed me hello. I hoped she'd slide into bed beside me, clothes and all. I remembered the details of the night before as I kissed her back. When she straightened up I couldn't help breathing out and shaking my head in slow amazement as I remembered *all* the details. I laughed, awe-inspired by our stupidity and our audacity: our drunkenness. What in god's name would have happened if we'd been discovered under the High Table of one of the largest and richest and least forgiving of colleges with half our clothes off? With a sudden and horrible clarity I could imagine our desperate struggle to drag them back on as the door to the dais creaked open, warning us. At the very least we'd been trespassing. Would we have been dragged before the dean of the college undone and unbuttoned? Would the story have leaked out somehow, as these stories mysteriously always do? Would we have been the best joke of the year, of the University, openly discussed in all the Junior Common Rooms to the accompaniment of throaty guffaws and slapping of knees? Would we have been sent down? What would I have told my *mother*, for crying out loud?

"What?" said Ginny, smiling down at me, "What's funny?"

I shook my head, trying to dispel the nightmare images, more intensely relieved than words could express that we'd been allowed to get away with it. "You know," I said, meeting her eyes, conveying to her, I thought, exactly what was running through my poor old drink-muddled mind, expecting her to return a conspiratorial smile, to bite her lower lip with the same excruciating combination of delicious fear and childish smugness that was causing me to grin a little too widely. Instead she smiled indulgently as if she had no idea what I was suggesting and, disappointingly, moved across the room. "Do you mind if I open a window? It's a little *high* in here," she asked over her shoulder, "I know you like it nice and stuffy, but you can have too much of a good thing, don't you think?" It was her usual gently ironic tone, but I was puzzled. Didn't she want to talk about last night? Was she going to come the prude on me? I leaned up on my elbow and looked at her a little uneasily. The window latch was stiff and required force. Ginny knelt on the window seat and tutted over it. "Bloody thing," she grumbled. I watched her and loved her more than ever. I also wanted her, now that I knew I could have her. I would have been game there and then to repeat last night's performance, perhaps this time a little more slowly. I'd always assumed that our physical intimacy would deepen in a series of plateaux and ledges; we'd trek across the first and jump down the second every so often. Now it seemed that we'd jumped hand in hand but Ginny had scrambled back up pretty sharpish. Disappointment was primarily what I felt. Somebody had nicked my toy pistol and chucked it out the window, thrown my ice-cream on the sand, scribbled on my Beano Annual. Then questions began to form in my mind as I woke up and sat up. It occurred to me that Ginny's clothes were bothering me. Where was the black dress, the hug-me coat?

"Ginny," I asked cautiously, "Have you been back to your room?" Obviously she'd been back, since she'd changed her clothes. I asked not to hear the obvious answer but because I badly wanted her to volunteer an explanation. The relevance of her leaving me early in the morning to go back to her room, change, shop, whatever she'd been doing with herself was not clear to me, but it *felt* dangerous. When had she ever slipped off like that before? It was certainly not what I'd expected after the great consummation scene. I'd wanted to wake up with her beside me.

"No," she replied easily but with some surprise, turning back towards me, "I wanted to see you. I'll probably go round in a while. I'm expecting that essay back. I *did* stop and get us some breakfast, though." From one of the bags she retrieved croissants, a pat of butter, a carton of milk, a bunch of bananas and a bag of apples, all of which she dumped unceremoniously on the window seat. "Although midday is a bit late for breakfast. I've decided our diet's appalling. While I was," she paused, "While I was back with my family they forced decent food down me. I realised my body was craving for a piece of fruit." She stopped and folded her arms in a sudden defensive gesture, looking not at me but at the floor. "Simon," she stated with an unfamiliar seriousness, then paused, leaving me at a loss to know what was coming, "I know I told you I'd explain my family – my god, how could you *explain* my family! I mean I told you I'd explain when I got back; and I will. I'm not putting it off – well, not much; just let me have something to eat. I got up so early..." She trailed off, then quickly added, "I'll make tea."

I was too confused to speak immediately. I didn't give a toss about her family. I wanted to know why I couldn't work out what she was going on about. I followed her movements about the room as she filled the kettle and buttered croissants with my penknife – "Damn. I could have brought back a knife with me if I'd remembered. And some plates." – then balanced them on the empty plastic carrier bag.

"So you didn't go back to your room?" I asked eventually.

"No."

"What have you done with that black coat? That dress thing?"

"What black coat?"

"So you didn't go back to your room?"

"No!" she remonstrated, stopping what she was doing and staring at me in semi-amused exasperation, "I'll have you know I got the most ridiculously early train I could just to hurry back to you. I told you I'd try to stay the one night. *That* didn't go down particularly well in the ancestral home, I can tell you. Mum and Dad had assumed I'd stay 'till Sunday. And I was going to tell them all about you but they were just too wrapped up in all that other..." Her eyes shifted away. Her voice took on a bitter edge I'd never heard before, but which I was to become familiar with over the next weeks. "... All that other stuff. They haven't got a second to spare for anything that's happening to *me*. God, I'm sick of it. Anyway, anyway." She slowed herself down, her hands spreading out in a gesture that quite beautifully gave visual expression to the mental process. Normally I would have been fascinated.

"So you went to see your parents after all? You went yesterday?" I opted to suspend understanding of the bits of Ginny's speech that made no sense until some rational explanation presented itself. When Ginny had emerged from the Porter's Lodge to save me from myself the night before, I'd assumed – if I'd had the coherence to assume anything – that she'd aborted her trip home, spent the day working or sleeping or shopping or god knows what. Her trip home would have been a two train journey; one train into London, another out in a different direction. If she'd been home the day before, it followed that she'd have just about managed a couple of hours with her parents. "You met them for lunch somewhere? Yesterday. That's what you did, isn't it? Did you meet them in London for lunch?" I was quite pleased with this idea.

Ginny stood loosely, staring at me, the penknife dangling from her hand, her left hand actually: Ginny was left-handed. Finally she said, "Simon, what do you mean? What are you suggesting? Where do you think I was last night?"

It suddenly came to me that the only rational explanation to all this – there had to be one, I *knew* I'd think of one – was that Ginny was pretending to herself that we'd not made love the night before. Some peculiar process of denial, perhaps. I imagined young girls were prone to playing these sort of games. Then another brilliant idea occurred to me. "Ginny," I asked urgently, ignoring her question, "Are you a Catholic?" You see, even these grim scenes had their comedy. "Are you a Catholic, Ginny?" I really did say that. I was quite sure I'd hit on the answer: religious guilt. Maybe she'd have to go and confess. Maybe we'd have these fun and games every time we made love. Maybe she'd feel too guilty to make love with me ever again.

"Simon," said Ginny coolly, "I am not a Catholic."

"Oh God, of course you're not," I continued, before she could, "You couldn't be because you're on the pill."

"I'm not on the pill, Simon."

"You *told* me you were on the pill."

"Why would I? Why would I say that when I'm not? When did I say that?"

"Oh, my God. You're not on the pill?"

"I'm not on the pill. I've never been on the pill." She added tentatively, "I was *thinking* of going on the pill."

"Oh shit."

"What are you 'oh shitting' about?"

"You might be, ah," I moistened my lips, "pregnant."

Ginny laughed. I didn't. The laughter went on for too long. Sideways and shy, she finally came out with, "Look, Simon. You can't get pregnant doing what we've been doing. It isn't physiologically possible."

I was sobering up by the second, but it wasn't clarifying anything much. I rather wished I'd not finished off the whiskey. "Ginny," I began, firmly.

"Virginia," Ginny interrupted.

I willed her not to be flippant. There must have been something in my expression that convinced her I was genuinely worried. She put the penknife down on the desk, then came a step closer. She didn't, I noted, as she might have done this time last week, lay herself down beside me.

"You've been having one of your wacky dreams again," she cajoled, trying to lighten things up.

"No."

"I wasn't here to wake you up out of it."

"You could be pregnant," I said.

"How?" she asked, giving me a look that was so clear, so honest it took my breath away. As honest, she looked, as the Virgin Mary. She crossed her arms as if I were beginning to irritate her. Nothing in my past experience had prepared me for this conversation. I might have a few notions of the whimsical deceit of the average *femme fatale*, gleaned from films I'd seen on the t.v. on Saturday afternoons, but I'd never fitted Ginny into the *femme fatale* slot. Anyway, this was something else.

"If you sleep with someone, you've got at least a chance of it," I said with more sarcasm than I'd intended, avoiding that heavy word *pregnant* a third time out of a superstitious dread of breathing life

88

into it. A pregnant pause. Only think of it. *The most terrible thing that could ever happen.* Only think if – but then: don't.

"Simon, Simon," she said more gently, "Really, really I couldn't be. You have to, well, you have to make love. You know." Ginny could seldom bring herself to use what my grandmother called *language.*

"We did."

"We haven't, not completely, not yet."

"We have."

"We really haven't."

We stared at each other incredulously. Ginny breathed very deeply a couple of times and looked away. I couldn't bear to stay sitting any longer. On the other hand, I'd gained a sudden reservation: I didn't want her to see me naked, not at that moment. By way of compromise I hauled myself out of bed to sit on its edge, bringing the sheet with me. I tried again. "What about last night?"

"Well, it was pretty awful and I've said I'll tell you about it.."

"What do you mean you'll tell me about it? Is there something I did that I've forgotten?" Oh my God. Had I *done* something to Ginny, something that had got swallowed up and washed out of my memory by the wine? Was this an explanation, the very worst explanation, for her bizarre denial? Yet would she be standing before me, if that were the case, running her hands over her hair and looking at me with a perplexed stare? Perhaps *this* was how women behaved in that circumstance. How was I to know?

"Simon, I don't understand what *you've* got to do with last night. I've not even told-"

"I can't handle this," I muttered almost to myself. "Okay," I went on, trying at least to handle it, "Okay." I placed my hands palms down on my knees as if to straighten my thoughts. "Okay. Last night we made love, we went all the way. We fucked. Okay, I admit I was rat-arsed yet again, but I wasn't so pissed I can't remember that." I couldn't look at her while I said it. "And look, I thought you wanted to do it. I know I, ah, wanted to do it." I was positively light-headed with the effort of such unaccustomed self-expression. In front of me I could hear no sound from Ginny. I concentrated on feeling surprised at the hand-shaped sweat stains my palms had left on the sheet draped over my knees.

When I finally looked up it was to see her shell-shocked and immobile. If she had received news of the death of a parent she could hardly have looked worse. I did nothing at all, but became overly aware of the distant hum of the building's generator, of the carpeted silence of the corridor beyond the unlocked door, of the day waiting behind the green curtains. For the first time I wished I were out of the whole damn sticky business of *relationships*, that twee little word, out of the room in the damp and grey world beyond and away from Ginny.

Remember the climax of *Psycho*, where you find out that psycho Norman Bates' dear old mum is actually a petrified corpse? – and you don't find out gradually, either. She swings round in her dear old rocking-chair and *arghhhh* screams the voice inside your head as you recoil with a surprise that is complete and a disorientation that has you spinning back through the plot, rewriting. Well, there was Ginny standing in the middle of my carpet: she'd walked through the door a known quantity, then she'd turned herself inside out so I couldn't recognise her. Had her hair really been so badly cut the day before? Had she had those dark rings round her eyes? Had her freckles lain just so? Her nails been that long? I thought about androids and clones and Midwich Cuckoos.

After an indeterminate length of time Ginny very slowly sat down on the floor and started to cry, hiding her face. I was paralysed. I found myself staring miserably and impotently at the top of her head, my gaze circling endlessly round the whorls of her uneven hair cut. After another stretch of time I thought to reach over to the desk for the box of tissues, and hand them to her, or rather place them carefully by her knees, as if I were feeding something wild. After yet another long moment, she saw them. "Thanks," she said thickly. I was relieved that she obviously didn't hate me so much she couldn't thank me. I waited.

"All right," she said finally, after blowing her nose, wiping her eyes, adding those tissues to the heap already forming on the carpet like a strange fluffy mole-hill, "I'm going to tell you what I did last night. I'm going to tell you about my family. Will you just, please, listen? In the end you'll see, you'll understand. Please, Simon?"

"Uh, sure." I patted my knees, as if I were in a tutorial, agreeing to consider some controversial theory on Charles II's sexuality or the impact of the dissolution of the monasteries, "Sure."

"Yesterday I was at my parents' by lunchtime. You probably weren't out of bed by then." The last sentence was said with an attempt at humour that emerged as a ghastly desperation. I marvelled at the distortion of her face the tears had provided; the blotchiness and puffiness. Unhappiness made her ugly.

I am sorry, Virginia, so sorry.

"They'd made a fancy lunch which none of us could stomach. We spent the whole afternoon, the whole evening, talking and talking, endlessly repeating ourselves. The bloody dogs yapping every time somebody went by on the road..." She gave a breathless laugh then continued, "Since I've been here, I mean at university, they've been heavily editing how things have been at home. They wanted me to have a good time, you see? To settle in. At least they say that's why they didn't tell me what was going on. So every time I've rung it's been 'Oh, fine, fine.' I *knew* it was all too good to be true," she said with sudden anguish, "Sometimes I just hate the whole lot of them. I wish I could just-" Her hands couldn't stay still. "No, no, I don't really. I don't really." She pulled herself up short. "I went home because Dad finally wrote to tell me they needed me. Apparently Mum had been ringing and ringing the college, but never reaching me, of course." I expect that at this point her eyes sought mine; and if mine had not been restlessly fixing on first tissues, then floor, then sheet, I expect her eyes would have met mine, and there would have been a brief moment of understanding. Granted, I was still sitting there, wrapped in my sheet like Caesar, but in my mind I could see an image of myself, backing away from the odd lit scene of the boy and girl talking, backing away down a long corridor, the sound of my footsteps muffled by carpet, my speed increasing as I made my escape.

"My sister has run away." As Ginny spoke the image in my mind slid into that of an Alice in Wonderland child running scared down the same corridor, silk blue dress bow fluttering behind her. I roused myself to an appropriate response.

"God. When?"

"Well, this is the terrible thing. They didn't tell me. She's been gone at least two weeks."

"My God. And what do they..? I mean the police?" I imagined Alice abducted, molested, chucked in a canal, golden tresses floating on the surface among the flotsam. No wonder Ginny was behaving oddly.

"The police listened, I suppose. Took all the details down, as they do." She shrugged. "Theoretically she's entitled to go where she wants."

The picture of Alice shrivelled. "How old is your sister?" I asked.

"We're very close in age. She's nineteen."

"But how can a nineteen year old run away?" To me nineteen seemed entirely adult. Here was I coping (I thought) with independence at seventeen.

"Believe me, nineteen doesn't necessarily mean *all right to be on your own*."

I didn't like what I took to be Ginny's assumption of a superior understanding of the world and its ways: her smart-arse tone. There was a whiff of something rotten in the air. I had an ill-defined presentiment of where all this was leading.

"Have your parents heard from her?"

"No. Nothing at all."

There was a pause. "I'm getting dressed," I said quickly. Actually sitting still was giving me a feeling of oppression; and I suspect I wanted both to cover myself up and to put off the rest of the conversation, which had, I could see, by no means played itself out. I moved slowly around the room, gathering my crumpled clothing, stepping carefully around Ginny. Our breakfast croissants sat untouched on the plastic bag on the window seat. While I dressed we didn't talk. Once I'd finished dressing I reboiled the kettle and made tea in cups I had to track down and then wash out in the basin. At least we had fresh milk; something of a luxury. When I handed Ginny the tea I had to repeat her name twice before she noticed me or the tea. I sat myself in the armchair and found a cigarette to smoke. Ginny shuffled herself back against the bed and hugged her mug like some old soak with a bottle of cider.

It's so tempting to rewrite this part, especially this part. It would be so easy to let myself remember how I got up and went over to her and held her close so that she didn't feel alone. I can't bear the thought of her feeling so alone. But I didn't get up. I sat and smoked. Eventually she continued:

"My sister is different."

"Different?" I prompted, when she seemed to have dried up.

"She was never just plain average."

"Do you mean she's some kind of genius?"

"Oh no. If anything she sometimes comes across as almost, oh, subnormal. As a child you wouldn't have noticed anything odd. Sometimes she could be unpredictable. I remember a lot of notes home from school. I rather enjoyed it. I could always be little miss goody-goody, play myself off against her. I suppose that made things worse." Her attention wandered away from me, travelled back again. "I had to have *some* way of diverting a little attention my way, you know?" I nodded, more because I could see she expected it than because I was getting her drift. She went on, "It was when she hit adolescence that she sort of *exploded*."

"Are you trying to say your sister's, uh, insane?

"Not exactly that."

"Delinquent?"

Ginny half shook her head. "I really don't know. I don't know. She's erractic, horrifically selfish. I think she might be amoral, and good at hiding it."

"I don't understand," I said, hoping uselessly that somebody would wave a wand and make the whole sorry scene evaporate. *Take Two.* Girl walks in expressing delight at erotic experience of night before. Boy invites girl to repeat it. They repeat it. Love blossoms. Life continues in sane orderliness. "Didn't you take her to a doctor?"

"Oh, we did all of that." Ginny's quick dogmatism told me I'd stated the obvious. "Absolutely all of it. She went to two child psychiatrists. We had family therapy,"- this said with an emphasis I didn't understand- "For a while there was talk of autism. We were put in touch with an organisation for the families of autistic children; I remember the newsletters they used to send us. My sister used to read them from cover to cover locked in the bathroom so we wouldn't know, and then ham up the symptoms. It would have been hilarious if it hadn't all been so dreadful." She gave a dreadful laugh. "She was never quite clever enough. And it was always so obvious when she was acting a part. She was always acting parts. The school tried to encourage her through drama, you know; self-expression? My sister acting a full-blown autistic... Then that theory went out the window and they played with the idea of schizophrenia." I looked up at this and saw with a nervous fascination that Ginny was nearly rigid with anger.

"Your sister's schizophrenic?" I couldn't keep the horror out of my voice. I might not know what the word meant with any accuracy but I knew enough to be aghast at my sudden proximity to abnormality. I'd seen 'One Flew Over The Cuckoo's Nest'.

"She's not schizophrenic. Well, *I* don't think so."

"You don't?"

"Nooo."

"So?"

"So what's wrong with her?" She grimaced. "Perhaps she's just *different*. Perhaps some people just are different."

"Mad?"

"Not mad. Maybe a bit mad."

"Evil?"

"No. Although sometimes the things she does have that effect. She's very cunning. Canny, you know?"

I gave up. "I don't think I understand," I said rather coldly, stubbing out my cigarette.

With a sudden burst of energy Ginny was up and pacing, speaking loudly, wildly, unevenly, "She just ruins everything. It's always been like this. Whatever I do, whatever I want, she's there too, right on my heels. I thought I'd got away. I really thought I'd managed to get away. Everything I value she takes. Do you know as soon as I'd moved up here she took over my bedroom? All my things? And my parents *let* her. Do you know she's been telling anyone she comes across that she's off to university to do English?" She was almost shouting. "I think I lothe her. Oh, I don't really. She's a sick child. A sick little girl. But this is too much. This is the thing I can't forgive."

Just as suddenly all the animation drained from her and she leaned against the wardrobe, face hidden in her arms, rocking gently.

You see how terrible this is, that I can't go back and hold her?

Histrionics had always scared me. My family – my mother, my grandmother, me – had bickered and griped, but we'd gone in for long silences rather than door-slamming in the event of any real upset. This outburst finished me off. "Right," I said shakily, "I want to know exactly what you're talking about."

"She's always wanted to be me," muttered Ginny into her arms.

"What?" I said sharply, fighting not to believe the madness of what she was about to suggest.

"She's always wanted to be me," she repeated more distinctly.

"How could she do that?"

"She used to ring up my friends and pretend to be me. It didn't fool them of course but it did drive them away. Nobody wants to be friends with somebody who's got a mad sister."

"You said she wasn't mad," I said.

She'd slowed down, exhausted. I had to concentrate to catch all the words. "When I cut my hair – it used to be right down to my waist, you know – so did she. She used to, oh, she used to copy all my catch phrases. I used to look up when I was eating and she'd be staring at me, trying to eat left handed and she's *not* left handed, she's right handed. I used to think she was doing it to rile me. I took it seriously, but not that seriously. I used to change myself as often as I could, to keep ahead. It became a bit of a game, really; we all used to think she was messing about, but it looks like it's more serious than that. Maybe she hates my guts. Maybe she wants me to crumble. Maybe she wants me to be as weird as she is. If she goes on like this maybe I will be."

"How is it *going on*?"

"Simon, you must know what I'm trying to say by now."

"No, I don't."

"Don't make me say it."

"I don't understand."

After a while she turned round, wiping her cheeks with the cuffs of her jumper in a gesture that was pure playground. Her face was bleak but she seemed more composed. "She's here somewhere,

Simon. It's obvious really. Of course she would have followed me. She knew exactly where to find me. Why shouldn't she? She's got to you, Simon. She got to you before I could." She began to rock gently back and forth. Then she added fiercely, "And I wanted you. You're *mine*."

I stood up. "For god's sake let's get out of this sodding room. Come on." I grabbed my jacket and made for the door. After a second's surprise, she followed.

In dreams I return to this conversation. I am making love with Ginny in the innermost chamber of a vast and complicated mansion. The room drips with rococo decoration, maybe, or is stuffed with the precious artefacts a later age collected: mummified cats and golden death-masks, narwhal tusks and Chinese boxes. The sanctity of the place comes with the profanity of the act. The room has been found only by chance, we may not be able to find it again in the layers of rooms and corridors of the mansion, and our privacy is only guaranteed for a short while. Gather ye rosebuds; seize the day: for the fabric of the chamber and all its contents are a compression of all things ancient, valued and loved. Usually Ginny and I have found each other only after a long rigmarole; telephone calls and secret messages and rambling searches. It's a question of *now* and *finally* and *at last*. It's terrifically and almost excruciatingly exciting, laced with wet-dream tension. Ginny and I in a four poster à la Trusthouse Forte Short Country Break or in my narrow student bed or in a sleeping-bag or on a sofa: all of these. I am happy with a poignant childlike happiness and then: before the moment of consummation everything spins off course; the record jumps, the wine's off, the milk's sour, the picnic's a washout, the holiday's cancelled, the child is stillborn. Ginny smiles to reveal a mouthful of rotten teeth, or I notice scabs on her body and realise she's giving me some gross sexual disease, or I look at her face and don't recognise her, or I look at her face and recognise its features but see that the eyes are completely mad. A dream of things spoilt, of an irretrievable past.

Christchurch meadows were populated, but sparsely, with track-suited figures distantly jogging to the river. On one of the playing fields a game of rugby was in progress, but all that reached us was an intermittent prehistoric roar. We marched side by side as if determined not to miss a train, sticking to the broad walk, which was very broad, and thereby giving ourselves plenty of room to sidestep the rest of humanity; the late flocks of tourists with matching umbrellas, the joggers. The wide gravelled path ran from road at one end to river at the other and for some part of its length skirted a gaunt Victorian block belonging to Christchurch itself. Ginny had paced in my room. Now we writ the movement large. When we reached the end of the broad walk, the length of which couldn't have been more than a quarter of a mile, we'd turn round and march back over our steps again. I remember it was spitting and that the light was half-hearted. It was one of those Autumn afternoons when the light begins to wane before it's waxed properly. A sodden landscape. A time of day that I'd always thought of as purgatory; in between whatever work I'd managed to achieve in the morning and the more solid and alcohol soaked evening.

For two lengths of the path we were silent. Ginny stared grimly ahead, while my mind practically ached with the effort of its machinations. When I'd worked out my strategy, I spoke.

"How would your sister have recognised me?"

"I've been thinking about that," Ginny answered. We half looked at each other. Ginny reached out and took my arm. Despite the day's lunatic turn, my body responded to the touch. See? After all that she was still my honey pie. I tucked her arm under mine. "And I'm not sure. As I said, she's canny." She shrugged. "She could have been here for two weeks. I bet she came straight here as soon as she left home. It's not the first time she's run off; though the times she's disappeared before it's only ever been for a night or two. She's probably using her building society account. I dare say she's found herself a cosy little room somewhere." Sharp edge creeping in. "She doesn't lack a sense of self-preservation."

"You let her have money?"

Ginny shrugged again. "She's not an out and out lunatic, Simon. Mum and Dad are still hoping against all the odds that she'll come round. 'Come round': that's how they always talk about it, you know, as if one day she'll wake up and it'll all be all right. *She'll be coming*

97

round the mountain when she comes... But then, wouldn't *you* hope?"
I was supposed to give a grunt of assent here, but in all honesty I
couldn't. I couldn't acclimatise to what was actually happening, the
conversation I was apparently having, never mind empathise with
the angst of a middle aged couple whose bare existence I couldn't
really grasp. So on she went, unstoppable, "They've tried to give her
the occasional bit of independence, fooling themselves that she'll able
to hold down a job 'once she's sorted herself out'. *Sorted herself out.*"
Snort. "Trying hard not to admit that it's difficult to think of her
living away from home without making a mess of things or getting
into trouble. Though she's never done anything, oh, I don't know,
illegal. Most of the time she's just a little strange. You can't quite
put your finger on it. She's never done anything like *this* before."
She looked away and an image flashed through my mind of the
luminous whiteness of breasts against black material, of the smell of
polish from the varnished boards of the floor and the underview of
a great oak dining-table, of the hidden stares of a hundred prurient
oil-paint eyes and of dim light filtering through stained glass in
heraldic designs. Ginny continued edgily, "I expect she followed
us. Horrible idea, isn't it? Being watched by someone who could, I
mean- maybe who wishes you harm, or else maybe-" Another shrug,
a restless grimace. "Somebody who could run up and hug you or
push you under a bus. Do you understand? " I raised my eyebrows
non-committally and this hyper-earnest version of Ginny deflated,
slowed down to a more recognisable pace. "Finding *my* room would
have been easy enough. I've written home; she'd only need to note
the address. It probably puzzled her that I was never *in* my room. I
mean- my god." She stopped dead for a minute, pulling me to a halt
with her. Then we started walking again more slowly. A couple out
for a Saturday afternoon stroll: how nice. "I mentioned in one of my
letters – I wrote a grand total of two, you know – that I'd made a
friend in your college. 'Friend'. In which case, all she had to do was
hover around until we emerged from your room. I can't bear to think
I made it so easy for her."

"She'd have had a long wait."

Ginny shrugged, "I'm only guessing."

I waited a space before I asked the next question, as if I were absorbing what she'd told me. "But you're not twins?" I asked.

"No, I told you, she's older." She made a *moue* with her lips to express perplexity at my obtuseness, while I watched them with a desire that had grown cautious. "You know, one of the psychiatrists put that forward as a theory, an explanation for her, oh, problems. That she'd only been a year or so when I was born. I suppose it might fit. By that time, though, they were really clutching at straws."

"So you're not identical in appearance?"

Ginny's arm stiffened against me, smelling out the challenge. She spoke carefully, "We're similar in appearance, not identical. But Madeleine always cultivated the similarity, you see? The hair. The clothes she tended to screw up on. Somehow she never can get them right. God, she's got terrible dress sense." She shook her head slowly, almost, well, *affectionately.*

"Okay," I said in as neutral a tone as I could manage, "Let me put it like this." We walked fifty yards before I continued, "You're with me almost every minute of the day for a fortnight. You go away for one night. I mistake somebody else for you and I-"

"Simon," Ginny said in distress, "I don't think I can bear to hear about that bit."

"Okay," I said. I'd had no intention of going into details anyway. "But look, how could I be that close to another girl and think it was you? How could I?"

"I expect you were very drunk," said Ginny bleakly, "And I expect she wore those stupid sunglasses she's so proud of."

It seemed to me that I'd said all I was going to say. My word quota for the day, the week, had been used up. We walked quickly on. The drizzle had seeped into our clothing and lay on our hair. I looked at Ginny and felt a surge of pure love and anger; mixed, though I hardly recognised it then, like sugar in boiling water, the sugar dissolving slowly in the water until the two are inseparable. The rain had darkened the red of her hair, yet her skin showed extraordinarily white in the failing light. She looked truly wretched. Half way through our transit and near the path leading out of the meadows she stopped.

"I think that we should not talk about this again. We can't change what happened. I don't think I ever want to know exactly what you did with her. Maybe she'll just leave us alone now. Maybe she'll just go home. Maybe that's what she wanted. She couldn't have taken much more from me, could she?" She turned her face fractionally from me with a gesture so fine-tuned in its despair that I reflected that, whatever the incomprehensible guilt that was making Ginny act out this ridiculous scene, she had the skill of a Liz Taylor. The eyes just moist enough that you know tears could fall but are being withheld, the shoulders rigid, the chin a tad too high. The face an angelic frozen oval. "Why don't we just.. I know we can't pretend it didn't happen, but couldn't we just not talk about it?"

"Fine," I agreed gravely, nodding, "Fine by me."

Automatically we turned together down the narrow pathway which led to the iron gateway out of the meadows. The next time I walked along it, and every time, I'd bring to mind the image of my fallen angel, Ginny with halo askew.

I didn't believe a single word of Ginny's story. How could I entertain for a second the rescripting of the last night's events I'd have to undertake if I did? Could she really expect me to shrug off with a rueful grimace the image of the monster this would make me? Could she *really* think I'd tolerate the first suggestion of the idea that my first fully-fledged sexual experience had been with a nobody I'd dragged off the street? There was something a little too close to the image of the soldier-rapist in it; you know, anybody's sister will do – though I hardly allowed my imagination to glance at *that* one. Then there was the taint of madness: I refused point blank to agree to a version of events where I'd come closer than close to madness, where I'd come, and come adrift, right in the heart of darkness.

It was a sheet of lined A4 that could have come from the pad of any one of the individuals in the college and it had been stuck firmly to the outside of my door with a largish blob of blu-tack. Though my room was at the end of the corridor and only my nearest neighbours would have had cause to pass near enough for it to catch their eye, the distinct black felt tip and block capitals of the message could easily have drawn the curious from further afield.

The message was large and central on the sheet of A4:

Neither a borrower nor a lender be
For loan oft loses both itself and friend
And borrowing dulls the edge of husbandry.

That was all. It was, of course, unsigned.

There's always something disproportionately nasty about the anonymous letter. It leaves so much to the imagination. Standing in front of this little piece of spite (or this echo of conscience, whichever you like) with the rain evaporating gently from my clothing and, I was sure, Ginny's puzzled eyes on me, I had a strong and sudden sense that *this wasn't fair.* My imagination had already been overloaded that afternoon. It wasn't *fair.* Remember I was still perilously close to childhood, to the stamped foot and the outraged wail. If Ginny had not been there I would probably have gratified myself by following the impulse to give the door the kick it deserved.

"What do you reckon it's doing on your door?" Ginny asked, with restraint and, I imagined, a knowing irony.

I shrugged as I pulled it off the door and folded it. "Good bit of blu-tack," I said, as I pulled that off too, to keep.

All the rest of that long day I simmered, my mind open as a can of worms and my mouth clamped firmly shut to make sure nothing escaped. To Ginny's occasional comments and questions all I could manage was a yes or no or perhaps. In truth Ginny was quiet enough herself. She'd regained her usual rather brisk air and I daresay I missed the effort in her control and calm. For myself, I felt steely with resolve. I never doubted that Dave Shannon had been responsible for the quotation on my door – Fitch was far too well-mannered to have come up with it – and I stoked myself up for revenge as if I'd been Hamlet himself, thrashing around in impotent rage as he plots the death of his father's assassin. Ha ha! I'll get you! Rant and rave. Do nothing. Somehow I'd track Shannon down, *prove* he'd written that bit of bitchery, show him up, knock him down. Most of all I wanted to land one on him.

I see now, as I saw then, after a year or two, that Dave Shannon was the last person to do such a thing, to flick through his 'Complete

Works' to spot a pertinent quote, to fiddle around disguising his handwriting by thickening its peculiarities with a felt tip and capitals, to sneak around with a blob of blu-tack in his pocket. There was nothing about Shannon that was or wanted to be anonymous. If he'd wanted to humiliate me about the Knotsworth I'd borrowed from Jules Fitch he'd have waited 'till he ran into me fishing my mail out of my pigeon-hole and he'd have brayed some comment loud enough to be picked up on the other side of the quad. Yet from my perspective it *had* to be Shannon, because Shannon was the one who knew Fitch well enough to have known about the Knotsworth. I lived a few yards from a hundred other people but in near isolation. I never gossiped; I never had anything to gossip about. I couldn't lock into all the circuits of communication that flowed all the time all around me because I had only the dimmest notion of their existence. Sure enough I observed the endless groups of friends in pubs spinning conversations out of thin air together, but I imagined they were playing an elaborate game at which they'd become expert, that the competitive tone I could hear revealed the whole ritual to be no more than a sparring match. That they might be making links of any real importance did not occur to me. If I had known that Shannon and Fitch and Purvis and Beverley McKenzie and Caroline Funnell and Stephanie Zielinski and a dozen others had chewed me over, that every time I appeared they added another episode to the soap opera they'd written round me, if I'd realised that Shannon's defence of Fitch against my meanness would have entailed broadcasting the episode in the college bar or over the dinner table, if I'd appreciated that I could not make others ignore me merely by ignoring them and that, if anything, such a course of action served to make me more visible, if I had understood all these things, then I would have been truly appalled.

* * *

We're spreading ourselves over our small share of the lawn that slopes away from the Royal Pavilion, backsides on the grass so we don't have to pay for deck-chairs. The Pavilion sits there with its frivolous curves and its Taj Mahal wink while the seagulls wheel overhead screaming in competition with the ambulance just now shooting past on the one-way system beyond the gardens. Drowned out by *that* is the busker twenty yards away on the path wooing the tourists with his saxophone and his cassette-player backing-track. We've eaten the rice-crispie cakes from the cafe-kiosk and now Alex is trying to eavesdrop on a neighbouring conversation, Henry is trying to effect an escape and I'm trying to stop him. Then it starts chucking it down.

"Oh, sod it," I cry and leap to my feet.

"Language," cries Alex back.

"Sod it. It's supposed to be July, for God's sake. We're supposed to sit here and enjoy it." I start scrabbling for jackets, back-packs, feeder-cup, carrier bags, Henry.

"Shall I put my hands over Henry's ears?"

"No, but you could help me get the bloody stuff together. Look-grab his hand and don't let it go."

"But we can't *go*, Dad, because we're going to meet Mum here."

"Head for that tree."

"But-"

"Look. I'm your father and you're supposed to give me unquestioning obedience at all times. Now stick that on your back."

We sprint over the lawn and Henry thinks it's a hoot because I've got him loosely on my hip and he gets thrown up and down in loose rhythm. It's like the four minute warning: the entire lawn is covered with people shrieking and snatching belongings and running for cover. Not that the tree we've chosen gives us much cover. We stand with a dozen others watching the rain find its way through the leaves and onto our heads. The trees line the edges of the gardens.

Alex says, "The people under that tree over there aren't getting wet."

"Perhaps it'll fall on them," I say.

We stand there a time longer and I shift Henry around on my hip but don't want to put him down in the mushy grass with his newish canvas shoes on and, anyway, if I do he'll be off. He blows raspberries because he's just learnt the trick and a young woman behind us makes a few isn't-he-adorable noises, but I fail to play along because the odd dribble of baby spit is reaching my jacket

– not that it makes a huge difference as I'm stationed under a branch that appears to be acting as the main conduit for the rain. It's that generous kind of summer rain that falls in soft dessert-spoonfuls, the kind that turns a pavement from light to dark grey in thirty seconds. Suddenly Alex says, "What *is* a poison pen letter?"

"Why are you asking me that *now*?" I grouch; but can't avoid – never can avoid – the kick-start, knee-jerk memory. There it is in front of me, the honey-coloured wood of the door of my room, the sheet of A4 with pale blue lines and black felt-tip, the loathing coming out of every neatly written word. I never did find out whose loathing. But just think: if I really could be there before the honey-coloured door, all I'd have to do is move my hand twelve inches to my right and I'd touch the rain-damp hand of a Ginny I'd not yet betrayed.

* * *

That night there was nothing for it but to drink. Probably we went out, but the cell storing that particular piece of information in my brain was obviously one of those the alcohol subsequently pickled. In the early hours we crawled into my bed and adopted our usual position. To have done anything less, to have suggested time off, a night alone, would have been to admit that our honeymoon was over. To have done more, to have made love would have been unthinkable for me, and unthought of for her. Even my body agreed with me on that one: no rocket ready for launch, powering up on the pad; more a damp squib, attempting a little fizz now and then in the grass. I got my first taste of sleeping on an argument, though it had not exactly been an argument, and the proximity forced on us by that narrow single bed just served to underline the fact. Not that I slept a great deal.

I will make an admission. Until the night before I had been a virgin. Only just. At seventeen I had real trouble admitting that, and I see even now, following the old reflex, I've deferred mention. God knows why. Now seventeen seems laughably young. We can't *all* be like Mick Jagger: I read in a Sunday Supplement that *he* claims to have lost his at the age of thirteen.

The next day was Sunday, usually our best day, the day we might legitimately have done no work. Effectively *I'd* stopped working altogether anyway. We walked. *Roamed* might be a more accurate description. We simply took directions randomly, letting the routes take us. We went and looked at the deer in Magdalen deer park, walked through the town – damp and dead – and ended up, as it started to rain, in the Pitt Rivers museum. We couldn't be apart and we chafed against each other: *the* topic we had agreed not to discuss settled between us like a malevolent chaperone. Walking at least meant we could have the comfort of a held hand without the need to look in each other's faces. And we had tense little exchanges – hardly conversations – that the week before would have been impossible. In Magdalen deer park, leaning against the link fence in parallel and pretending an intent interest in a small herd a hundred yards from us:

"How come I've never seen your room?" Simon asks.

"You never showed the slightest bit of interest in my room."

"I'm just saying it's strange I've never been there."

"You can go any time. But you'll find it disappointing."

"Why don't you like it?"

"It's all right. It's cold. Nice neighbours."

"Why have we never spent the night there?"

"You never wanted to."

"I wouldn't have minded..."

"We'd never have got away with it, anyway. The atmosphere's quite different from your college."

"How is it different?"

"It's a girls' boarding school in disguise."

"When did you last go back to your room?"

"Thursday."

"*Did* you?"

"Well, yes. I go back every couple of days."

"*Do* you?"

"Of course. I ruffle the bedclothes and move things around on my desk. Sometimes I ask the girl in the room next to mine to go in and mess things up, lend her my key."

"Really?"

"Really. I don't want the scout to shop me. I expect she knows, really, but I'm counting on her turning a blind eye. I don't want to lose the room."

"You never told me any of this."

"You never asked me." Finis.

Or trekking along by the river up to Folly Bridge:

Clearing of throat. "How old were you, Simon, when your father died?"

"Nine."

Pause. "Do you mind talking about it?"

"I don't mind." Lie.

"What was it? I mean, how did he...?"

"Cancer of the oesophagus."

Pause. "How old was he?"

"Only forty odd. But he smoked two packets a day."

"And yet you smoke."

"Not two packets a day."

End.

Or in the Pitt Rivers Museum, leaning together over a table-case full of amulets and charms – a cloth heart pierced with pins; the forefeet of a mole; the tiny effigy of a man and woman clutching each other in coital embrace; hair and nail-parings:

"I should have rung home. Why didn't I ring yesterday? Mum and Dad have got to know."

A twitch of irritation from me, hidden, I hope.

"And the police should know. Perhaps now they'll take the whole thing a bit more seriously."

Simon remains silent. What to say? There is nothing for him to say.

"I'll ring as soon as we get back. Or there's that phone box along St Giles."

Simon reads label under baked clay figurine, trying to block present voices with those from the past: *figure of man and woman buried in the ground as a fertility charm, La Paz, Bolivia, 1919.*

"What really gets to me is that she always wins. Here she is, the centre of attention yet again. The police sticking her on the missing persons list. Mum and Dad *sick* with worry. Us..."

106

Simon marvelling at Virginia's dissimulation, and feeling way out of his depth: *pair of forefeet of mole, cut from animal while alive (which is then allowed to go away).*

"She just spoils everything."

Simon finally speaks. "You didn't tell me you had a sister, before yesterday."

"You never asked." End.

It was my third visit to the museum. I loved it. From the outside it looked like a mainline station: big and bold, Victorian red. Inside the natural history section, fantastic wrought-iron palm-leaves supported the ceiling and stone-carved flora and fauna encrusted the tops of pillars; but it was the further chamber, a tall cube of a room stuffed with ethnographic artefacts, that called to me. This Victorian collection seemed intact, and so did the Victorian presentation. That was the best part, the gloomy lighting and the lack of space, the clutter. Such a sense of solidity, of constipated certainty. Great oblong cases like tropical fish tanks.

I wandered off and managed to forget for at least five minutes the horrible sticky human mess into which I seemed to have been sucked, by staring resolutely at a wooden handloom. Five minutes I managed, lulling myself with the wheels and the strings of weights, wondering if it had been moved by foot peddles, reminded of my air-fix models; and then I caught an alarming glimpse of a sharp eye through the loom's intricate angles; the sharp eye and the quarter of a face I recognised. *Oh shit.* Stephanie Zielinski. Damn Friendlies seemed to get everywhere; common as woodlice. She'd seen me, of course. I even had the uncomfortable feeling she'd been on the opposite side of the case for some while.

"Keeping out of the rain?" she said, sliding round to join me for the seemingly inevitable chat, "I was just over the road in Keble visiting with an old friend. I can't *believe* it can be raining again. This place has the weirdest climate. And of course I came out without my umbrella." Of course Stephanie would have an umbrella, probably one of those retracting ones my mum thought state of the art. It was only common sense. "Just as well they put this museum here. Pretty handy, hey? Saved *me* getting soaked, anyway."

"Yep," I said.

"What an amazing collection, don't you think? The lighting's a-bom-min-nable, though." Ghastly bonhomie.

"Mm."

"Neon strips is what you need."

"Neon strips?" In here? What a *philistine* suggestion.

"Absolutely. Then you'd actually be able to see what you're looking at."

"If the light were any stronger," I said, I hoped crushingly (shut up and go away), "all the delicate colours of the costumes would fade."

"Good point," Stephanie agreed, quite unperturbed, and with such an unexpected element of *don't mess with me* that I looked at her. Her slight, sharp little face tilted up at me from at least a foot below. Raindrops had settled all over the hair wisping away from it. She looked like a vengeful pixie who'd brushed with a cobweb. She went on purposefully, "Actually I'm glad I ran into you. There was something I wanted to say to you."

"Really?" I said flatly.

"I tried the other night, but you weren't exactly in a fit state to listen."

I waited.

"I reckon," she went on matter-of-factly, "that you've got a kind of duty towards Jules."

"A *duty*?" Who the hell did she think she was?

"Yes. I think that you could, well, you could help him a lot."

"And I suppose he really needs my help," I said, not bothering to conceal the sarcasm.

"Maybe. He certainly needs somebody's. Perhaps it wouldn't do any good, but anything's worth a try, don't you think?"

"And how am I supposed to help?"

"You could talk to him."

"You want me to talk to him."

"It might help." Stephanie had to crane her head back to look me in the face. Either that was giving her a crick in the neck or else she was sounding tense. Her rather long lashes blinked too often.

"What am I going to talk to him about?"

"Well, anything. You know, a chat."

"I don't chat."

"I'm coming to realise that."

"What's supposed to be wrong with him, anyway?"

"He's working far too hard."

"We're all working far too hard." Not strictly true of me, but a sound enough point in general, I imagined.

"Look, Simon," she sounded as if she were using my name under duress; and I'd just as soon she'd not used it at all, "It's not only that he's working too hard, though that's some of it, he is terrified of, well, *failing* I suppose, especially with Prelims. coming up so soon-" Those words, *Prelims, failure* certainly found a ready response in me. 'Prelims' was the fancy word for end of term exams. "-and he seems to think he's going to let everybody down, his family and Frank Passmore..." I hadn't seen Stephanie hedge before; it would have been diverting under other circumstances- "The root of it all, really, *seems* to be that he's got a bit of a crush on somebody. As far as I can gather." The last sentences hung there, incomplete.

"You've been *gathering* quite a lot, have you?"

"Pardon?"

"Of information. About Jules. You know what's best. For him."

"I'm trying to help."

"Oh." *Condescending. Interfering.*

"I can't just stand by."

I bit back the next sarcastic rejoinder and asked instead, "Why would he want to see me? I hardly know him. I have nothing to do with him."

She shot me a speculative look. "He likes you." She couldn't stop the slightest curl of her lip, a curl which added the comment: I have no idea why.

I might have shrugged and escaped then, had not Ginny found us. She looked a little happier, as if the dulling warmth of the place had soothed her. "Hello," she said to Stephanie.

"This is Stephanie," I said dryly.

They smiled at each other. Stephanie visibly relaxed. I wondered not for the first time why everybody appeared to warm to Ginny without her having to make any effort. She hardly had to open her mouth. Jealous: I was jealous of that. "And this is Ginny."

"Virginia." More smiles, Ginny's coming up a little wistful.

"You both do English," I added, "So you'll probably have a lot in common." Then I shut up. Sure enough the two of them fell into an easy chit-chat routine, Anglo-Saxon this and George Eliot that. In fact I felt annoyed with them both, annoyed with the world, annoyed with Stephanie not only for sticking her nose in but also for reminding me of the end of term exams, annoyed with Ginny for the last forty-eight hours and, though I couldn't admit it to myself and had absolutely no right to envy her in an area where I had so little ambition, her charm. That's the trouble with wobbly self-esteem: it seems quite happy to exist side by side with cockiness, and it seems positively to foster intolerance. I stopped listening, stared into the mechanisms of the loom and was actually becoming convinced I'd worked out how the thing might have been operated, when Ginny prodded me. "Simon? Was it?"

"Was what what?"

"Was Jules the boy who came to your room? The one I've met?"

"Yes," I said wearily, and added quickly, before Stephanie could crank herself up for another assault on me, "We'd better get going. I've got to start revising for those prelims." Quick exit. Stephanie's suspicious look gliding after me.

And on the way home through the dying light of a town that seemed buried in sodden leaves another exchange:

"Did Stephanie mention her worries about Jules Finch to you?" There was a kind of liveliness about her, as if she were pleased to be able to worry over *something else.*

"Fitch. Yes."

"What do you think?"

"About what?"

"Would you be worried about him? Do you think he's cracking up? That's what she's suggesting, isn't it?"

"God knows."

"God knows whether he's cracking up or god knows whether she's suggesting he is?"

"Both."

"Simon," tightly, "Could you try to be a little less obstructive?"

"Well, honestly, who does she think she is?"

"Stephanie?"

"Stephanie bloody Zielinski."

"Is she somebody else you don't like?"

"Yes."

We reached the phone-box and Ginny made a great palaver about phoning home to 'tell Mum and Dad about Madeleine'. Actually Ginny referred to her as Maddy. While she talked, her profile moving animatedly, she looked so transparently anxious that I had to remind myself I doubted her, I kept *forgetting*, damn it, that I didn't believe her. So I speculated. What was she saying? Was she actually ringing her parents? Was she actually ringing anybody? For all I could see through the graffitied glass, she could have her finger on the receiver button. I smoked and wondered what to do about all of this, about fictitious 'Maddy'. The name even: some kind of a joke? And above all the question: why? What for? Why was Ginny doing this? Finally I saw the receiver replaced and Ginny emerge drained of energy. "I feel better now," she said, though her appearance belied her words. I decided to try and catch her out. Surely if we talked about Maddy long enough she'd slip up? Then perhaps we could go back to the way we'd been. As if that's ever possible.

"Were they surprised?"

"In a way, no. It could have been predicted, that she'd follow me."

"Were they shocked? About what *Maddy* did with me?"

Ginny shot me an unfathomable look. "I didn't tell them any of that. How could I? What would I have said?" She seemed appalled. I was appalled by her skill in playing the part she'd chosen.

"So what *did* you tell them, Ginny?"

"That you'd seen somebody who looked a lot like me. It was enough for them. They know what she's capable of."

"So you told them about me?"

"Almost. A good friend, I said."

"Why didn't you tell them the truth?"

"Look Simon," she said gravely, "if you were in my situation *you'd* want to hold some things back from your family."

"O.K." I conceded, but I was thinking: nobody has ever been in your situation. Not even you.

111

She changed the subject. "Shall we drop in on Jules now?"

I was in the process of lighting another cigarette. I paused with the spent match between my fingers. "I'm not going to go and see Jules. I'm probably the last person he wants to see, apart from anything else. And I don't *want* to go and see Jules."

"Why 'the last person'?"

I couldn't think quickly enough to deflect that one. I flicked the match and watched it skip into a puddle.

"It wouldn't hurt you." She sounded like my mother.

"Yes, it would. I'd be bored stupid. Jules wouldn't have a clue why I'd come. Or else he'd smell a rat and be insulted. He doesn't need nannying."

I had no intention of letting Ginny anywhere near Jules. I could imagine too vividly the comment he'd let slip about his difficulties at the History Department library. I could imagine Ginny working out the meaning of the message left on my door- if she hadn't already. I laboured under the impression Ginny loved me in ignorance of my faults. The truth was probably more nearly that she loved me despite them.

"Where's his room?"

"Oh, I don't know."

"I'll ask at the lodge."

"Ginny..."

"*I'll* go and see him. You don't need to come."

Imagine the scene. Jules' gorgeous eyes filled with melancholy as he reclines on his bed. His hair lightly tousled. Ginny bestowing the gift of her optimism like some Victorian lady. The chair piled with clothes so she has to perch on the end of the bed. Jules turning on that gentle charm, the charm that teases out female adulation. Laughter. She cheers him up. He touches her lightly on the arm. She reaches out to brush the hair from his brow. He. She. Then he. She.

"Okay," I said rapidly, starting back towards college, "I'll go."

Jules' room was not the orderly antithesis to mine that I had imagined, neither did it approach anywhere near its squalor. It was pretty ordinary; a gentle disorder, a few clothes, a few books out of place, a couple of posters on the wall (a print of a late Picasso, an Amnesty International promotion), a scattering of more personal objects – an antique clock on the mantelpiece that he must have brought with him (why?), a framed photograph of a middle-aged man who bore him a striking resemblance. The carpet was threadbare and the electric fire unlit. It was freezing.

My arrival seemed to have energised Jules. There'd been a dead silence behind the door when I knocked. Now Jules moved rapidly around the room, clearing a seat, sweeping the hair from his face in what was palpably a nervous gesture, fiddling with the copy of Bede he'd presumably been reading before I came, small-talking as if somebody had overwound him, making coffee. I had, as they say, thrown him. Yet he seemed pleased to see me. You might even have said *thrilled*.

"I'm sorry it's so cold. The fire smelt incredibly of burning so I stopped using it. I just pile on more clothes." The outermost of these was a dressing-gown. It was noticeable, or at least, I noticed that the layers of clothing which would have made many look ridiculous were transformed by the fine proportions of Jules' body almost into fashion statement. I could imagine a shoot in Vogue- "Hey, let's do the impoverished student look."

"But wouldn't the, er, Maintenance men mend it? If you asked?" When Ginny wasn't with me I found opening my mouth a trial. At least the coffee was superb; proper coffee: a luxury. Perhaps it tasted so good because it warmed me up. It was the only thing I was right about as regards Jules, that he drank filter coffee.

I sat in the only chair.

"Oh, well, I expect so."

Then that was it: he'd wound down. As the silence grew I cursed Stephanie Zielinski and even Ginny. Jules added to my discomfort with his restlessness. He seemed incapable of sitting in one place. He ended up standing by the window, through the twelve panes of which could be seen the medieval perimeter wall of the neighbouring college and, above it, very twentieth century undergraduate rooms stacked like gulls' nests on a cliff. Those windows which were lit revealed their inhabitants' every move. And if you had thrown up the sash and leaned out, you would have had a clear view of my own accommodation block, fifty yards down the road. I quite envied

Jules his odd-shaped shabby old room, with its creaking floor boards and its greying whitewash. I felt like a squatter in my own room, exposed by the expanse of its picture window, but this would have suited me.

Finally Jules turned to me. "I didn't think you'd come," he said, more meaningfully than I thought the sentiment warranted. "I really didn't think you'd come."

"Well," I said.

"How's the work going?"

"On the whole, it's not." We were on thin ice here. I held my breath, waiting for him to accuse me of plagiarism. Instead he raised an eyebrow, gave a shade of a smile.

I wondered how long I'd need to leave it before I could decently leave myself. I was just coming to the conclusion that perhaps I'd better make sure I had something to report to Ginny, that I'd better force myself to ask a few questions along the lines of *how's it going*, when Jules began to talk. His tone was so different that I met his eyes and then found I was unable to disengage my own from his. His gaze was too enigmatic, the brown eyes a puzzle that I was compelled to solve. He spoke more slowly now, as if exerting great control or in significant fear, and in the glacial temperature of the room faint clouds of condensation accompanied his every breath: mine too, I suppose. The voice froze me in my chair and I listened with a kind of mesmerised alarm. "I have always felt a kind of affinity with you," he began, "Simon." Then he said the name again quietly, as if he enjoyed saying it, "Simon." He gave an odd half laugh. "If I don't say this now I never will. It's all too difficult. I *thought*, oh, weeks ago that I felt something coming from you, a kind of response, an *answer* if you like, but I was never sure, and the risk was too great." He paused and swept the hair from his eyes *again*. "This term has been hell. I haven't said that to anyone. I feel as if I'm being expected to perform miracles: walk on the water or – I don't know – *prove* myself every minute of the day. And I've felt so *lonely*." In the background there was the muffled slamming of the front door, laughter, talk: somebody taking a friend back to their room. I visualised myself running down the stairs, pushing by them to get out the front door, their surprised expressions, the damp of

114

the lane outside. "Shannon, Dave; he's been great. But there's such a hell of a lot I've had to *hide* from him. He's, well, he's a *lad*, isn't he? You'd hardly expect him to..." In the lane there would be groups straggling along to the warmth, couples and cyclists weaving round them. Over in the New Block Ginny would be making more tea and reading her book. She would have put Madness on the record-player. "That night in the quad. It was such a relief, even though I *did* make such a fool of myself. You were incredibly drunk." He gave a laugh that I realised, with a paralysing chill, was affectionate. "But some of the things you said...made me understand. You'd said so little before then. I had no idea what was going on in your head and then, that evening, you actually *knew* what I was talking about. And I realised why you, to put it bluntly, *take* things from me. That sodding book, Simon. That essay. Do you know how long it took me to come up with those ideas? The flask. You know, that flask must be one of the most precious things I have...had. But you can keep it. I want you to keep it. That night I..I cringe to remember Purvis taking me home." He shook his head slowly. "Never to be repeated. But it was relief, you see? Sheer relief that you didn't despise me, that you *wouldn't* despise me because you knew what was going on in my head. It was the first time I'd even *let* myself entertain the shadow of a possibility that you were," he breathed out as if to steady himself, "that you were like me. The amazing possibility that you might *like* me, my god." Quickly he walked over and to my horror knelt down in front of me. "However you want it to be, Simon, that's how it'll be." He laid his head on my knee.

He laid his head on my knee and I jerked myself clumsily out of the chair. If he'd bitten me it would have had the same effect. My knee crashed into his cheek and he reeled back. I hate to think of that, that he never knew I'd not struck him intentionally. I can't visualise the look that I involuntarily shot at him, but I saw its reflection in his face. He cried out. Then I left.

Here I am at my Virtual Reality game again. That room and that time and that brief confrontation can never, it goes without saying, be conjured up exactly. Apart from anything else, it was the freezing cold that defined Jules' rashness and my disgust. My approximation just can't recapture that, and I find I sneak objects into the room to fit it to my middle-aged conception of 'a student room of the late 'seventies'. I keep hanging a duffle-coat on the back of the door. As a matter of fact, there were a few duffle-coats lingering then – but Jules Fitch would never have worn one. And I keep trying to groom Jules a little too much, to give him a more decent haircut than he ever had, to age him because I can't *believe* how young we all were, to put him in a silk dressing-gown when I'm sure he was wearing one of a much more mundane design. Probably I'm slipping into the straight man's error of camping him up, Oscar Wilde-ing him. Then again, duffle coats don't fit with silk gowns and I can't have my cake and eat it and all I end up with is something never quite right.

I try anyway. Jules finishes his breath-taking declaration and kneels down on the threadbare carpet and lays his head on my knee. I feel the weight of it, watch the longish strands of blonde hair spread over my leg – you can get that effect with Virtual Reality, can't you? sensor pads or whatever – and I shake him gently by the shoulder and say, "Hey, Jules. You know that girl you saw in my room? That's my girlfriend. Didn't you realise? Who'd you think she was – my *sister*?" And than Jules stands up stiffly, red as a fire-extinguisher, and I say, "Don't worry about it. You screwed up, that's all. Join the club." And Jules looks unconvinced, no, devastated, and I go on more urgently, "Look, we're even now. I've got one on you, and you've got one on me," – plagiarism, theft: I can't make myself be more specific – "We'll just agree to be, uh, discreet. Look, let me buy you a pint." Crude and ham-fisted, maybe, but probably all I could have managed at seventeen. Jules mutters something incoherently, won't turn to face me, then says I'd better go. I refuse to leave, I insist on Jules coming with me, won't take no for an answer, pull him down the stairs after me. Ginny just has to put up with me turning up half-cut three hours later. That night Jules and I fashion a tenuous kind of friendship from the raw material of our embarrassment that over the next few weeks firms up and over the next few terms sets into a concrete shape. What's more, it's just about feasible that without the tarnish of my real-world meanness rubbing off on me that evening, I don't feel so much of a bastard so I don't act so much of a bastard the following day, that with one of my Snakes-and-Ladders counters

116

dropped down the floor-boards I never get to hip-hop them all home; that, oh god, *I let Ginny be.*

* * *

Now, Jules would be the sort of person who occasionally drops by for an evening drink. We've been having the hottest days this summer, days when you long, really *long* to be on the Downs lying sprawled on the short grass of a shallow hillside. The evenings are the best, balmy, Mediterranean, cossetting. They lend themselves to the pokey back gardens we have in Brighton, to the white-washed walls and multi-levels, the steps up or down, the pots of red geraniums. The occasional evening we stay outside until eleven, eleven-thirty, sharing a bottle of wine with a handful of friends, talking lightly and with the incorrigible facetiousness of our generation, letting the minor frustrations of the working day dissipate. Jules could be there among us, my old college friend: why not? I imagine him based in London, Fulham or Greenwich, or why not have him down in Brighton? He's working as a Conservator for the Pavilion or for English Heritage, some occupation that combines an aesthetic instinct with an immersion in the past. For some reason I don't place him in academia: possibly I judge he wouldn't have been able to hack the competitiveness. Such a *romantic*, our old friend Jules. But then I can't talk, can I?

He's aged well. A light tan on his forearms, a slenderness around the middle that suggests the work-out, crinkles around the eyes that add obscurely to his appeal. He sits at our Habitat garden table on our Habitat chair, beneath the grape vine we planted five years ago now. Later in the year we actually get grapes from this, though they tend to be acid. The table and chairs are in a rather delicious blue, the lapis lazuli blue of medieval religious icons, mother Mary's robe, a deep aquamarine. Jules has on a brilliant white shirt of a very simple but perfect cut above linen trousers in a pale greengage, a look I decide to copy, though I will probably pay far less for my clothing and the shirt's more likely to come from Gap than Paul Smith. He drinks his white wine and absent-mindedly works his way through the bowl of olives while I pick his brains about the Pavilion.

117

Jules is very relaxed. He lounges in his chair and leans his head back to laugh. It's a good few months since we've seen him, so I leave off talking about the Pavilion and in a meandering fashion we catch up on the small events of our respective lives. That teenage hesitation, the hint of a stutter he used to have, has long gone. Yet I still find it too difficult to question him on the subject of his personal life. There was that incident between us so long ago... Sometimes he drops the odd comment, and one name begins to crop up more often, 'A colleague of mine, Richard...' I speculate. The 'eighties were difficult for him. He lost several close friends to Aids. For a while he worked abroad. But now he seems to be easy in his skin.

What huge liberties I have taken, extrapolating from the thin slice of Jules Fitch that I saw when we were young. For all I know he would really have gone into accountancy, ended up working for Shell in Nigeria; but I prefer my version. We were all so unformed then, rough substance that could have been manipulated over the years of chance and event into half a dozen different shapes. I like the Jules I've conjured up, sitting on the blue chair, the one with the chip in it that Henry made with the trowel he should never have got hold of, in our garden, beneath the vine and by the French windows, drinking the wine I've poured him and being greedy with my olives.

* * *

It took me till the Monday morning to discover the letters Ginny had dropped on my bare middle on the previous Saturday morning, and whose arrival had been upstaged so completely by her freaky story. The weekend just finished – the strangest weekend of my life: no competition – had straddled the middle of the eight week term. Now I was on the home run, so to speak, catapulting towards those end of term exams and the Christmas vacation. *The Christmas vacation?* Home seemed distant and improbable, as set and dead as the reconstructions in the local Museum of 'An Undergraduate's Room in Christchurch in the 1770s' or 'The kitchen of a terraced house in Cardigan Street, Jericho, in the late 1880s'.

Ginny had left soon after we'd got up around eleven; and if I'd wanted proof of the passing of a wind of change it was in my own sneaky sense of relief at being left alone to try and make sense of her. That's just how it seemed, that the wind had changed and the faces we'd been pulling had set rigid.

The letters might have lain forgotten for longer yet, had not I been baffled by what Jules had said about the hip flask, that I'd taken his. I diverted my attention away from the other things he'd said with this, almost ingenuously bothering myself with the question of why I'd have had my hands on his flask at all. Why would I have wanted it? And above all, why did he see my hypothetical theft of it as flirtatious? In truth I had no memory of a hip flask of any kind; and I suppose I was hopeful that if I could debunk the existence of the thing I might be able to bury the existence of the other things he had suggested (what had I said to him in the quad that had given him hope? What had I done? Had I *done* something?). As soon as Ginny was safely down the corridor I began a systematic ransacking of my room in search of the flask. That's when I found them. The letter from my mother and the note from Frank were both beneath the bed, presumably where they'd scooted when I wrapped myself in the sheet that other morning. I flicked the dust from them. Sheila's thorough clean the other day had obviously not been *that* thorough.

Frank's note spoke volumes through its envelope already, so it was cowardice that made me open my mother's first. She'd written on decent notepaper and her lines were dead straight because she always used the ruled sheet they give you at the front of the pad.

Saturday. Dear Simon, she wrote, *It's beastly cold and I'm sitting on the side of the bed steeling myself for the dogwalking and/or washing clothes, shopping or house cleaning – I must do it all. The dog has had her cup of tea and is not pleased that I am not sharing my coffee.*

I expect you have heard they've already arrested two men for Mountbatten's murder. It beats me how people can do such things. Lord Mountbatten always had a bit more about him than most of the Royals. Shame.

Celia and I are having lunch at the Green Man on Sunday – it will be good to see her. I might try and leave Nan behind this time, get her a cold tray or something, though she will moan about it. She talks about you a lot and keeps saying "He's such a good old boy" – not to be taken literally (the old bit) as if it were said about me! I worry about her sometimes as she seems to get confused. She was always so on the ball. I'm sure she would appreciate a letter from you if you can find the time to write. Not a lot happens to her.

I'm beginning to wonder if Bess isn't losing her sight, cataracts maybe. I know she's always been a bit short-sighted but she runs into things now. It would be funny but I try not to laugh as she is such a dear old lady. I think she misses you as much as any of us, she's asked to be let into your room numerous times and gives me such a look when she can't find you.

Wednesday. Talk in the staffroom has much to do with the U.S. hostages in Iran and the possibilities of war. Why on earth the Americans thought they had to let in the Shah I do not know. They should keep well out of it. I'm getting so paranoic about the Russians I see their hand in everything. Where are the revolutionaries getting their money from?? If the Russians get into Iran we've had it.

Thanks for ringing, though it is a while since we heard anything from you! You will say I am nagging, but we do worry if we don't hear. Is it all work and no play? I hope not. You are such a conscientious boy.

Dorrie moves this coming weekend and I shall go and help her unpack the following Monday afternoon when we have a holiday. Lots of love. Take care and keep sensible. Margaret/Mum XXXX

Folded inside my mother's letter was one from my grandmother. It had been typed on the back of a letter from Bassett's apologising to my grandmother for the fact that she'd had no blue and pink jellies in her pack of Liquorice Allsorts, and hoping that the postal order for £1.59 1/2 p, equivalent to the cost of a bumper pack, would go some way to making up for her loss of enjoyment.

Dear S, she'd typed, I have given you time to settle in before I bother you with a letter well that's what your mother told me to do anyway. Trust your work or whatever you call it is going well, also hope you like your students or teachers or whatever you call them.

I have managed through the Red Cross to get you a very nice dressing-gown, I have told your mother to let you know but she is very busy with school and might forget, hence this note. I do not get to shops so this year I shall not be getting cards presents etc., Could ask your mother to get them but she is busy etc. and the expense.

It is quilted, navy blue with a red lining, very nice and I think the right size, it fits me with a large winter coat on and finishes at my feet and its brand new, it has a makers name in it , forgot it, and it also gives washing instructions inside also, you wash it in soap flakes, rinse and drip dry, so thats easy. At the moment it is spotless, so my suggestion is, altho you do as you like, but to use the thick one I gave you at begin. of Autumn and washed, mended etc for second best and use this one for visitors coming or you calling outside or to go to the door etc., so now I have got three for your mother, two for you, so I think thats it.

Only write when you can spare the time from your work, I trust you are liking your room and fellow students, also the ladies??? By the way at weekends NEVER PUT AN EXPENSIVE STAMP ON ANY LETTER? JUST A CHEAP ONE? THEY GET THERE THE SAME TIME. THIS IS AT WEEKENDS AND WOULD SAVE YOU 3p.

Cheerio, come along the spring and nice cheery days. Nan.

P.S. Its terrible here today, rain and perhaps snow I hope not, Bess would hate it, she is a dainty one and would hate putting her feet into cold snow.

Cheerio. I am very proud of you, am sure you will do well. Make the most, life is short or so it seems.

I sighed. That was it: my family history summed up on three sheets of paper.

The moment had come to read Frank's note. I lit a cigarette, then cautiously slid it from its (good quality; a waste) envelope.

Simon, he wrote in generous, swooping letters, *I suggest you see your way clear to appearing in my room at twelve on Monday the 12th, to discuss your work. We might also take the opportunity to discuss your lackadaisical approach to my previous note. Frank.*

It was five to twelve and certainly Monday. The twelfth I'd have to take on trust. I stubbed out the cigarette (more waste), pulled on a pullover, shoes, spun round to locate my key, nearly scrabbled for my gown then remembered Frank didn't insist on it, grabbed my pad of A4 – to have a prop, to look alert? – and ran.

121

It could have been worse. Frank was lothe to intervene in the way his students chose to plan their academic careers. Yet it was also the case that he had some form of pastoral responsibility towards them, not to mention the, should he say, vested interest he held in the fulfilment of their potential. I had, as of course I realised, won my place at the college against considerable competition. Did I realise, however, just how much I had achieved? For every successful candidate, another seven were disappointed. Was it not the case, moreover, that I had further excelled myself by achieving an Exhibition? He was at a loss to understand, therefore, the extent to which I was proving myself to be disorganised in my work. The chance I held in my hand was exceptional. He had very high hopes for me. He also wanted to be justified in his choice of me over all those other – gifted – candidates. There were some undergraduates who made the transition to full independence a little shakily. It seemed I was one of those. He hoped that my sloppiness was an aberration. He suggested that, if I were to have a decent chance of showing the full extent of my ability in Prelims. *which were in a mere three weeks*, I get myself back on course within the next week. "Now," he wound up, "Is there anything you wish to tell me? Any specific problem?"

I gazed at the half full mug he had been using throughout as a means of emphasis, wondering if he had chosen its rather Marks and Spencer floral pattern himself. I asked Marks and Spencer for inspiration. "I have been ill," I said finally, and realised as soon as I said it that there was an element of truth in the lie, "I think I'm still ill."

"Well, for heaven's sake, why don't you go and see a doctor?" Frank blustered, "That's what they're for, I believe."

"And," I forged on, inspired, "I'm concerned that my girlfriend might be..." I paused, momentarily distracted by the change in Frank's expression to an oh-my-god ghastliness as he thought he understood. "No, it's worse than that, really," I muttered, "I think she's schizophrenic." That was a lie too, but as I said the words it suddenly seemed to me I might be right.

That shut Frank up for a while. Absent-mindedly he drained the cup, though the dregs of his tea must have been disgustingly cold.

I'd never seen Frank at a loss before. He stared into the empty cup as if reading tea leaves. Then he looked up. "Well, Simon," he said, "That might be something you could bring up when you visit the doctor."

* * *

Alex said to me the other day, "Did you hear the one about the schizophrenic who couldn't decide whether to get married?"

I'd already said "No-" before I realised that I had.

"He was in two minds about it."

The mention of schizophrenia always brings back to me Frank's tall-ceilinged room with its view of the bare branches of the college garden's huge copper beech and Frank staring into his empty cup, and the tall, spare, lying boy standing before him. And everything that spun out of those lies drifts out of the image and has to be re-viewed before it will lie down again.

"Actually that joke's sexist, isn't it, Dad," says Alex, "because it just assumes any schizophrenic's going to be a man, doesn't it?"

"It's quite an old joke."

That joke was doing the rounds when I was revising for my A levels. It would have done, in fact, as a summary of my knowledge of the psychological condition at that time. When I told Frank Ginny was schizophrenic I was talking out of a deep green ignorance: hey, look – Jekyll and Hyde; hairy faces, ravings, melodrama, the terrifying suggestion that the mind, your mind, my mind, could change colour and go psychodelic as a sixties' album cover. I hadn't thought before opening my mouth: but I took his silence as a kind of confirmation. He hadn't said, "Don't be so ridiculous, you stupid boy," had he? Why hadn't he?

The doctor took me seriously, too. He was called Dr. Fell; really. **I do not love thee, Doctor Fell/The reason why I cannot tell;/But this alone I know full well/I do not love thee, Doctor Fell**. (Thomas Brown). As he introduced himself to me I slid into a kind of vacant panic and distracted myself with a silly internal monologue on the necessity of some doctors bearing the name Fell or Foster or Body, just as some lawyers must be called Crook or undertakers Death or demolition experts Reckitt. We sat in his roomy surgery with its skewed view of the facade of Magdalen seen through discreet net. I could even see one end of the skip to which I had consigned the Knotsworth. No black bags bulged over its upper edge and I guessed it had been emptied. I imagined the Knotsworth sliding down one of the hummocks of domestic rubbish at the municipal tip, wherever that was. I wondered how quickly mildew grew on damp pages, how much maltreatment it would take to loosen the binding.

The doctor cleared his throat. The smell of shower gel and aftershave had to be coming form him. *Clean* summed him up, or maybe *healthy*. Sitting in front of him made me feel like a dosser. I'd chosen the wrong moment to spring the revelation on him. We'd been through all the preliminaries. He'd asked the right questions, ummed and ahhed, felt my neck, taken a blood sample, postulated a virus. Now he'd just finished fiddling about with the swab he'd used to scrape a swathe of furry yuk from the back of my throat, writing something on a label with a pen that wouldn't work properly. As soon as I'd spoken, hesitatingly, almost inaudibly, he straightened up and gave me a sharp glance. "What makes you think that?" he said with all the caution of the professional.

I felt foolish. "She thinks she's two people." I shrugged with embarrassment.

Dr. Fell eased himself in to his swivel chair extremely slowly, as if a sudden movement would make me bolt, but said nothing. The old 'make them fill the silence' trick that I know so well *now*, that I use, *now*, myself. Then I felt the whole weight of the doctor's ten year head start on me, and imagined I was as transparent to his superior gaze as a glass of water.

"She's fabricated a sister."

He nodded.

"But I think she believes in her."

"Go on."

"That's all, really."

"Well, now. There must be a little more you could tell me," he said evenly, and added, "Mr. Donaghue."

I knew he thought the formality of the address would flatter me, mist over his real opinion of me as a spotty little kid. I asked myself what I had ever thought this conversation might achieve. I felt as displaced in Dr. Fell's surgery as a fish in a sugar-bowl. I imagined myself and Dr. Fell sitting in our comfy-consultation-room chairs opposite each other but on different planets: the doctor over there on the orange planet with two rings, me over here on the green one with three moons; him speaking the language of the Zargs, me the language of the Xarps. In truth I'd hardly thought of how the conversation might go. My sole motivation in coming could well have been to show willing to Frank, to give my excuse to him more substance: to cover my own back. This last, of course, was my absolute priority. "The sister does things ... acts in a way ... she wouldn't herself."

"For instance?"

"Things that my girlfriend would consider ... bad." That was all he was getting. This time I let the silence stretch.

"So," he said eventually, "Are we talking about reported events? I mean is it simply that your girlfriend *tells* you about this sister?"

I thought I could hear condescension in his voice. *I* knew what 'reported events' meant; I didn't need him to explain to me. I kept my mouth shut and shook my head.

"So she acts out a role, is that what you mean? Have you actually seen-?"

I nodded quickly.

"Are you entirely sure it's not a, well, a game or even a, oh, I don't know, a flirtatious gesture?"

I was nodding vigorously.

"It would help if you'd feel able to give a little more detail."

I shook my head. I started to put on my jacket. Nothing could have kept me in that room any longer. Xarp flees Zarg.

"Simon," said Dr. Fell, surprised out of the 'Mr Donaghue' lark by my rapidity, "I want you to keep in touch. Right? Now you'll have to ring in or drop in for the results of the blood test. I want you to book an appointment, come back in a week or two and tell me what's happening. Will you do that, Simon?"

125

I nodded vaguely as I hoiked my arm into the sleeve of the jacket.

"Simon," he repeated, "Will you?"

"Yes," I said, "Absolutely."

There is one other event that must have happened that week, fifth week, though it has cut itself adrift in my memory. I find I can slot it in where I want. I think of it as out of time, an irregularly shaped bubble floating around in darkness, overlit like an operating theatre or a landscape of snow, a one act play of the fringe theatre variety. The light is important. Getting out of bed so late, I'd grown used to missing the part of the day that might claim brightness. Those November afternoons were dominated by smudged half-lit skies that dictated a mood of apathetic deprivation. Suited me. I cut out more of the light with those lined green curtains. Swimming round my room from bed to basin to desk to bed-basin-desk to bedbasindesk I was the goldfish who forgot about the repetition.

Habitually we slept poorly. Maddy the Mad slept between us, wedging us apart even though we lay as we'd always done, because I had become convinced that my snap diagnosis of Ginny was uncannily accurate. Without noticing, I'd slipped into treating her with the cautious placatory false intimacy we reserve for the very old or the mentally ill. The idea of her illness terrified me. Whenever I tried to direct my feet to the college library I'd find them veering one hundred and eighty degrees off course and leading me the extra five hundred yards to Blackwells bookshop, where I'd end up in the Psychology section. Here I could confuse myself with all the contradictory mass of references to the condition, a condition whose name took on the identity of a thing, or even a creature, a bubbling quatermass of a monster, tentacles and dripping saliva. Here I read of cases, dozens of different cases under the weight and variety of which any definition became impossible. It started out as a morbid fascination with the word I'd used as a conjuring tool, picking it up in my ignorance like the Mickey Mouse sorcerer's apprentice in *Fantasia* – the first flick of the wand's quite fun, the second brings with it the first tremor of unease, the third's terrifying. Because I was looking for it I found confirmation of my worst fears; I read of personalities so shredded they fractured into ten, eleven, twelve persons, vying to dominate the body they inhabited, vying to use its airwaves and broadcast from its mouth. And though each new fact gave a new twist to my nightmare, given half a chance I'd be back for more. The assistant behind the cash desk eventually took me for a Ph.D. student and started to suggest 'good reads' to me. Worst of all, I began to imagine I could feel parts of myself sliding around a little. Contagion, I fully believed, was a possibility.

The effort of keeping up appearances, Ginny and I each of us to the other, was exhausting. We made excuses, or rather the same old *work* excuse, to dodge each other for the greater part of the day, our day, which did not quite correlate with anyone else's. By degrees we'd become semi-nocturnal, getting into bed some time before dawn, getting out of it some time before dusk. Then the nights, our nights; the nights were always waiting like a bandit force, to truss us together.

The difference about the day in question was that we were out in it, and its appalling brightness. That perfect winter blue that seems more delicate for presiding over the frost that tends to come with it, that hint-of-turquoise blue that really does make you feel you're on the inside of a giant egg-shell. It dazzled me. I was a cave dweller thrown out onto the plain.

The scene always begins in one of the hothouses in the Botanical Gardens. Don't ask me what we're doing there, why we've opted to spend time together for once, whose idea it was, what the day is, what the time is, because I can't tell you. All I can tell you about is the perfect blue outlined in every oblong pane of the sloping greenhouse roof. Wrought iron scrolls figure somewhere. We stand a little apart but closer than friends, as if those bandits had only half untied us. Ginny is wearing a black shirt and my coat, which I've wrapped her up in as nurses wrap invalids. I don't know what I'm wearing. Ludicrously, tall palms tower over us and I expect to hear the chatter-cheep-caw of Tarzan films kick in over the quiet respectful murmur of the other visitors' comments to each other. There's a good steamy smell of earth and ozone and the temperature matches that of my room. Perhaps we've ended up here just to keep warm.

"Come and see my room," says Ginny.

"Sure," I say, because I agree with everything she suggests these days.

"Well, come on then." She doesn't make her ironic little asides any more. She talks blankly, like an assistant in a shop, and simply, like a Junior School teacher. I take this to be another phase in the cycle of her illness. I see evidence of instability in her every twitch.

"Sure," I echo, taking the hand she offers me and allowing myself to be led out into the startling cold and along under that damn sky. We've never been so close to her college before and I assume she wants to look through her pigeon-hole or find some clean socks – or I assume all her decisions, even trivial ones like this one, are erratic and meaningless and *mad*. It's only a few minutes along the main road, the cars and its stream of cyclists flying in parallel to us with assembly-line regularity, the rooks suddenly flying up from the trees beside the road making Ginny swerve towards them in alarm, so that even I notice how strung out she is. We don't talk (see what sparse dialogue this part of my fringe production has) until we're well within the grounds of Ginny's college and we've crunched our way over the gravel skirting a manicured lawn to arrive beneath the darkened stone of a long multi-storeyed Victorian block.

"Looks like a hotel," I comment. Ginny hums assent. It does: just like one of those whacking great big seaside hotels thrown up to accommodate all the Victorian families who spent their summers by the sea and never dreamt of going abroad. Windows and blank windows staring politely straight ahead, gables and drain-pipes and a hundred other big, solid protuberances. *Uncluttered entrance.* Where are all the bikes, the ones that are piled three deep against the walls of my college? Where's the Porter's Lodge? Notice boards? Pigeon-holes?

We're sucked in through large polished swing doors and down corridors that still remind me of hotels and I realise it's the kemptness of the place and the carpeting and the thoughtful lighting that is pointing the resemblance. There are *landscapes* on the walls, for God's sake. I have a moment of panic when I wonder if Ginny's madness has brought me into some private building; a conference centre belonging to American Express, for example. Supposing that, once again, we're trespassers? So far we've not seen a soul: and we

128

don't, not at all. This thought takes me along the entire length of a corridor, but is erased as Ginny digs her key from her trouser pocket and lets us through the final door.

We're standing in a brilliantly whitewashed room with several pointed Gothic windows. There is no sense of its occupation, which is not altogether surprising under the circumstances and damn it all, it *still* looks like a hotel. It even smells like a hotel, as if there's a room freshener hanging in the wardrobe. I remember Ginny saying she comes here every few days to rumple the bed and disturb the objects on the desk and I glance at the bed which is in apple pie order and I look at the desk which is one of those reproduction jobs that always seem to appear in book club advertisements and can't help noticing that it's completely clear and I resurrect my fear that I'm really in the conference centre. Ginny's alter ego has stolen a key from behind the reception desk on some previous occasion and she's brought me here to... I suddenly realise why she's brought me here, and I wait.

"This room really looks like a hotel room."

"Yes," says Ginny, as we stand and shiver and Ginny doesn't take her coat off.

I wander with assumed calm over to one of the Gothic-horror windows and see I'm looking over the lawn we skirted. Straining my eyes, I scan each degree of my view to pick out either a young female in a college scarf or a middle-aged delegate carrying suitcase and briefcase. All I see is the immaculate lawn which glistens emerald in the unfiltered winter sun. When I turn back into the room, window shapes dance in purple before my eyes and against the whitewashed wall. I can't stop my imagination transforming all this chilly whiteness into something ecclesiastic, monastic, under the suggestion, I suppose, of those windows. Ginny stands in her crow-black like a nun in her cell.

"This is it," she offers, with a little shrug and a look around, "This is all there is to my room."

"It's very..... spartan," I agree, obligingly looking around too, then up. "It's lit by a *neon* light? Isn't that rather rough in the mornings?"

"I can't remember," she replies, apparently without coyness.

We stand around for a while longer.

129

"Is it completely unheated?" I ask, just to hear someone speak (notice how the tables are turning).

"Oh, the radiators are *on*. Feel." She walks across to me and takes my hand and draws me across the room to a bulky old radiator I've not noticed before and places my hand on it; and keeps her own over mine. Under my hand I can feel the most tepid of heats. Above it Ginny's fingers are icy but through them I begin to let myself be moved by the old impulses. My honeypie, my glacial golden girl. What happened to my golden girl?

"Simon," she says, and that deliberate way of talking, that slightly low voice spark all the old responses and I see that I am lost because some part of me has locked itself to this mad girl, that I think I've pulled away but that last bit of skin's still stuck in the zip.

"I want to break her spell," she tells me, as if I'll understand. I understand only the part that means we take off our clothes like children undressing for gym, and climb between the stiff clean sheets of the smallest single bed in the world. Ginny leans over and reaches a packet of Durex out of the bedside drawer and explains needlessly, "I bought these." She's tense as a coiled spring and rigid as a doll as she hands me the packet with a smile that is both desperate request and provocation. I can't bring myself to admit I've not used one of the things before so automatically fish one out and use all the common sense I can scrape together.

The cold is a kind of challenge to the nerve endings: they respond with an electric shiver. It is the oddest embrace I ever experience. We never warm up. Cold as cod, we press closely together. Ginny clings to me which is in part a necessity given the width of the bed but also the gesture of a passenger scared to death of being thrown overboard. It is infinitely disturbing and intensely exciting as we lie sideways and I immediately enter her as if the nights of proximity have been all the arousal we needed. For me, my God, this is certainly true. Ginny buries her face against the side of my neck and I realise she's *smelling* my skin which I do not understand but don't dislike. The rhythm of the thing is rapid-fire, the tone Mick Jagger, definitely more of a *Let's Spend The Night Together* than a *Red Rooster*. We speed and skip and rock and roll; too young to die, but we do anyway. Well, I do.

As soon as it's over the urgency of the thing seems incomprehensible. There's a terrible sense of having made a mistake. Something nun-like still clings to Ginny's body and I feel as if I've trampled on a baby. Ginny starts to cry and seems unable to stop. I stroke her hair, tentatively, scared that in some mysterious way I have damaged her, that all that intricate female paraphernalia inside her has been jumbled up.

"Poor Madeleine," she sobs. My hand slows and halts, lies still over Ginny's ear. "She's so vulnerable. I never looked after her. I was so awful to her. How do you think she's coping now? She *can't* be coping. Maybe she's sleeping rough. Do you think she's sleeping rough? In this cold?" I watch the way her head indents the pillow, which has an outdated design of super-bold turquoise flowers, and carefully avoid revealing my exasperation. Ginny rattles on. It's like watching someone haemorrhage. I dislike the mess but can't stem the flow. "She could die of exposure. She'll be *used* by people." A quick glance up at me which, can it? implicates me in this last. She can't be, can she, in her wacky way, *blaming* me? I'm to be held responsible for the downfall of some fictitious character, the shard of a split whole, is that it? Just so Ginny needn't take... But she's trotting on, "I know I said she's canny, but that's only some of the time. Sometimes she's got the sophistication of a ten year old. And she's so stupid with men, setting up situations she can't cope with. All that low neckline crap which men fall for like guppies. Like, oh, I don't know, dogs." Another little glance. "I don't suppose for a minute she's on the pill, stupid girl. She probably thinks it sounds *knowing* if she says that. Can you imagine her bothering with the pill? Really? 'Oh dear, mustn't miss a day. That wouldn't be sensible.' She's probably throwing herself at all the weirdos she trips over on the pavement. Poor little Madeleine. I should have looked after her. She *is* my little sister. My big sister. I should have, oh I should have... done something."

At this point a stunning but stunningly obvious idea comes to me, like a gift. Clumsily I try to apply all my mish-mash knowledge, the rags and bones I've picked up from my sneaking missions into Blackwell's Psychology Department. Ginny uses this sister rubbish as a cop out, shifts all her anxieties onto a fairy-figure. Ginny worries about getting pregnant; heigh-ho she spins a sister up to worry about it for her. Ginny gets uptight about sex; oh, dear, Maddy can't cope. It still sounds pretty mad; but at least it has a kind of logic to it. I am amazed with myself for noticing the connection. In these situations, I wonder, should you challenge the deluded individual, refuse to let them get away with all the fantasising? Or should they be treated like a sleepwalker? In all the pages I've waded through in Blackwells I've never come across the chapter I've hoped for, the one which tells the curious reader what the hell to *do* about it, how to wave a magic wand and make the madness go away. They say, don't they, that it's dangerous to wake a sleepwalker, just as they say that the dream of a fall which ends at the bottom of the cliff ends in the real death of the dreamer; though there's no way of proving *that* one, is there?

I decide to begin a tentative debunking of Ginny's story. I will no longer clap my hands to revive Tinkerbell as she swoons and threatens to die. I begin to stroke Ginny's hair again. It's a little long now. No doubt Ginny will be getting out the scissors soon. "Isn't it odd," I say quietly, as Ginny settles against the palm of my hand, "It's something of a coincidence, don't you think, that your parents chose the name Madeleine?"

"What do you mean?" She uses the pillow to wipe away the wet from her cheek as she speaks, and she sounds genuinely curious. She shifts around so she can lie facing me and she touches my face as if experimentally: eyebrows, temple, cheek, stubble, lips.

"Well, you know, Madeleine, Maddy, mad." As soon as I've spoken I see Ginny's face change. The portcullis comes down, the drawbridge snaps up. She draws back her hand as if I've bitten it, then very deliberately rolls out of the bed. I don't have the sense to see I've said something fatuous. I feel probably as alone as I ever have. I watch her slender white body dress in a shaft of sunlight and disappear beneath layers of clothing. I'm appalled by the dead expression around her eyes and mouth but don't have any idea what to say to bring her back.

Later when I get out of the bed myself I notice that there is blood on the sheet and, though I am shocked by the discovery, do not understand the significance of what I'm seeing. I spend a fair proportion of that time not understanding.

* * *

My little Alex – not so little now, five foot six – is quite a puritan. Whenever she catches me with a glass in my hand she lights up with malicious glee.

"My dad's an alcoholic," she'll tell the company, or the room, if there's no company.

"There's nothing wrong with alcohol, as long as you use it moderately," I'll say; and even I'll be conscious of the hypocrisy.

"It pickles your insides."

"I'm sure."

"Like pickled onions. Don't they use alcohol ... hey, hang on a minute, Don't they use alcohol to stop bodies, you know, *going off*?"

"Formaldehyde."

"Is that alcohol?"

"Probably. I don't know. You're the one who's supposed to know that. Anyway I could do with preserving."

Then if we're on our own she'll lollop over me, making friends, and she'll say, "Can I have one little sip? Just to see what it's like?"

"Don't let your mother see," I'll say, and give it her.

* * *

Back then, back in the Ginny days, I'd stand in Oddbins comparing the proof of different bottles, then buy the highest I could find. I moved on from wine pretty rapidly and usually opted for gin, because it rhymed with *sin* and echoed *Ginny*, and because it seemed a miracle that anything so pure and transparent could so instantly sharpen up the senses – before it dulled them. I chose to believe against all the evidence that gin left no hangover. I lined up the empty bottles along my window-sill and was surprised how quickly it filled up. That's how it came about that I operated most days through the magnifying lens of the gin. **Little nips of whisky, little drops of gin / Make a lady wonder where on earth she's bin.** (Anon).

The gin was relevant to how events unfolded. Perhaps I could even shift blame onto the gin. If it hadn't been for the price of gin, so excessive my dear, I'd never have started to receive letters from the bank, I'd never have had my hole-in-the-wall card withdrawn and I'd never have had to resort to using my college tab. In the college bar and in the dining hall you could use chits and meal-tickets for which no payment was required 'till the end of term. If I hadn't been forced to use these, I would never have had to come out of my room and into the life of the college, never have run into Shannon, caught the gossip.

I thought the gin helped me to see the world in sharp focus, a friend lending me an opera glass. In actuality it was the equivalent of forming an understanding of world events through reading the official newspaper of the Nazi party. I overheard Beverly McKenzie as I waited – alone, Ginny who knows where – in the dinner queue.

"Did you know," she told Caroline Funnell, "Dave Shannon's got himself a new girl-friend?" *Hum it and I'll see.*

"So he's moved on to fresh woods and pastures new, has he? Do you mean the top-heavy girl? Blonde?"

"No. *She* lasted about two minutes. She got the old heave-ho. Well, that's Dave's version anyway. I suspect it happened the other way round. No, *this* is somebody he met at his film club."

"We're not good enough for him, I take it? He has to look elsewhere?" Caroline attempted lightness of tone, but achieved instead something rather heartfelt.

"Dave's not too bad, really. Just a bit full of himself. I'm not sure why Stephanie dislikes him quite so much."

I was surprised Stephanie disliked Shannon. I'd wandered into a conception of college life as a distant party, static and superficial but always genial. And ten minutes later, as I crunched coleslaw, sitting apart and staring resolutely at the portrait of the college's founder which hung over the hall's large fireplace, the gin suddenly lit up another interpretation of those words: *film club.* I forgot to eat. I saw that Shannon and Ginny were seeing each other behind my back, I saw that Shannon was using Ginny to undermine me, that he was trying to unhinge me with notes left on doors and by convincing Ginny to spin me stories of mad sisters. Then the light went out and I un-saw it all. But that lunchtime *did* leave me with the quite illogical sense that some kind of understanding existed between

Shannon and Ginny, that given half a chance he'd snatch her from me: as if Shannon and I were two seagulls and Ginny a titbit, as if Ginny were there for the snatching.

If I'd watched Ginny cautiously up to that point, then from it I observed her as closely as a specimen. I tried to dissect her with hidden glances. I entirely avoided mention of *Madeleine*, but instead set up situations where I could put her to the test.

"Let's go to Evensong," I said, over the record blasting out. 'London Calling' it was, *The Clash*.

Ginny laughed. "What?" she mouthed, and put her book down beside her on the floor. I walked over and flicked the needle from the record, though it went against the grain to curtail it.

"Let's go to Evensong. Really. I'm serious."

"Where?" she challenged, a puzzled half-smile playing round her lips.

I named the college which had seen our game of run-and-see through its hushed corridors, which had seen Ginny and I make love under the table from which its president ate his supper. I watched her eyes for the merest flicker of cognizance. There wasn't one: or I missed it.

"Why?" she said.

"Why not?"

"But why *now*? I can't remember the last time I stepped inside a church."

"All the more reason," I countered, feigning flirtatiousness. I stood over her and placed my bare foot on her stomach. "It's in fifteen minutes."

She sighed, yawned, pushed my foot away, stood up and started to pile on the layers. When she thought her face was hidden from me, as she did then, it altered. It crumpled or contracted, I could never decide which, but its lines suggested an odd blend: of suspicion, of misery, of indecision. Suddenly she looked round at me, and very nearly caught me observing her.

"But I haven't rung home yet," she said. It had become her habit to ring home each evening 'for news' from the 'phone situated in the entrance hall of the accommodation block, from where anyone within a radius of fifty yards could hear the business of the caller as it echoed around the stair-well. I never went with Ginny when she 'phoned. Anyway, there never seemed to be any 'news'.

"Ring when we get back," I answered impatiently. I was fuelled by an unkind enthusiasm to get Ginny into that college under any pretence so that I could observe her reactions. I must still at this stage have been hoping against any expectation that Ginny would blush, break down, laugh, cry – anything – just so long as she'd admit to me the whole pretence of her ignorance of that episode was just that, a pretence. I wanted Ginny well and whole again. I wanted to walk back through the days to the beginning of our affair. I wanted to love her without the anger towards her intruding.

I made sure we approached the place from the same direction as we had done that night. I even staged a pause beside the gateway of my own college and kissed her as I had done then.

"I thought we were late," she said.

"We are," I countered, remembering how dark it had been then and how difficult it was now to pick out anything much on her face in the shadows. If the lane had been deserted before, this time it echoed with the voices of friends recognising each other, while bikes spun sideways across the tarmac and were thrown unceremoniously against the wall onto the communal heap. Finally a delivery lorry started to back around the corner.

"Oh, sod it," I said, and pulled Ginny along after me.

"Sod what?" She sounded surprised. "What's the matter? I thought this was your idea. We can go back if you –"

"No." I marched her along the lane and through the grand back entrance of the neighbouring college, just as we had done that night, and across the quadrangles, just as we had done that night, and damn her she never flinched or wavered or blanched or flushed or whatever I had hoped she would do. Instead she seemed to go out of her way to react differently. The library was an imposing oblong of Corinthian columns and balustrades. High windows under carved semi-circles of stone were eyes opening in surprise through which your own eye was drawn upwards to the exquisite ceiling of its brightly lit interior – a distant vision of twirling plasterwork shining with the blind whiteness of snow. The library, which had shone just in this way the last time when we scurried by it like excluded peasants skirting a mansion, but which had drawn from her then no comment, not even a flicker of interest; this building sent her into raptures of admiration. For a few seconds I could imagine this was the old Ginny, the uncomplicated one.

"Look at the ceiling," she exclaimed, in that slow way she had, "Just look at it. The lights? Can you see the chandeliers? They must be worth......there's something so exciting about it. It would look brilliant as an illustration, or in a film; you could play around with the contrast of the night, the pitch black up there and that sharp clear *white* light. No stars tonight, are there? A few stars would look even better. Can't you imagine it, Simon? What do you think?"

"Nothing. I don't think anything. Let's go."

She turned her head towards me and fell silent. It was a movement that can't have taken more than a second, but it held the deliberation of the swan swivelling to note the trespasser on the river bank and, when I remember it now, I can't get it faster than the speed of an action replay; or worse, the faltering, slurring deceleration of the film spool jamming. When I remember it now, it repeats itself half a dozen times so that I have no option but to see the various doubts she's having about me minutely alter the curve of an eyebrow or the width of a lip until the face finally comes to rest more set, more hopeless. She fell silent. It was a silence we maintained until the end of the service.

The college chapel had the proportions of a small cathedral. Our breath drifted up against the thick pillar in front of which we sat. The congregation numbered perhaps thirty, and as I looked at the variety of individuals, only united by their resort to bulky winter clothing, I registered mild surprise that such variety still existed. I'd fallen into a feeling that all the world was eighteen, and the whole universe a grid of ancient streets lined with ancient buildings and dotted with pubs filled with eighteen year olds. Ginny and I looked carefully ahead, into the aisle and away from each other.

I remember only the singing, which pulled me out of myself and dragged me through the freezing air up near the impossibly ornate ceiling and which even I in my antagonism to it could feel conveyed, oh, something. The choirboys who had scuffled and chattered in muffled voices as they assembled behind us conveyed nothing, the cathedral was nothing more to me then than dead stone built around too much space, but the notes, just the notes manipulated something out of me that I had not realised was inside. I found myself thinking with maudlin fondness of *home*, that little modern semi tucked on its estate of identical semis behind the village. What came to mind was the plastic-mould fishpond my mother had installed slap in the middle of our tiny lawn. I could see it in unbelievable detail, the thin layer of ice that would lid it, the goldfish lurking in stupid hibernation at the bottom above all the sludge, the blades and curves and twists of all the water plants my mother had nurtured and fussed over and moved around and tweaked and fingered. I could conjure up Bess, our old black dog, who'd be snuffing along the pond's edge in a short-sighted haze, outraged that she'd had to leave the warmth of her spot by the radiator in the kitchen. And as the notes spooled out one by one, ruthlessly, they forced me, like a paternal hand in the middle of the back, towards the disenfranchised figures who should have been peopling this little drama of home all along, but who had been shoved backstage by the shirty director. There was my mother, filling in the final piece of her latest jigsaw, with the telly on, worrying about the Russians, and me. There was my grandmother behind her, getting up, sitting down, disappearing out the door, coming back in again, fidgetting around with the curtains until my mother wouldn't be able to stop herself saying, "For heaven's sake sit down for a minute, can't you?"

After the final words of the service we sat frozen for a while as, slowly, the rest of the congregation realised it was all right to cough again, and shuffle off their pews. Ginny's thoughts must have spun off into strange corners, for she turned and said to me, in a small, chilly voice, "I read today that there are *five thousand* languages in the world. Now. Today. That's not counting dead ones. Would you have guessed so many? *Five thousand*. Think of all that.....scope for misunderstanding."

The warm, worrying images of home were still fizzling out and I must have looked dim.

"Five thousand languages, Simon Donaghue. We even talk the same one, don't we, but it doesn't seem to help us much." She got up quickly, and we left.

Outside the gateway of my college I gave her the room key and told her I was going to the bar 'for ten minutes'. I didn't ask her to come with me, and she didn't offer. I felt as if I needed some time on my own to sulk a little about the failure of my ploy. So I used credit in the college bar to buy a double gin and, because it was reasonably crowded, managed to sneak out the glass under my jacket (*strictly no glasses beyond this point*). I headed for the T.V. room, a first floor room with leaded windows overlooking the quad, which I calculated to be the most under-used communal space in the whole place.

There is something undeniably comforting in the atmosphere of a room with the lights turned off and the television turned on. *Then*, boiled eggs in front of *Blue Peter*, later homework avoided in front of *Top of the Pops*; *now*, a nice little whiskey in front of *Newsnight*. That night I was in luck. In the T.V. room the television played to empty ranks of oddly-angled arm-chairs. Each one of the twenty or so was of a unique design, a shabby individual relic of a particular period, and together they stuck up out of the near-dark like a collection of geriatric refugees waiting on the quay for news of a sailing. I sprawled myself comfortably front row centre, a kiddie at the cinema, and guzzled my gin. *The Waltons*. Do you remember *The Waltons*? That's what was playing on the television as I settled down. The colour was tuned too high and John-boy's face was Edam orange. The camera panned out to show the whole family sitting at table saying grace, their faces a long row of gently bobbing Edams. I chuckled away to myself, then became quite absorbed in John-boy's ambitions to become a writer and one of his sister's crush on a boy and his mom's fretting over.....

"Fairy-cake," stated a voice from somewhere in the shadows right at the back of the room. I yelped and spilt gin down my t-shirt. It was Shannon, of course, lurking in the dark and so low down in his chair I'd taken him for a discarded coat. The bastard must have known I'd not seen him, must have enjoyed the peculiar power that viewing the unwittingly viewed gives.

"Shannon," I returned, flatly, talking forwards.

"Enjoying the show?" he taunted.

"It wasn't me that chose the channel." I replied.

"You could have switched it over."

"I don't particularly care which channel I watch."

"Neither do I."

"So why are you skulking in here?"

"I'm not skulking, sonny Jim. I was dozing, as a matter of fact. Sleeping off a bloody good supper."

One of the Walton boys had just learnt a lesson about life, and was admitting he'd made a mistake and John-boy was telling him that you learn through mistakes. Their voices sounded suddenly inordinately loud and I could feel the old anger rising, but I was damned if I was moving for Shannon. If he chose to sit here all evening I'd out-sit him. All night. After the telly had shut down and the reminder tone had come on, if necessary.

"Had an argument with Virginia?" he started up.

"None of your business."

"No need to get narky. I was only enquiring."

I remembered the conversation I'd overheard in the lunch queue the day before. "I hear you've, uh, been having a little trouble in that department yourself."

"Oh?" he said dangerously.

"Well, you know, you hear things." Offhand.

"Oh?"

"But I don't repeat gossip."

"That's right, Fairy-cake," he said, "Gossip's for queens, isn't it?"

I was deciphering this one when he continued with the unexpected, "Did you know Jules is bent?"

"Yes, I did." I finished off my gin, remembered just how Jules' head had weighed on my knee and the pattern the straight blonde hairs had made on the fabric of my trousers, and blinked to erase the image.

"It takes one to know one."

"What?" My heartbeat grew audible to me.

"I said, it takes one to know one. It's a colloquial expression indicating that in order to recognise a certain condition it helps if you're familiar with it. That you share its characteristics."

"What are you talking about?"

"Now *I* had no idea about Fitch until this afternoon. Not that it changes anything. Well, not much. But it certainly explains a fuck of a lot."

"Does it?" I asked, though I didn't want to know.

"A fuck of a lot." Shannon obviously enjoyed the way that particular phrase hurried off the tongue. I could hear him shifting about in his chair, getting settled for a long explanation. *Enjoying* himself. "Now I just couldn't understand why Fitch made such a fuss about that book. At first."

"Which book?"

"Oh, *come on.*"

"I returned it to the library. It was a simple loan. Fitch lent it to me. I took it back for him, for Christ's sake. What was the problem?"

"You didn't return it."

"I absolutely did."

"When?"

"God knows. One evening."

"When the library had shut?"

"I put it in the book drop."

"So you walked over to the History Library, and- Did you have the book in a bag?"

"What?"

"Did you have the book in your hand? In a bag? Pocket?"

"God knows."

"Was it dark?"

"Yes."

"Was it raining?"

"Look-"

"Where's the book drop?"

"The History Library-"

"Which side of the building? On which street?"

"Why should I remember that?"

"What does it look like?"

"You know; it's just a flap in the wall."

"Like a letterbox?"

"*Yes.*"

"How big?"

"For Christ's sake..."

"Is it twelve by twenty? Twenty by forty?"

"It's just a hole in the wall."

"Brass? Steel? Iron? Does it open inwards or outwards?"

"It's a compartment for late returns."

"And that's where you put the book? You slid it through and you heard that satisfying thud and there it was, in the compartment reserved for late returns?"

"Yes. The book drop."

"The History Library," he said lingeringly, "does not have a book drop." How he was enjoying himself.

Embarrassment kept me quiet. I should have stayed quiet, but eventually I couldn't bear the smug silence behind me.

"It was one sodding book."

"But it wasn't, was it? Not to Fitch. As you well know. Don't pretend you don't know. I don't care what the fuck you did with the fucking book, Donaghue. But I'll tell you what the fuck I do care about and that's what you fucking did to Fitch."

"Finished?"

"No. You see, I just didn't understand why he couldn't stop mentioning the book-"

"Don't you mean the *fucking* book...?"

"Don't arse me about, Donaghue. Until this afternoon, I just thought you were mean. A kind of trivial character who was sloppy with his promises. A kind of *careless* character who didn't give a toss if other people had to pay fines for books they couldn't return. Actually he didn't get a fine, he was just debarred from using the library for two weeks."

"Shannon," I said, "What exactly gives you the right to hog all the moral high ground?"

He ignored me. "Which wouldn't have mattered to you or I, would it, Donaghue? You're a stranger to the joys of academic slog, aren't you, sweetheart? You only leave your room to buy supplies-" I didn't like this. How did people *know* when I was in my room? "- and I know ways and means of avoiding the place, but *Fitch*..."

"It was only-"

142

"Oh, spare me," he said sharply, "Not to put too fine a point on it, Fitch is thoroughly screwed up. I don't pretend to understand what's going on in his head and I've tried to shake him out of it." For the first time he sounded helpless. "God knows why he can't just-" He exhaled quickly, in exasperation. "You'd think he could just-"

I used the chink in his defences. "Why does everybody think I'm somehow....*responsible* for Fitch? He's not even a friend of mine. First of all I've got Stephanie bloody Zielinski on my back, acting as if I'm his psychiatrist. Now I've got you going on as if....." Something struck me. "What happened this afternoon? What did Fitch say to you this afternoon?" It was difficult to sound only moderately concerned, when wild images of myself labelled *bent* were spinning in my imagination. Everybody in those days thought they'd erased their prejudice because they never voiced it, because they used the word *gay* not *queer*, because they opted for a colossal not saying instead of cracking jokes about *minding your back*, but I could see how it would be. My masculinity rose up as a towering Colossus of Rhodes from which chunks threatened to fall into the water and between the legs of which members of the public threatened to sail so they could throw their heads back and guffaw at the inadequacy under the tunic.

"You sound worried, Fairy-cake." Shannon was back on form.

"You were the one who brought the whole subject up."

"What I can't stomach," he said hard and fast, "is deliberate cruelty. I don't care if Fitch is bent. I don't care if you're bent. Each to his own-"

"I'm not bent. I've got a girlfriend."

"Oscar Wilde had a wife."

"I'm not bent." I stood up and faced him. Damn him, he was still slouched in his armchair, as if the conversation were routine, a chat.

"I don't care if you're straight, bent, fucking *triangular.* I wouldn't care if you walked in here in a swimsuit and a tiara. I wouldn't care if you were wiped off the face of the earth tomorrow. What I can't stomach is the way you've deliberately messed Fitch up."

"Unsay what you've just said."

"You deliberately let Fitch think he was in with a chance. You deliberately-"

"I am not bent. Unsay it."

"You quite deliberately allowed him to develop his ridiculous infatuation with you. With *you*-"

"Unsay it."

"Fuck knows why he chose you. And what satisfaction did you get out of it? What was the thrill in tormenting the poor fucker?"

"Unsay it." I wanted to hit him. I couldn't have cared less if he thrashed me in return, just so long as I could get in one good solid punch, feel the resistance.

"Oh, be quiet, Donaghue, and go back to-"

The door opened with a fast swing, and six or seven loud Third Years spilled in, oblivious to the part they'd taken on as Chorus in our opera of antagonism.

"Oh sorry," said one, switching on the light, "There's normally never anybody in here."

"Anybody mind if we turn over to the Results?" another asked, addressing a point midway between Shannon, half out of his chair at the back of the room and me, poised ready for a fight like a character from *West Side Story*.

"Are we interrupting?" somebody with a little more insight questioned.

"No," I barked, and found my chair again. I glued my eyes to whatever it was they were watching, looked neither right or left and grimly stuck it out.

During the next couple of hours the door opened and shut twice. It had a piston closing device, but this was broken and the door slammed both times so that I had no way of knowing whether it was Shannon, leaving. I refused to look to see if it was Shannon, leaving. When finally the channel shut down for the night I let myself stand up and turn round slowly, expecting an ambush. I was stiff with tension. If Shannon had been there I would have been just as ready for him, but it was only the remnants of the group who met my eye and I was forced to leave disappointed- or it could have been relieved.

Hate is not an emotion I can easily feel now. I don't hate the bank clerk responsible for writing the letter which accompanies the bounced cheque, though I swear when it arrives. I don't hate the neighbour who comes out as I am parking to watch my back bumper so it doesn't scratch his Reliant Robin. For him I reserve a kind of pitying irritation. I don't even hate the monsters who commit atrocities on children they have plucked from the streets, children like Alex and Henry (touch wood, *never* them). They don't rank as people. They're half-formed things, aberrations that I box with malignant untouchable forces- killer viruses perhaps; bacterial infection.

Then it was dead easy. I hated Shannon with a generous uncensored indulgence of emotion. I loved hating him. When you're young it's pleasurable to hate: and useful, for you can tip any emotional left-overs into that one jam-packed container. Shannon had been so unkind as to reveal my unliberal self to me. It had taken him a mere few minutes to debunk the tolerance I'd always professed – "I mean, yeah, it's up to the individual, right? There's nothing *wrong* with, uh, being, uh, drawn to someone of, uh, the same gender." He'd had me on my feet, eagerly jumping into the camp of the gay-bashers – so terrified of the slur he'd cast that I was keen to let him rip me up with those rugger-hardened limbs. Not that I'd have expressed it quite like that then. I'd have said I hated him because he deserved hating. He was a wanker, wasn't he?

* * *

It's one of the worst.

I'm swimming along a sewer as wide as a motorway. Above is the weight of an underground city. We're so deep that daylight's a distant dream. The holocaust has been and gone and everything has been wrecked forever. Tower blocks set into the rock on either side, and suddenly ahead and above, are grim as a Moscow suburb, colourless as old footage; tenements full of hopeless people, whose washing hangs out of the windows and whose dozens of children are listless, dressed in vests. The water is so heavily polluted it's like thin mud. Flotsam's scumming up the shoreline and shapes bob past me. There's a terrible sense of my body out of sight under me, a prey to whatever's down there: could be any disgusting filth, could be rusted iron sharp as a knife, could be life, gross as the element from which it's grown. I can't reach the shore. The tower blocks rise sheer from the sludge and give no hand-hold. I'm way out of depth. Eventually I'll get tired and my head will slip under. I'm straining to keep my chin up and my head's angled back. Ginny's behind one of the plate glass windows tapping at a type-writer, looking like a Sindy doll; tight suit and film-star glasses. Right up at the top of the block ahead is a balustrade and behind that is the only lit window and inside it I can see a plasterwork ceiling of brilliant white, and beneath it, though I can't exactly see them, I know my father and Dave Shannon are sitting smoking cigars together; fat cats in low leather arm-chairs. They own the place. My father gives Shannon a great Godfather kiss on the cheek, hands cupping his head, one cheek, the other cheek, the first cheek again. That's it, nothing else. All I can do is tread water and feel the stirrings of objects or creatures brushing past me under the surface. Against my foot is not so bad, against my hip is intolerable, against my neck....

I wake myself up this time. I've pushed the cover off me completely, but somehow Ginny's still asleep beside me. I can't shake the idea that I'm covered in sewerage and that the flow of it around my body is hope leaking down the drain. We've despoiled and ruined and there's nothing of any value left. Then slowly I wake up completely and steady myself. It's full daylight beyond the curtains and in the room above some kind of gathering's going on. No music that I can hear, just the mumble of a dozen voices in sociable mood. Ginny's very deeply asleep, long low breaths and a look of absolute self-containment. I watch the rise and fall of her diaphragm with hostility and I think, *you didn't even throw me a line; you could at least have thrown me a line.*

* * *

My grandmother was always one for bargain gifts. Her childhood of relative poverty had left her with an inability to part with money unless it was for things like loaves of bread or decent cardigans.

146

Presents were a shocking waste of money and the prices the shops in town charged *daylight robbery*. Consequently all the presents she gave me were from the Red Cross shop. I'd open them with dread, already planning the smile I'd fix as I picked at the sellotape binding the wrapping paper like swaddling. And the paper: retrieved, of course; holly leaves for birthdays and silver horseshoes for Christmas. Usually the parcels were soft and bulky and contained dressing-gowns. I'm not sure where her fixation with dressing-gowns came from. There must, after all, have been a first; she can't always have collected them – and given them – with such persistence. I'd managed to get away from home with only two, but as her letter had informed me, there was another waiting for me, no doubt already laid out on my bed.

Before I had left home for university she'd surprised me with a small hard package which she'd thrust into my hands as we passed on the stairs. She chose her moments. It took me three seconds to leap up those stairs, but it took her several minutes to edge down them. We met somewhere in the middle, like points on a graph. I remember the paper: it was pastel blue with repeat-pattern teddy-bears and the message *Congratulations* running in lines across it. Inside was an oldish compact camera, the kind that dads held at sixties' sea-sides to take snaps of their children building sandcastles or their wives in polka-dot swimsuits.

"You can take pictures of all your lady-friends," she said, winking, "We shall want to see if they're up to scratch."

"Thanks," I said, "Thanks. That's great."

There was a certain irony in what she said, though it only struck me much later. At the time I'd no intention of using the thing, though I had to stick it in the suitcase along with the dressing-gowns. The day before I left home she was in and out of the bedroom as I packed, my mother's attempts to entice her away a complete failure. After all, somebody packing was *an event*.

I did use the camera. In those days after we'd gone to Evensong and after my skirmish with Shannon in the T.V. room, I dug it out, bought a film from Boots and started to take pictures of Ginny. God knows why. Maybe I wanted to be able to stare at her image when she wasn't there, to search for clues, to pin her down. She didn't voice any objection but on every photo her face had the slight tilt she reserved for questioning, her eyes were invariably puzzled. *Why are you taking a photograph of me?* they clearly asked. I don't have these photos any more. I found them a couple of years on, and destroyed them.

The camera could only be used outside. When Ginny left in the morning, our morning, which was usually around four, I'd offer to walk her to the library, another change in routine which seemed to please and confuse her at the same time. Along the route I'd get her to pause. Out would come the camera, a quick shuffling into position with a pretence at framing a composition of some sort, then – *ready?* – it was all over. Ostensibly I posed her in front of *sights* or at some arty angle, but really all I was interested in was capturing her face, as if each new near-identical image might be the one to talk to me, to leak the truth the original was withholding. But the damn camera had no fine-tuning of any sort, the object had to be at least eight feet from the lens and every time I tried to force it to take anything at a more intimate distance I knew that it would come out as a fuzzy blur. After three or four days I gave up, took the couple of films I'd worked through to Boots for processing and chucked the camera back in the suitcase.

Here are the words that Ginny used that finally made me make my decision about her, about what to do.

"Simon, it's her."

That was all that was necessary.

It must have been the Saturday at the end of sixth week. Two weeks to go till the Christmas vacation and one week (and a bit) to exams. I'd been to pick up the processed films, paying by cheque-fairy money; since there was nothing in my account it didn't really exist. That would get the bank-manager hopping. I hadn't been out for a while and I felt like a peeled prawn, underdressed and overexposed, protected only by the thin coating of separation the gin provided, disoriented by all the people who seemed to move too purposefully round the edges of its chilly glow. Completing my short orbit and coming back down to land, I walked along the corridor and was surprised to see Ginny sitting on the floor beside my door waiting for me.

"You decided to give the library a miss? I said.

"I was lonely," she said. She looked cold and pinched, a down and out in a doorway.

A weird disjointed feeling welled up inside me, but "Yeah...?" was all I said.

While she made coffee I fished out the photos and dropped them on the desk, and then realised my mistake: I'd been hoping to keep them to myself.

"Oh, you got the photos, did you? Well, let's see them."

She walked over to the window and briskly drew the curtains to let in the last bits of light of the day.

"Do you have to?" I protested.

"But it's so dark. And you won't be able to see the photos if I don't."

I had the feeling *she* didn't particularly want to see them anyway, and was expressing interest for my benefit solely, but she did add, "It would be nice if there was *one* good one in all that lot."

We didn't get them out immediately. We sat on the window seat and drank our coffee. I watched a large group of Friendlies meander down the lane buzzing round each other in a friendly kind or way. Beverly McKenzie was there, Caroline Funnell and Stephanie Bloody Zielinski as well. Stephanie was carrying one end of a long, trussed object, a boy I recognised but couldn't name the other. Their difference in heights meant the object sloped at an angle of forty-five degrees.

"Oh god," I exclaimed, "They've bought a Christmas tree. Oh my god. A plastic Christmas tree. I don't think I can stand it."

"What?" said Ginny distractedly.

"They've all gone out together, like the seven dwarves or something for god's sake, hi bloody ho, and bought a plastic Christmas tree. Where the *hell* do they think they're going to put it? It's not even December yet, for god's sake."

Ginny made a half-hearted attempt to crane around to catch sight of them.

"It must be seven foot. At least seven foot."

"Oh well," said Ginny.

A disproportionate anger mounted in me. "Oh my god," I said.

"What?" asked Ginny.

"I know where they're going to put it. I bet they're going to put it in the corridor. I bet they're going to put it in this corridor. Outside Stephanie bloody Zielinski's room," I groaned.

"Let's look at the photos," said Ginny.

She laid them all along the window cushion in three or four lines, balancing them on the couple of t-shirts, plastic bags and bits of paper that had drifted there since Sheila's Big Tidy.

"What do you think?" she said, jollying me along.

I hated being jollied along. Nevertheless I made some attempt, leaning forward to look.

"They're all the same." She sounded disappointed as if, despite her reluctance to have them taken at all, she'd really hoped for some great snapshot. They were pretty much all the same. Ginny in front of old walls, Ginny in front of old bicycles, Ginny in front of old gateways, Ginny with her eyes shut (caught her blinking) in front of trees, Ginny in front of shops with a bag in her hand. Diane Arbus I was not. A good half were out of focus or too dark.

"No they're not all the same," I commented peevishly, "Some are even worse than others."

She hadn't heard. With slow deliberation she picked one out of the selection and held it close to her short-sighted eyes. She looked ill; sick at heart. "Simon," she said, "It's her."

Immediately I understood, but that didn't stop me fighting hard not to. "Who?" I said.

By way of reply she held the photograph so that it caught the light from the window and we could both see it. It was one of the blurred ones. Ginny stood at the top of the steps into the English and Law libraries, which shared a building. Concrete steps and sharp modern angles and trim prim clean lines, that building, as I reconstruct it in my imagination. The light in this photo was surprisingly good since I'd taken it on the one clear bright day we'd had that week. Ginny was patiently standing at the top of the flight of stairs wrapped in one of my jumpers but looked chilled nonetheless, a white plastic carrier dangling from her hand. *Why are you taking this photograph?* was vocalised in the curve of her back and no doubt would have been in her facial expression if it had been clearer. Behind her two or three badly blurred figures swirled around the swing doors of the building itself. The one whose hair swung out in an arc could have been a girl, but then again.... As for the others, one wore red and the other black and a college scarf. I stared hard at them for ten seconds, shook my head. I couldn't in all conscience even *pretend* to pick out *you know who*. I sighed with a kind of relief and looked at Ginny.

"Behind-" she began, and had to clear her throat as she passed me the photo. Even then the voice that came out had a curtailed quality: breathless. "Behind the door. She's behind the door." Her hands crept up to her face. I've noticed that since, that this is a sign of real distress. People nurse their faces, as if to hold themselves together and in one piece. When my grandmother died my mother developed the temporary habit of covering her mouth with her hand, as if she thought some awful indiscretion would fly away from her out of the hole.

Reluctantly I drew my eyes from Ginny's and looked again, this time behind the indeterminate girl with the frozen hair and her red and black friends.

That moment has become one of my vulnerable moments. I mean that, even now, images I come across can bring it back in all its strength when I least expect it, like a sharp clip round the back of the head. Recently I watched a documentary on T.V. on the subject of the Brontë Society, a group of enthusiasts who catalogue and wallow in each and every fact related to the Brontës, who try to resurrect them practically; well, even literally. One of them had taken a photograph of the Parsonage at Haworth. It was summer and the door stood open. Inside could be seen the distinct yet indistinct shape of a dark full-clothed figure crossing the hall. *But,* she asserted, *there had been no visitors in the house at that moment.* I didn't believe in *Madeleine* then any more than I believe in the ghost of Charlotte Brontë now, but it made no difference. When I saw on the photograph Ginny handed me a distinct yet wholly indistinct figure behind the plate-glass door of the library I felt the foundations of my rationality shoved to one side an inch. I felt that I was seeing something supernatural ('Is there anybody there? Knock if you're there. Oh, oh, the table's moving. Who's there? Who's there?'), something I shouldn't be acknowledging if I wanted the

Other Side to leave me well alone. Yet all that could be seen, really, was the shape of (probably) a girl wearing (definitely) a dark fitted coat who might (the colour was bad) have had red hair. The face was averted, as the figure turned from the doorway to walk further into the building. Fear is so infectious: the tremor in Ginny's hand as she passed me the photo had vibrated straight through its chemical and paper and up my arm, and the fear, which might have made me reach out for Ginny as I recognised its echo in myself, drove me away from her as surely as caries. "Simon, it's her," had been the final connection, the plus connecting to the minus and completing the circuit, tripping the switch in me. All the while I was putting my arm around her, patting her on the back like a child, skim-listening to the stream of conjecture and explanation that poured out of her, I knew the decision had been made and that it only remained for that decision to be acted upon. Already as she spoke in those fractured sentences into the hollow of my shoulder I was running as fast as I could, I was skidding over the sand-dunes and leaving her high and dry, stranded among the driftwood. I'd sold her down the river. I kissed her on the cheek and she laid her head against me.

* * *

When my grandmother finally died last year, my mother gave me most of the clutter from my grandmother's room. I suppose she didn't want it herself. Alex took charge of it, which was just as well: I'd have been tempted to stick the whole lot in the next jumble collection.

Alex shook out the contents of thirty-year-old carrier bags and forty-year-old shoe-boxes all over her bed. I'd stuck my head round the door of her room to say something like *the baby-sitter will be here in twenty minutes so can you brush your teeth/clean up this mess/finish your homework....* Sitting cross-legged among my grandmother's debris in a dressing-gown that had, it goes without saying, been retrieved from the Red Cross by my grandmother herself, Alex had been picking through the pencils, packets of needles and perished rubber bands in a biscuit tin on the lid of which Dalmation puppies cocked their heads and on the rim of which rust crept. She fished out a photograph.

"Who's *that*?" she said, making a face.

It was me. I was standing by the back door of my mother's house stiff as a mannequin. I obviously hadn't known where to put my arms and they hung oddly. I was staring straight at the camera with what was probably reluctance but came across as a Jim Morrison kind of arrogance – early Jim Morrison, before he turned himself into a toad, when he was still a brutally good-looking prince. I had a suspicion my mother had taken it the summer before I left for college; could have been before then, but it certainly wasn't after. It had that feel of being an attempt to trap someone in time, to remember them. She'd known it was the last summer I'd be hers.

"It's me," I admitted.

Alex was entirely expressionless for a good ten seconds, holding the photo before her face. "No," she said finally.

"What d'you mean, *no*?"

She shook her head at me. There was the faintest smile. "*That*," she stated categorically, "is not you."

I laughed. "Yes, it is."

She shook her head at me. The tip of her tongue protruded at the edge of her mouth, which meant, *I know what I'm talking about.*

"It is," I said, not sure whether she was joking.

"No."

"Yes."

"But look," she said, as if it was all that *needed* to be said, "The hair."

"What about it?" I said provocatively, knowing full well what she meant, "Long hair was in then." Not strictly accurate.

"But it's kinky."

"Do you mean kinky as in curly or kinky as in freaky?"

"Well, *both*."

I keep my hair dead short. I've only the occasional grey hair.

"That's just how it was." I shrugged.

She simply couldn't let it drop. I turned to go – I'd not changed yet, we were expected at eight – but she said quickly, "It's not just the hair."

I leaned against the doorpost.

"How come I've never seen a picture of you looking like this before?"

"I was camera-shy."

Still she wasn't satisfied. The tip of her tongue was back at the corner of her lip. She looked at me blankly.

"Look," I said, "Can I go and get ready now? Is the interrogation over?"

"It's just not your face."

"Yes, it is." Exasperated; late.

"No, it's not. I don't like this man," she challenged, waving the photo gently in my direction, "There's something creepy about him."

"You don't," I said dryly.

"No." She laid the photograph in front of her like Exhibit A.

"Alex," I countered, sliding out the door, "If it's not me by Granny D's back door, then who is it?"

"I don't know," she called after me, and I could *see* that decisive serious grin on her face, "But it's not you."

* * *

Several days passed before I acted. Then I returned to Dr. Fell's surgery, something I'd not intended to bother with. I hadn't made an appointment, not through sloth, but as a result of the kind of urgent distraction which was directing me through those days. Because it happened to be nearly at the end of surgery and because I simply stood in front of her until she'd finished ticking me off, the receptionist slipped me in. Dr. Fell looked surprised to see me, and more surprised when I opened my mouth and talked without prompting and without stopping until I had had my say.

I started with the photograph and worked backwards. I re-scripted the more lurid elements of my close encounter with 'Maddy', made it into a cup of coffee sort of affair. I'd talked with 'Maddy', I said, in my room one afternoon. It had been so obviously Ginny, I said, that I'd not even suspected Ginny's confusion till the next day when she denied even being there with me. I emphasised Ginny's confusion and distress, her dips into complete fantasy. I became nearly eloquent in my relief at shifting the burden off my back. As I talked, and as Dr. Fell continued to take me seriously, looked, in fact, alarmingly grave, *I* began to take myself more seriously. The certainty that I'd been right to come grew in that workaday environment, while the life Ginny and I had been leading by contrast began to appear grotesque, like the hallucinogenic dreams of addicts. I felt as if I'd stepped into the disinfected orderliness of Dr. Fell's weighing-machine-wall-chart-net-curtain universe from out of a *Lucy In The Sky With Diamonds* world in which Ginny was Lucy herself, twenty foot tall with telescopic eyes and a prismatic dress.

When I finally dried up, Dr. Fell was quiet for a few moments, then told me I was not to worry, that he would contact Ginny's college and through them the G.P. responsible for Ginny. He would *set the ball rolling*. Did I have any questions? No? And incidentally my blood test had shown positive for glandular fever and he would suggest that I get as much sleep as possible, drink a lot but *no alcohol mind* and try and take things easy. That might be tricky with- didn't I have exams. coming up? At least it was nearly the end of term and then I could have a good rest and go home to Mum and Dad and Mum could cook me a few decent meals. Did I have any questions about any of that? No? Was I sure?

So I had *set the ball rolling*. As I walked back the ridiculously short distance to my room the phrase rattled around in my head like a Party slogan or the catch phrase of an advert. Ball bearings like perfected grape-pips, marbles like cat's eyes, tennis balls, footballs, cannon-balls, snowballs, the massy balls that swing to demolish old buildings. I imagined a bowling ball the size of a house channelled at speed down the lane beside the accommodation block, coming towards me as I cowered, a Jerry trapped on the lane of the bowling alley as Tom releases his volley with a demonic grin on his face. My thoughts spun associatively, wildly, drunkenly; perhaps, with the virus, feverishly. *Tom and Jerry.....Of Mice and Men....Are you a man or a mouse?...Charles Atlas....Dave Shannon.* About the only subject my mind skirted was Ginny, what I had done to Ginny, how hard and fast the ball would roll and where it was likely to roll to rest.

If all that has gone before in this narrative has been played at normal speed, from now on it's all fast-forward: not the fast-forward of the video or the skidding cassette, rather the more sedate rapidity of the record skipping from 33r.p.m. to 45. That's what it felt like. Events came too fast for their consequences to be understood, conversations might just as well have been relayed in Martian for all I absorbed of them. So read it fast. Read it late at night, when you've just come in and you've had too much to drink and your mind's speeding along through all the lousy past choices you've made or buzzing with all the plans the drink's convinced you are still possible. Run a temperature and read it feeling like death warmed up, so only half makes sense. Read it after you've had a run in with your partner, so your pulse is a little too fast and your anger keeps leading you away into what you *should have said*. Read it to loud, fast and discordant music. How about *The Sex Pistols*? That should give it a 'seventies feel, help you feel the chaos inside my head.

Ginny said, "You never say you love me, you've never said it."
"What do you mean?"
"You've never actually said it."
"That can't be true."
"It can't be true but it is."
"I say it all the time."
"No. Never. Not once."
"We've slept in the same bed for weeks."
"You've never just said it."
"I'm lying three inches away from you now."
"That's not the same."
"How much closer could I get?"
"Saying it's different."
"I have said it. I'm always saying it."
"Say it now."
"This is such a cliché."
"Clichés are just real things that happen frequently. Please just say it."
"How can I, now?"
"You can't say it, can you?"

Ginny walked straight into it.

She said, "When I went back to my room yesterday I checked my pigeon-hole and-" Pause. Exhalation of breath. "there was a note in it from the college office saying that a doctor was trying to get hold of me, that she'd rung me three times no less. Dr. Blick." Tut. "Apparently she's our local G.P. What's going on, Simon?"

"How would I know? It's probably for some routine thing."

"Like what? Why would the doctor who covers for the college, a woman I've never even contacted – I mean I've never even been to see her for a sore throat – why would she ring me?"

"Maybe that's it. Maybe you were supposed to register with her."

"I did register with her. Everybody did."

"Well, maybe you filled in the form wrong."

"She'd write to me. She wouldn't ring *three times*."

"She might."

"*Simon*. Listen to me. I'm worried. I just keep thinking it might be something to do with Madeleine."

"Oh. Oh, right."

"Sorry. I'm sorry. I don't mean to sound as if I'm *blaming* you or anything. God, Simon, I don't know what I'd be like if you weren't here, if I couldn't come here and...lie close to you, but it's just that-"

"It's O.K."

"Supposing the police had found something out about her. Oh, I don't know, something *terrible*... I can't even bring myself to say the things I've thought. But I just keep thinking perhaps the police have found her...one way or another....and they've given the G.P. the job of, you know, *talking* to me. You know, *breaking news*."

"Oh, I see. I see what you mean."

"Poor Madeleine."

"Why don't you ring the doctor back?"

"I know. I must."

"Why don't you ring her in the morning?"

"I will."

"You should."

"I will."

Ginny said, "I rang the doctor."

"Aha."

"It was such a relief. I can't tell you what a relief it was."

"Yes?"

"Well, Madeleine's all right. At least no news is good news."

"So....?"

"Well, she was just concerned about me, the doctor, I mean. Although she was a bit cagey, actually, about who'd put her onto me. I thought it might be the college, but...I don't think it can have been. They never see me there but they probably all just think I'm tucked up in the library all the time or down the pub or something, and anyway... Anyway, she knew about Maddy. All I can think is that Mum's flapping about me. She's lost one, hasn't she? She probably wants to make sure the other daughter's all right. They don't know I've got you, do they? So all I can think is that Mum got the doctor's number from the college and–"

"What did the doctor say to you?" My voice came out way too sharply, but she didn't notice.

"Oh, you know, she just asked how I was blah blah blah... Actually I made a complete fool of myself."

"Oh?"

"I'm embarrassed to admit it. I got myself so wound up thinking about Madeleine that I cried down the phone. God, I hate crying in front of people. Except you. I've never felt embarrassed in front of you. Do you know you're the only person I've cried in front of since... since Hazeldene Parochial Junior school?"

"Hmm."

"And she was so, oh I don't know, *sympathetic* that I just crumbled. I probably sounded completely hysterical. And I have to admit to you, Simon, that I told her what happened between you and Madeleine."

"You did?"

"It's been so awful *not* talking about it to anyone. I know I said we should not...refer...to it, but maybe... Anyway, I did."

"How much detail did you...?"

"Well, very little, obviously, since, thank god, I know very little."

"Of course."

"It's over now, Simon. It's past. Let's not-"

"Right."

"We've got to get back to how we were before."

"Yes."

"We've got to try."

"Yes."

Ginny said, "Are you awake? I'm still awake."

"Hmm."

"I can't see your face. Are you really awake?"

"Probably."

"I went to see Dr. Blick."

"Oh?"

"Well, she asked me to."

"And what did you talk about?"

"It's so dark tonight, isn't it? Usually you can see a kind of sliver of light down that side of the curtain. I wonder if it's moonlight or lamplight or.... It occurred to me how I've always been so suspicious of doctors, and it's not been fair of me, really. God knows, all the doctors *tried* with Madeleine, didn't they? I can hardly blame them for not helping much. Probably nobody could have helped. Some things simply *are*, aren't they? And anyway, Dr. Blick seems better than average."

"*What did you tell her?*"

"A lot. Almost everything. I told her I think Madeleine's following me. The photo, you know? It was as if the doctor had given me a truth drug." Sad little laugh. "I suppose that's what comes of holding things back- for years. For years, Simon, I've held it all in check. I always had to be the child who was *all right*, the one who behaved. I've coped and coped and coped and coped on and on-"

"*What did you tell her?*"

"About the photo. That she's here in Oxford. All the time, somewhere just out of sight like some kind of Rumpelstiltskin, ready to pop up out of the floorboards and spoil things....trying to take over my life, trying to be me. Scary stuff. You know what I remembered the other day?"

"What?"

"Do you remember *The Exorcist*? What a stir it created?"

"You were too young to see that. It was X rated."

"I didn't see it. I borrowed the book from a girl at school and I locked myself in the bathroom to read it. It must have taken me hours. I wonder what they thought I was doing in there? Do you remember the green vomit?"

"Green vomit? No."

"Well, you know it's about a young girl who becomes possessed?"

"I know nothing. I didn't see it. I always thought it sounded complete crap."

"It was, but it was powerful crap. A young girl gets taken over by spirits. *We are legion*." The last sentence in a dalek voice. "And-"

"This isn't doing much for me, Ginny. I thought we were talking about Dr. Blick."

"We are. I'm telling you what I told Dr. Blick."

"You recounted the plot of *The Exorcist* to Dr. Blick?"

"No. I used it to try to explain what it feels like to be invaded like that. I didn't feel I was convincing her how frightening it is; she kept nodding her head and trying to look as if she understood but I could see she didn't. Which is hardly surprising. So I told her how reading *The Exorcist* gave me exactly the same feeling as being near Madeleine. It *is* like somebody trying to crawl inside you." Breath on my cheek so I know she's twisting towards me. "Did you ever try and terrify yourself with a Ouija board?"

"No. Well, yes, but, look, Ginny, this is making me uneasy..."

"That's the same feeling. That nothing is under control. That anything could happen. With Madeleine anything could happen. Anything *can* happen. She's out there-"

"*Ginny*. Stop it."

"See? Even *talking* about it spooks you. Imagine looking up and seeing somebody curling a strand of hair round her finger and realising that you're curling a strand of hair round *your* finger and that she's trying to copy all those little tics that make you *you* because she wants to *be* you. Try and imagine how that would feel."

"I can't and I don't want to. I think we should both shut up now and go to sleep."

"Okay. But she *is* still out there. Simon, what do you think she'll do next?"

"Perhaps there won't be a next. Perhaps something will stop her from doing *next*."

"What? What would stop her?"

"I don't know."

"Keep me safe, Simon."

There was the tutorial with Frank, the third tutorial from which Jules had been absent. I felt irritated with Jules for taking the initiative; somehow if he'd turned up I could have used the glandular fever and skived off myself.

Frank, boiling up his kettle for his inevitable cup of coffee though I could hear from its laboured hiss it hadn't got enough water in it, said twitchily, "Apparently Jules is not going to join us today. He is unwell." He continued wearily. "This tutorial session has the potential to become something of a shambles, don't you think, Simon? One of you with glandular fever and the other.." He raised his eyebrows. "And did you manage to address yourself to the task of preparing the passage?"

At the finish of what turned out to be an edgy session for me, with no one but me to answer all those canny questions, he handed me an extra reading list. "I'd be very grateful if you'd drop in on Jules with this," he said, fixing me in his sights like a sparrow, "Relay to him the tasks in hand. Oh, yes, and..." He strolled over to the book shelves and without hesitation pulled a hardback from its place. I realised with wonder and a dawning sense of the world as a place holding a far greater variety of individuals than I'd ever imagined that he must have his books arranged alphabetically. As he walked over to place the book in my hand and as I recognised its particular colour and bulk an eerie sensation came over me. "If you can give him this as well, there's a good chap. It's the Knotsworth, as you can see. Jules tells me he's had a bit of a problem getting hold of it.

Heaven knows why, you'd have thought the History Library would have been able to oblige," he ran on, unaware of the clamminess of the hand that I reluctantly offered, "Will you impress upon him that this is *my personal copy* and that if he loses it he will be in the deepest water he has ever found himself in? Hmm? Yes? Thankyou. And I'm relying on you to keep an eye on him – as are others, as are others. He needs an eye keeping on him. Yes? Good, good. Now. One more tutorial before Prelims, as you are aware. We'll discuss arrangements for sitting it – times, etc. – then. So: everything under control? Hunky-dory? Yes? Good."

I left, dangling the book at the end of my arm like a dead thing gone high, sweaty at the prospect of *seeing* Jules again, never mind at the prospect of being reluctant party to the sick joke of the Knotsworth. I considered leaving the wretched article in his pigeon-hole, instantly rejecting that particular cop-out on the solid grounds that Frank would be bound to see it sticking out as surely as if it had been lit by neon and that he would be less than thrilled to see *his personal copy* treated so casually. I considered for about an eighth of a second giving it the treatment I'd meted to the first. I even considered asking Ginny to take it over to Jules' room. *What a good idea*, I sneered to myself and at myself, *let Jules tell Ginny all about his crush on little old Simon and how he could have sworn little old Si felt the same way.*

I'd wandered into the quad. For the moment it was empty, save for a rogue scrap of paper scudding hesitantly over the paving in the eddies of wind; a renegade from the notice board in the Porter's Lodge, perhaps. In my indecision I was drawn to the sundial, homing in to circle it slowly.

Indulge me once more and once more only while I indulge myself with my Virtual version of what happened then, let me resurrect the eternal present of a simulated wish-fulfilment *might have been*. It helps. It doesn't take long, and it helps. This is it: after a couple of meanders around the sundial I decide to get whatever's coming over with quickly. Anyway I can hear the operatic volume of Shannon's voice growing from some hidden direction, so I snap the book up under my arm and stride across the quad towards the Porter's Lodge. As I step out into the street it starts to drizzle and the rain slants in streaks across the sandstone of the buildings and across the charcoal of the tarmac and the grey of the paving, steadily darkening the colour of them all. You can imagine how good the computer will be at generating this colour change, though it might fail to trap the peculiar softening of the air that comes with drizzle, the sharp smell, the subtlety of the changes in current and temperature, the deadening of sound which never fails to bring to mind and memory the interiors of theatres, the childhood pantomine. Because it's mid-afternoon everywhere looks pretty dead. One or two Second Years I've never talked to walk ahead of me chatting amiably and getting wet. I tuck the Knotsworth inside my jacket and follow them along the lane and round the corner near the 'sixties accommodation block inside which my own room waits for me in all its squalor. From here I have only a hundred yards to the short terrace of houses in which Jules lives. How shall I use that hundred yards? I'll use it wisely, walking with rapid steps beneath clouds so heavy and mobile they invite comparison with a dirty bedsheet shaken, along the lane narrow enough to stir faint claustrophobia. The first twenty yards I'll give to Ginny and the resolution to tell her how I've loved her, loved her. The second twenty I'll give to *home*, to writing in my head the letter that begins *Dear Nan, I am so pleased you've managed to get me another dressing-gown...* The next twenty I'll force myself to allot to *work*, the hunting down and flattening of the squat slug guilt that stops me actually *doing* anything about *work*. Then I'll get out the metaphoric differently-coloured felt tips and draft a *work* plan; blue for revision, red for reading, yellow for notetaking... The last forty I'll devote to directing my feet towards Jules himself. Now my route takes me close to the window of my own room, the lane I'm walking down passing at right angles to it, tucked as it is round the corner. I take the time to glance over my shoulder as I hurry and surprise, surprise there's Ginny sitting with her book on the window seat. Back early she must be, no longer avoiding the daytime me, so I can suddenly believe along with Bob Marley that *Everything's gonna be alright, everything's gonna be alright...* It's only a flash of window, Ginny, book, but it includes her smile as she sees me, her quick wave. What's more, I see she's wearing a dress in cornflower blue I've never even seen before which makes her look...which makes her look older, beautiful, different in a way I can't define because *I've not got there yet: I'll have to run to catch up...* Wow, I think with surprise, *she's shed the black. What else has she shed?* Then I'm into the last forty yards, the impressions of my first and last visit to Jules' room still uncomfortably fresh, able to tip me into a many-corridored doubt (*What did I say to Jules in the quad? Why did he think I wanted him? What did he see in me that made him full of hope? Could I be...?*). I almost jog the last few yards because some echo of a presentiment tells me I must hurry and then I'm out of the Virtual rain through the scruffy front door (plum-coloured: never noticed before), already starting up the stair before I have time to shiver in the chill damp of the hallway, hearing as I take the stairs two at the time the background noise of a conversation from another student room (good, good, there's help nearby), knowing as I reach Jules' door which I see is speckled with the ghosts of so many drawing-pins it appears to have terrible woodworm that the inexplicable dread I feel more strongly now is real and must be heeded. I don't waste time knocking or calling, but have my hand on the knob before the rest of me has come to a halt. The door sticks so that for a second I think it's locked, then I'm through into the shocking cold of Jules' room. Jules is lying in his layers of clothes on the bed, his back to the room, his hair slopped across the tartan blanket he's half-wrapped round himself.

"Fitch," I say, "Jules. Jules," my feet taking themselves over the threadbare carpet and my hand, still damp from the rain, reaching out to grasp his shoulder, "Jules. Jules." There's just enough time.

Unfortunately most of this did not happen. It began to rain as I circled the sundial. Rain seemed to be the natural backdrop for that place. Damp defined my Oxford then as brisk breeze defines my Brighton now. Yet at that age I hardly cared whether I got wet, I even quite liked defying the elements, so it was not wet that drove me through the Porter's Lodge and into the street, it was the operatic tone of Shannon dissecting the latest rugby practice as he emerged from the J.C.R. into the quad with Purvis and a couple of others. I shoved the Knotsworth beneath my jacket and legged it to the dying tones of "Fairycake..what joy...." out into the street, where I headed for the anonymity of the city centre.

164

How did I waste that afternoon, fritter away all those minutes that might have changed so much as if they had been no more than units of my student grant? I think it must have been that afternoon that I reached the bank just before it shut at three-thirty and attempted to withdraw money with my cheque-book, only to be told that this did not appear to be a possibility as the account was already overdrawn (without authority). That left me with the eleven pounds and twenty-five pence in my pocket to last till the end of term. I know it was that afternoon that I broke into this amount to buy a bottle of gin from Oddbins which, I swore to myself, would see me through till the end of term. It was that afternoon as the light failed, early, because of the dense sky, that I took myself into Christchurch meadows and along the circular path that hugs the wide, flat river, the only occasion I've ever seen a water rat stoically ploughing its way through the water; that afternoon that finally I found myself using the same route Ginny and I had taken on that other ridiculous afternoon to emerge out into the lane running by my college as dark fell. Back in my room I piddled about drinking coffee, playing my favourite tracks from my modest collection of L.P.s, picking at the remains of Chelsea buns that Ginny had bought the day before, wiping away the spots of rain that had somehow despite my care defiled the cover of the Knotsworth.

Then, and only then, did I put my sodden jacket back on, tuck the book once more beneath it and, leaving the door unlocked – there was no way this was going to take me more than a minute, *no way* – left to walk to Jules' room.

It was still raining and the evening was black and starless. Unsurprisingly the lane was empty of traffic and noise, though I could hear unmistakeably the rather slushy lyrics of Bryan Ferry's *Dance Away* leaking out of somebody's room as I lowered my head to stop the drops running into my eyes. Centuries separated the high wall on my left and the accommodation block on my right. If you had angled the camera one way I would have appeared just as I actually was, a dishevelled twentieth century student loping past the identical closed curtains of half a dozen undergraduate rooms, but if you had swung round and angled it conversely you'd have had me as something quite other, a young anybody from the deep past, a timeless preoccupied figure stuck in his timeless youth and inexperience, set moving against the uneven stones of the wall.

The door of the house Jules lived in opened as I reached it and spilled out the Nigerian graduate who lived in the ground floor room and some friend of his too nondescript to have lingered in my imagination. They held the door for me and I realised that it was usually kept locked and that, if I'd not met them, I'd have had to hammer on it enough to wake the dead to gain entrance. I noticed for the first time that it was painted plum-coloured, damson not greengage, a colour wildly unfashionable then but judged rather fetching now. The house was quite silent after the voices discussing, I think it might have been, the monetary systems of underdeveloped countries (nobody was polite enough to call them 'developing nations' then) had drifted off down the lane, and my steps on the stair – a creak for every one – sounded to me positively histrionic, as if I were treading on a dozen Sooties. It threw me when I came to Jules' door to find it slightly off its catch, ready to be pushed open with a finger, and a thin lit line showing at the edge, as if he'd slipped out to the toilet for a few minutes. I held the door steady with one hand and knocked with the other, juggling the Knotsworth, then knocked again. No answer convinced me I was in luck: he'd nipped out and if I was quick I could dump the book on his chair with a scribbled note on the back of the scrap of paper I was sure to be able to find and I could avoid meeting him at all. I even muttered 'Great' a couple of times to myself as I pushed the door open with the gingery hesitation of the interloper.

There is a difference between the stillness of sleep and the stillness of death. It is not a difference that the intellect notices, but a message that travels from body to body, organism to organism. That's how it strikes me. That's how it struck me. My eyes tracked across the gentle disorder of the room and stopped at Jules' hunched back and messy hair, the crook of his gently bent legs, the lie of his twinned feet in their mountaineering socks. None of these parts spoke *life* anymore. None of them seemed to hold individuality any longer. There was a thing on the bed.

Oddly, though part of me set up a kind of instant internal screaming, the strongest impulse was of a terrible imperative curiosity. Without thought, I walked straight over to the bed and I must have dropped the book or placed it somewhere for I never had it afterwards. I leaned over him and saw that his face looked quite blank and his eyes were shut. His immaculate immobility awed me and stopped me from any grand gesture. I didn't slap his face or shake his arm, though after a second or two I hesitantly placed my hand on his shoulder. I had made a voluntary connection; but I was not prepared for the intimacy that arose from it, the irreversible intimacy of being the first to touch him dead. I was aware of, but did not think on until a lot later, the sordid jumble of objects on his bedside table and I can never decide whether I really saw two brown pill-bottles among the screwed up handkerchiefs and rings of spilt squash or whether my mind, under the influence of television drama and subsequent knowledge, placed them there.

Then with a vengeance normality of sorts returned. "Fitch," I croaked, shaking him and watching with disgust the soft floppy way his hair lolloped around on the blanket, "Jules, Jules." I think I tripped as I made my way out of the room, I think I knocked something over, for later there was a rumour of the room being ransacked when he was found.

Outside idiot normality still reigned. The passivity of the street was chilling, the no-adrenalin, mild-heart boringness of the two or three irrelevant home-goers I ran past was wildly irritating. The road elongated before me, spun out as obstructive and difficult to negotiate as the linear course of some nerdish computer game. The awful responsibility of knowledge (nobody knows, nobody else knows) was the Holy Grail, the magic ring, the poisoned cloak I had to deliver before I could be released from the terrible quest and up to the next level. My only focus was the moment I'd stumble into the Porter's Lodge and shift off that responsibility, blurt out what I'd seen to the porter, as if that would be the end of the whole episode, as if that would erase Jules Fitch from the whole game.

I told people. I told the Porter, who couldn't stop saying 'Oh dear' with a gravity that wiped out the banality of the phrase completely. I told other people, people looking through their pigeon-holes, reading the notice-board. I don't know who I told. I felt I'd shouted the information from the highest point of the college; I became the centre of a whirlpool of activity. Someone ran off for the master key in their panic, though I tried and failed to tell them the door of Jules' room was open. People came and left. Some of them tried to make me sit down. I remember shaking my head, shaking off a hand on my arm. After a length of time that never had a definition I looked round to find the whirlpool eddied away and myself standing beside the posters for plays that dominated the wide notice-board in the Lodge, their badly stuck corners flicking gently in a draught of air. In all this jumble of impressions the one clear detail is the stark design of the nearest poster. It was for *The White Devil*. There was a mug of hot sweet tea in my hand and at a little distance the Porter was shaking his head, punctuating the damp silence between us with an occasional fading 'Oh dear'.

Read this next bit to the music of somebody like Michael Nyman: something skewed and unsettling.

By the time I was walking out of the Lodge once more and onto the street I was able to notice things again, that it was still raining and that I was cold and that there were suddenly more people about, but it was an oddly lobotomised kind of noticing, sliced away from any reaction I might have felt to what I was seeing. I felt nothing much, not even when finally I reached my corridor and immediately met the six foot plastic Christmas tree that had been erected and lavishly decorated, then placed in a handy alcove twenty foot from the end of the corridor and my room. As I passed it slowly I noted without curiosity the tinsel, the little wooden figures of candy canes and boxes of toys and rocking horses, the golden baubles. I couldn't even quicken my step when I saw that something was obviously going on *in my room*. The door was open inwards and a mixture of voices travelled towards me muffled by the lowness of the corridor's ceiling and the carpeted floor. It was like being a child again, never knowing what scene to expect next, never knowing quite where the adults would be or what they would be talking about, who might be in the room you were walking towards and whether you would be allowed to stay in it. Imagine that corridor through my eyes, as in a film where the shot is suddenly that of the handheld camera, exaggeratedly swinging with my slow tread, tracking the magnolia walls with a drunken roll, making you feel, what with the movement and the 40 watt lighting, just a little claustrophobic, longing for the nice sensible static overview again -the adverts, a cup of tea. Imagine you can see the odd strand of hair swinging into the side of the frame, my long hair, and that you can pan down to take in my hands loosely swinging, quite large hands, hands that ought to be capable but look helpless.

I walked the short length of the corridor and as I reached the door of my room a middle-aged woman, smart with short-styled hair and ear-rings that suited her, in some kind of trousered suit, stepped out to meet me like a genie from a bottle.

"Simon? Are you Simon Donaghue?" she began, and went on, but I heard nothing at all more that she said. I let her hold my arm as I looked past the strained calm of her expression through the doorway. The room was lit only by my desk lamp and there was the impression of a crowd. Beside the window stood the dean of the college, elderly, bald and clean-shaven, grossly embarrassed, looking as incongruous in my room as a zebra. A man older than I but a lot younger than the dean hovered beside the bed, passé in denim, more self-assured than the dean but hardly happy. Squatting before the desk was another woman, whose low voice, I realised, had been consistently audible beneath the intermittent contributions of the others as I'd walked towards the room. I remember her for her woolly, unrestrainable grey hair and her large face, her brightly patterned clothing and the green shoes that were obviously supposed to match. Her entire appearance worked against her and yet – her air of command: she seemed to be in control of events. Beyond that, I was dimly conscious throughout of *explanations*, of the smart middle-aged woman at my elbow explaining, explaining, then questioning me. A waste of breath. All I could take in properly, and I took *her* in with a dull and heavy aching, was Ginny.

My desk was of the design that had a row of drawers either side and a central gap for legspace. It was in this narrow gap that Ginny had huddled herself and into it that the grey-haired woman directed the flow of her words, lulling; trying to mesmerise. As she spoke Ginny shook her head and made small dismissive gestures with her hand, but kept her head tight-pressed against her knees. She nearly didn't fit at all and it would have been an easy thing for the grey-haired woman with the help of, oh, the younger man to pull her out, but they were trying persuasion – first. Ginny's red hair looked brown in the shadow of the hole she'd crawled into but the skin stretched over her knuckles as she clung on to her own knees for anchorage were white as always. Somehow I couldn't bear the fact that her feet were bare, as if she'd been at home and relaxed, reading on the window seat, when they came for her.

There we all were. The curtains were open to the night, though all that could be seen in the wide pane of glass above the row of empty gin bottles was a deadly-clear reflection of the bizarre scene in the room, with its highly contrasting dark and light and its lunatic poses. Then the dean remembered himself and drew them, fussily. Aside from that, it seemed nothing could change and I felt I might always be here with the smart woman's hand gently restraining my arm and her urgent incomprehensible voice in my ear.

Then Ginny raised her head in a gesture of despair. For the first time she saw me. Hope lit her up.

"Simon," she said with an appalling clarity, "I don't want this to happen. Simon, they don't believe me. Tell them what they're doing. Tell them they've made a mistake. Tell them about Madeleine."

"I have," I said faintly.

"Do you know what they're trying to do with me? You've got to tell them everything." She half wailed this and stared so hard at me I couldn't look away. For how long I don't know, but I saw changes of expression remould her face like a fast-changing sky as her understanding raced ahead of her and, finally, she saw what I'd done.

"You bastard," she said, and the disgust in the voice was the worst thing yet, "You complete bastard." She refused to look at me again. She refused to talk to any of us, right up to the point that gentle pressure – if that's possible – was used to prise her from her priest's-hole of a hiding place, right up to the moment they led her past me in a part embrace, part hold, while I shrank back against the wall of the corridor. Then, a throw-away, last-ditch attempt to sabotage uncontrollable events:

"I think I'm pregnant," she cried, too loud, as if she hoped the rooms along the corridor were occupied and I might be shamed by the assertion.

"It's okay, Virginia, it's okay. We can have a long chat about that at the hospital," said the grey-haired woman breathlessly, too old for this kind of exertion, "You're safe with me, Virginia."

But the smart woman at my elbow turned to me questioningly.

"She can't be," I said blankly, "It must be a kind of a...of a..." I trailed into a sick silence. The smart woman loosened her hold on my arm, but eyed me speculatively for a few moments longer. Then the dean came out of the room and joined us, dabbing at his cheeks with a clean and pressed white handkerchief, and I met his eye by mistake, recognising in it my own cowardice.

The strange little trio of the grey-haired woman and the denimed man with Ginny sandwiched between them, her determination not to co-operate giving all their movements a spastic jerkiness, edged along the corridor until they were abreast of the Christmas tree and then it became obvious they were together too wide to clear it. Yet on they went as if they had fused to become one unruly organism with only one instinct: to move forwards. With a ghastly fascination the three of us watched the three of them as the grey-haired woman's wide and weird shawl-like top caught a straying plastic branch. In slow motion the tree followed her as she went, leaning on its flimsy stand until it could lean no more. Then over it went, with a discreet *shush*. None of them even turned round. The tree flattened itself against the floor as if felled, rocked over to one side and came to rest almost blocking the corridor. One single plastic bauble rolled across the carpet and stopped at the feet of the dean. There was a fire-door at the end of the corridor. The tri-part animal got it open somehow, clumsily pushed through, and disappeared from view. The fire-door eased shut after them with its familiar thin whine. Until then the sound had hardly registered; now it just hit that nails-on-blackboard note.

The dean's relief was palpable. He breathed out lengthily, rather the way cows do. He said, "We shall have to get the maintenance men to see to that door." There was a significant pause. Without consultation, but with one impulse and the ephemeral camaraderie instant upon disaster, the three of us set about resurrecting the tree. We moved slowly: post-adrenalin. I, for one, felt enervated, as if I'd been thoroughly pummelled by some rugby player. The smart woman gathered up the baubles and the other decorations and, when I had helped the dean right the tree, handed them to us. Only then did I realise that she must be Dr. Blick.

So it was that I decorated a Christmas tree with the dean of the college. Later on, when I was called before him, this helped.

We'd nearly finished when Dr. Fell pushed through the fire door they'd taken Ginny through, hesitantly, as if he weren't sure he'd found the right place. When he saw us gathered round the plastic Christmas tree his confusion increased. By then, I was beyond surprise. If Dr. Fell wanted to join us, well why not? Now that Ginny was out of sight, my reactions were once more cauterised. I felt light-headed, hilarious even. I only just stopped myself handing him a bauble.

"Ah," he said, recovering himself, nodding recognition at Dr. Blick. There were the usual preliminaries, which flowed right over me. I nodded and smiled vaguely, intent on the bauble which would not stay on the branch I'd chosen. I think I only began to hear what he was saying when he drew me a little aside.

"...to see if you're all right. Now Dr. Blick's rung her parents, though perhaps you'll want to do the same....obviously very concerned...they understood the difficulties of the decision....apparently this has been going on for many years...you'll probably feel very confused, guilty even, but...right thing...help her....please contact me if....*Simon.*" I focussed on him, and he continued more slowly, "You do understand that Virginia has been committed for twenty-eight days, don't you? This is just an assessment, so that everybody can decide where to go from there. It's the minimum period. We'll help her in any way we can. You can go and see her at any time."

I nodded because it was expected of me, but my thoughts disintegrated as soon as they were half made. The number *twenty-eight* danced around in my head. I visualised it in a psychodelic 'sixties typeface, cartoon style: I gave each number a Disney face, goofy grins, Mickey Mouse gloves, hula skirts, and watched them gyrate. Twenty-eight days was a lunar month, a rent book month, a menstrual cycle.

"I suggest you spend what's left of this evening with friends," advised Dr. Fell before he left, "Don't underestimate how up and down you'll feel. Take things slowly."

Once the fire-door had slammed behind him, I was alone with the Christmas tree, the other professionals having obviously exited at some unnoticed moment. *He's off course about the up and down*, I thought to myself dreamily, taking one of the chocolate decorations from the tree, unwrapping it slowly, eating it slowly, for as the door slammed behind him I'd been flooded with the sweetest relief. Before I went and tucked myself up in bed with my – very last, yes indeed – bottle of gin, shunning the good doctor's suggestion of an evening with friends (who, exactly?), I worked my way through every single chocolate decoration, letting the silver wrappers fall to the floor and come to rest where the roots of the tree should have been.

* * *

That should have been that, the hiatus between *then* and *now*, but I see I've disingenuously elected to skip an episode. A whole chunk of the events of that grotesque afternoon has slid off the whole. All along our Sussex coastline frosts and winds loosen the fracture lines of our chalk cliffs and throw chunks into the sea, bits of land that hold memory, that people walked on, farmed on, squabbled and kissed on. Entire buildings teeter on the edge, empty and hole-eyed, for years, but come the winter with the most ferocious gales... My memory's not so large a segment, cannot compete with the three hundred years of history of those flint-built farmhouses, but the geography of this narrative's inaccurate without it; and I want an Ordnance Survey, not a mappa mundi, all vague shading and out of scale porpoises. Besides, there are one or two uncomfortable facts that won't make sense without it. Why else would I have had to go and see the dean at the end of that term? Why else would I have been fined? Why would I have only narrowly escaped being expelled?

It's an Iggy Pop of an episode, pure mischief and aggression.

It says something for my state of mind that I was shy of going back into the room which had just witnessed Ginny's downfall, even though it held the plastic carrier that cradled the unopened – the last – bottle of gin and even though my body, trained to expect its shot, craved it. I think I even left the door of the room gaping. What did I care? Things seemed to have fallen apart with a swift efficiency.

There weren't a great many choices of venue. I couldn't spend money. It was a soaking weekday evening. I had no intention of speaking to another human being. I could *feel* – well, *feel* conveyed nothing much to my marshmallow of a mind. I concentrated on motor co-ordination. Unsurprisingly I ended up in the woolly dark of the T.V. room, mercifully on my own, and there I decided to stay until some other punter walked through the door.

The T.V. was already switched on and relaying its chat in an overloud fuzz, despite the notice that asked undergraduates to turn the set off on leaving the room. The order of programmes was as familiar to me as the routine of getting up in the morning, just that fag-tea-teeth was replaced by Nationwide-Tomorrow's World-Top of the Pops, though it was a while since I'd viewed it and I found that T.V. now meant a childhood that had shrivelled away into nothing, meant baked beans on toast on my lap, meant my mother asking me if I'd done my homework, my grandmother's querulous complaint that the performers on TOTP sang out of key and, any road, she couldn't tell the girls from the boys. I sat in the front row of armchairs and pulled my seat even closer so I was too close and so that I could hear the faint echo of my mother telling me of the rays the screen would be beaming dangerously into my skull. The way I remember it, a couple of hours edged by with the easy images on the screen bouncing around harmlessly on that bed of marshmallow inside my head, probably along with all those dangerous beams, like a random assortment of objects being chucked indiscriminately into an old rucksack. So it was that I only gradually became aware of my name shouted in the background.

I thought it was Jules. Through the muzz came a clear visualisation of his figure lurching under the window of the T.V. room in the quad. I could see his dressing-gown flapping open and his feet freezing on the flagstones, the puddles of rainwater soaking their grubbiness up through the mountaineering socks. His hair flopped over his forehead and the hand he used to sweep it back was inept, the tremulous hand of senility or addiction. My name thrown up at the window was raw and brusque as a crow's caw.

Slowly I pulled myself from the low chair and walked obediently to the window. I thought the dim T.V. light and the thin curtain I half stood behind would obscure me, but I had to lean near to the small leaded panes to see him. Even then the angle wasn't sufficient. Abandoning caution I stretched over the deep sill and twisted the handle of the window, a thin, elderly iron twirl, and gave the window the shove it needed to open. I needed to see him: whatever.

"Donaghue." With the window open and the damp air instantly creeping into the fug of the T.V. room, the voice below carried square and clear. I met the imperative stare of Dave Shannon. He was wearing a large shirt over denims I could see were grossly faded even in the reduced light of the quad. A shirt large enough to seem large on Shannon was a large shirt. There was something unnervingly impressive in the simplicity of his clothing, as if he'd put on stage costume, as if he'd dressed for an event. Hamlet, Othello, Clint Eastwood, Darth Vada. All the revenge plots of any relevance rushed into my mind together. I woke up, and realised he'd come to get me.

"Donaghue." Shannon's bellow failed to bring the porter running. He must have chosen his moment, ensured he wouldn't be interrupted. The event was staged. I told myself he was just pissed; though why that would have been less dangerous I don't know. In any case, he was sober, as sober an avenging angel as ever was, as angry as a god.

The third and final 'Donaghue' was a recognition: 'So you're here', it said. God, how he hated me. It was a hate that won me over at the time: I accepted his right to it when I believed his reasons for it. If I'd not reeled under my unwilling connection with Jules I'd have seen clearly enough to see that Shannon's motives were as murky as mine. Jules had *something* to do with his hate, but not *everything* by a long stretch. Over the space of that term it had grown like an odious baby. He loathed the length of my hair, just as if he were some troop-inspecting military man. He loathed my lassitude. He

175

was outraged that a girl like Ginny had even looked at me. Most of all he reviled the part of me that Jules had wanted.

None of this could have occurred to me then. I stared belligerently at his upturned face and was glad the drizzle was dampening all that brutish handsomeness. I thought of besieged castle-defenders pouring scalding oil on the heads of their enemy, then following it with any and every scrap of filth they could lay their hands on. It was his only vulnerability, our difference in heights.

"Hallo, sailor," I goaded. Terror made me flippant.

"I hold you responsible." He sung it out, playing to an audience that may have been just out of sight; I don't know. At least I know that everything he said he said at volume. He wanted to be overheard.

"What for?" I drawled.

"I told you I'd hold you responsible. I hope you feel guilty as hell."

"I don't know what you're getting so uptight about, Shannon." I imagined Shannon literally bursting with fury, the anger inside him tightening into an I.R.A. contraption of timing-device and semtex. Simon throws the switch and thirty seconds later *whoomph* Shannon is fragmented over the quad, hard tissue rattling against window panes, soft tissue coating the flagstones. Shannon reduced to something to skid on. I wondered about ramming one of the armchairs against the doorknob of the T.V. room, but somehow I couldn't leave the window. We were locked into this.

"Oh, you know, Donaghue. You know. You may be a complete tosser, but you know what I'm talking about."

"I don't think I do."

"What you're going to tell me," he said deliberately, "is exactly what you did to him. I want to hear you admit to it."

"What? Confession? Penance? Absolution? Who the hell do you think you are?"

"Why were you in his room this afternoon? Just tell me that. If you had so little to do with him- You're pure as the driven snow, but you just happen to be the one who finds him after he's... You're in this up to your scrawny little neck, Donaghue. Were you a regular visitor in that glacial room of his? Were you? Did you teach him all your tricks? What did you do to him, you bastard? What did you say to him? Why did you pick on him to play your stupid little games with?"

"You don't know anything about me."

"I don't give a shit about you, Donaghue. I don't give a shit about what you think or don't think. You're just not going to get away with this."

"*Get away with this*? I didn't *do* anything."

"If you weren't on this earth, Fitch still would be."

I stared at him. It felt like the truth. His stance told me he expected me to come down to the quad so he could rip me up. "You're not in some fucking melodrama, Shannon. Don't be such a drama queen." I lengthened the *Shannon* into a sneer. A fucking melodrama, of course, was exactly what we were stuck in. Our age dictated we played it like this; and maybe it's a better way to play it. Adult compromise (mediation-conciliation-moderation-negotiation) can be so fucking boring. But I was wrong to start Shannon off on the swearing. He could outswear the pants off me.

"Don't fuck about with me, you fucking little worm. You're not fucking here to give it. You're fucking here to take it. Is that fucking clear? And I've just told you that you're not fucking going to get away with it, and you're fucking not. Is that clear?"

"Leave me alone, Shannon. I'm bored of this."

"Get the fuck down here."

I said nothing.

"He wasn't queer, you know," said Shannon, finally lowering his voice to a more normal level, "Not until you came along. You turned him."

I looked down at the self-satisfied crease around his eyes and the jut of his jawline and the crotch-promoting spread of his rugby-player's legs and that's what it took. I turned. I didn't even hurry that much. I knew Shannon was immoveable, would wait down there for what was coming. I walked over to the television on which Freddie Mercury's skinny form waved, and turned it off. An illogical gesture, considering. I unplugged the set, tugged out the aerial and, bracing my back, lifted it up against my chest. It was heavier than I'd expected. I shifted it so I didn't drop it and manhandled it over to the window. I could see it would only just fit, sideways, through the opening between the wall and the central mullion, but I was entirely determined. Just then I felt I'd have been able to shift stone so long as I could have it the way I wanted it. *I did it my way*, as Frankie would say.

Easing the set half way over the sill, I climbed beside it to look at my target. With delight I saw Shannon fixing his gaze on the doorway out into the quad directly beneath me. He thought I'd disappeared to come down and be slaughtered by him. He thought the world bent to his will. He thought he straddled it, feet in opposite continents, haunches in the ether, head by the stars, angled down in judgement.

I laughed. He looked up. I tipped the balance of the television and it jumped as if on its own accord out of my hands and straight down. An inelegant rushing fall. Shannon's face had time only to look vacant, but, damn it, his body saved itself. He stepped back, neatly, as if merely avoiding the brush of a stranger's shoulder, and watched the set smack into the flagstone on which he'd been standing the instant before. The screen came out and spread glass like scree for a distance at every side, showering his shoes, while the body of the set remained intact. The noise, though, was terrific. If I gained any satisfaction it was in that, the noise, like a motorbike crashing against a brick wall, a gut-churning multi-layered smash; and in the look of profound surprise that sprang onto Shannon's face and wouldn't leave it.

It was at that point that the porter shot wheezily out of the lodge. I was too far from him to hear his exclamation, but I knew what the words forming on his lips would be: *Oh dear.*

I am so sorry, Ginny.
I am sorry, Jules.
I'd do it all again, Shannon.

* * *

Under the apple trees I've gathered the newspaper, a packet of biscuits, a packet of fags, a pile of paperwork I'm supposed to have read and a chilled bottle of Becks. Thank god it's Sunday. Work tends to distract from these moments, *work* is a series of too long interludes between real life, and real life is here, in the garden with my daughter. Henry's bedroom is the little one at the back of the house and we can see his curtains sucked out of his open window by the breeze, then sinking back in again. The moment he wakes we'll hear him.

Alex is even more organised than I. She's dug the newest deck-chair from the shed and erected it so that her head is in shade, resting on a cushion from the sitting-room, and her legs in sun. On her lap lies a fan, which waits unused for the second she should start to perspire. An upturned flowerpot does for a sidetable. Rather ostentatiously she leans over to it every now and then to take a sip from the glass of lemonade she's balanced there, lemonade that is home made by Alex herself and which has a dense scum of peel floating on the surface.

"Would you like some, Dad?" she asks. She's grown out of the Australian soap opera intonation.

"I'd love some later." I aim for conviction, and seem to do well enough, because she gives me a quick flash of a smile, less sardonic than her usual.

We settle into a companionable semi-silence, a rustle of paper here, a clink of glass on terracotta there, laid over the mildly threatening buzzing of a dozen wasps in the apple tree, the one that we planted when we moved down here, the one that's supposed to reward all our fussing by showering us with fruit but never has yet.

"What's that plant there?" Alex interrupts, shamelessly flicking the pages of her paperback like a razzled old poker-player dealing in a cowboy film.

"Lavender." I'm pleased with myself for getting it.

"Nooo," says Alex facetiously, waving the book in the right direction for my benefit, "that red thing next to it."

"Oh." I make a wild attempt at maintaining my position of authority; "Dahlias? Delphiniums?"

Alex raises her eyebrows at me. "Dandelions? Daisies?"

"You'll have to ask your mother when she gets back. You know I'm not the gardener."

"Oh, you're no use." She gives an exaggerated sigh.

"You shouldn't flap that book around like that; it's not yours to ruin." I counter.

As she bends back over her book I realise how *old* she's looking today and that it's intentional, a cultivated look. As long as I know she's unaware of my gaze, I take it in. Everything she's wearing is brand new, because she's off on a school trip to Italy at the end of next week and has been *treated*. There's a brimmed straw hat with miniature scallops by way of decoration, from under which her newly-bobbed hair bushes out rather like the grass at the edge of our sheet-sized lawn. The dress she's wearing is long, with the slinky-silky movement of synthetics. It has a tiny floral print.

The dress would fit a small woman. It is cut to accommodate hips and breasts. Its v-neckline, however modestly, waves the idea if not the reality of a cleavage under your nose. These observations, coming together, make me realise with a jolt that Alex is a small woman.

Alex gives a huge yawn and catches my eye. "What?" she demands, "You think I look silly, don't you?"

"As a matter of fact," I improvise, "I was trying to imagine you tripping through St. Mark's Square, wowing all the boys."

"*Father*," she rebukes, looking caught out yet also faintly pleased, as if she had been entertaining hopes and fears in that direction. To cover her tracks she takes a sip from the glass of lemonade and pretends to be involved in her book. I know for a fact she's not particularly enjoying this book, which is one of those gushy teen reads imported from the U.S., spilling over with boyfriend dilemmas and letters to God and *sleepovers* and *how far should I go*? Poor old Alex, so desperate to be one of the crowd, has borrowed this manual from a school-buddy and is grinding her way through it to prove to the friend, to the world and even to me how *regular* she is. She might as well give up now. Alex will never be one of the crowd. She's going to be too tall, she *is* too prickly, too offbeat, too intelligent, damn it, ever to be accepted into the girls' club. Sometimes it strikes me, as I see the echo of my rather definite jawline in Alex's face, how much of me there is in her.

Forced to leave off my scrutiny, I dutifully adjust my gaze downwards to the paper, the glare from which, in this strong light, is almost too much to tolerate. I even read half a paragraph of some flip analysis of middle class manners before the image *I've* conjured up begins to intrude.

Imagine my little Alex, fresh as a daisy in her brand new dress and sun-hat, meandering across St. Mark's Square with all the other daisies, not all of whom, however, are sweet little meadow daisies, just sprung, but might even be some jaded big-blossomed know-it-all variety. Imagine all her bright-eyed excitement and her too-slow steps, her wide-open face, broadcasting her inexperience from one side of the square almost to the other. Imagine the clutch of Italian lads homing in on them, on her, spotting with well-trained eyes the touristy innocence and the lack of guile. Imagine their insolent eyes sliding over the tiny floral pattern moulding Alex's shape, unpeeling the frock of which she's so proud from her skin without even looking at it. Imagine their young-boy's sweat springing into their swaggering armpits as they shout their comments to each other, knowing they won't be understood. Imagine their sturdy young-boy's bodies, groin led, circling my little girl while she stares up, mesmerised by some architectural scribble. Just imagine the violation of even *one* of their stubby, hot fingers on the pale freckles of her forearm, one mouthful of their cajoling, seducing breath on the perfect curve of her cheek.

I imagine myself, improbably airlifted to the same spot, pushing past the droves of tourist groups with their swinging cameras and stuffed shoulder-bags, fighting against the flow of the crowd to reach my baby, finally breaking through the last fleshy barrier to vault towards the frozen pair and yank him off her by the hair, to prise his fingers from her arm – on which they will leave a series of red marks, slowly fading – and to shake him till the teeth rattle in his casanova head.

I clear my throat and realise I've been gritting my teeth together. I shift around on the grass and feign nonchalance. Alex sniggers at something in the book. A cat leaps onto the flint wall dividing us from the next garden with the improbable ease of a film run backwards and, with the swiftness of frequent practice, I reach for a fallen apple-twig and flick it at the animal.

"Scat," I hiss, "Cat. Bingo! No- damn; I thought I'd scored."

Alex doesn't even see the cat, so rapidly does the film run the right way, snatching the cat back over the wall, its tail the flicker of a hair on the celluloid. *"Dad,"* she says anyway, "that's so cruel. You shouldn't hurt animals."

"Damn cats," I mutter, unrepentant.

"They can't defend themselves."

"Oh, I expect it'll find a way of revenging itself on me. I can think of a way-"

"Yes," she interrupts, enjoying herself, "I bet one day they all gang together and come and get you. You'll wake up and see all their slitty eyes staring at you in the dark." This puts her in mind of something else. "Do you know what?"

"What?"

"In a video we saw in Science it said that, wherever you are, you're never more than ten metres away from a rat. Isn't that sick? I mean, really *scuzzy.*"

We both sit and think about this for a few moments. Finally I can't resist saying, "What about in the middle of the Yorkshire moors?"

"Well, you *could* be," she replies defensively.

"What about in the middle of a tower block?"

"You could be," she cries triumphantly, "What about all the air vents or whatever they are? You know, the drains? Ha. Got you."

Actually even to me that sounds not improbable and I concede with a shrug and a 'hmm', but not before Alex has got in a couple more 'ha's. We subside into the next semi-silence. A light aircraft flies overhead, just like a larger version of the wasps droning in the apple tree.

When it comes down to it, I can't begin to imagine the kind of boy I could tolerate within twenty feet of my daughter. Look at her now. A leaf's floated down off the apple tree and landed on her shoulder, where in a minute she'll notice it and tut as she flicks it to the ground. Her bare toes are tapping a silent rhythm on the grass. The sun has brought out a new scattering of freckles across the bridge of her nose. When she yawns I can see so clearly beneath the rather square structure of her face a long-gone, rounder structure and the sudden yawn of the two year old. The shutter lifts for a moment and I begin to make links between *then* and *now*, something I usually try strenuously to avoid. I go back to my first term at university and by mistake take Alex back with me. Events start to roll: we have to go through them all, from A to Z, from prelude to postscript, though I'd love to fast-forward. This time round Alex takes the leading female role, though she's really too young. I'm a kind of Dad-Director at the periphery, only one all the actors ignore and run rings round, standing helplessly by as Alex-Ginny goes and falls for a boy just like me, a boy who steals all the joy out of her. That hair, slopping over his face like a bunch of dead grass, so patently obviously a barrier between him and the world. Couldn't you just take a pair of shears to it? What can she see in him? The girl's not *safe* with him. Can't we just *cut*?

My god, how I hope my little Alex never meets a boy like me.

* * *

That's the knot tied on *then*. I didn't say there were no loose ends. In fact, there were a dozen or more, and I tripped over them for quite some time: years, even. Yet somehow that's where the past ended and the present began, the instant the television set smashed against the slabs of the quad, the instant I tried and failed to assassinate Shannon. I slipped off a skin, leapt a canyon, crossed an ocean, pushed open a new door. I could bury it in metaphor. It's better than dwelling on it. When I'm feeling gloomy, it crosses my mind that most of my life may have been the dull exhaustion that follows a rush of adrenalin. Months go by now without event, or big event: Henry gains a tooth, we try out a new restaurant, we visit my mother and I prune her pear tree because the top's too high for her, we have a flurry of anxiety at work because the budget's been cut again, friends divorce, and so on and on: and on. I sometimes wonder if all the true excitement of my life was distilled into that autumn when Ginny, Jules and Shannon were the massive figures that filled the screen entirely. When Alex drags me down to the front row at the flicks and I have to slide my backside right down in the seat and, even then, Minnie Driver or Robin Williams or Brad Pitt has a twenty foot face that looms so large over me I can almost tell what they've eaten for lunch on set, *that's* the identical sensation. I loved Ginny – I'm more sure of that now than I ever was then; I hated Shannon; what I felt for Jules is anybody's guess. Those scenes that I've replayed and rewound and, I dare say, edited are just as vivid as they ever were, as disturbing as a freeze-frame from the climax of a Jacobean drama, as over-coloured as an advert. Not one pastel shade in those months, only purple, crimson and black.

Some of the loose ends were tidied up quite quickly. I had to reimburse the college for the television, and a fair whack was added to the amount by way of a punishment fine, though I avoided *rustication* – in ordinary language: expulsion.

The replacement t.v. was a far better model, I noticed, than the one I'd wrecked, which had always had a picture that stretched people's foreheads so they looked like the forerunners of futuristic super-brains. Actually, my mother paid the fine for me, if you can imagine the stickiness of that particular transaction. In theory it was a loan, but my mother was too soft ever to claim it all back; and, anyway, I was in debt to the bank for so many years it all became arbitrary. It was my chum the dean who dealt with discipline and on whose leather-upholstered seat I had to hunch waiting for a verdict. He was lenient, though feigning severity. It takes one to know one: as our glances met for the second time only, I could tell that he remembered the Christmas tree and the tenuous camaraderie of that moment. If he had realised that I was quite unremorseful, that I still regretted Shannon's quick step back, if he had not been able to slot my murderous intention out of sight behind laddish slapstick, if he had not assumed that both Shannon and I had been nothing more than drunk and disorderly, that I had been traumatised by the discovery of Fitch's body, he might have shoved me out from under the protective wing of the college to face less archaic forms of justice. As it was, Shannon colluded with me, inexplicably almost *covered* for me, as if he were still following some boy's own code: or as if he couldn't stomach the role of victim, even at the expense of missing watching me hang by the neck. For the rest of the term, well, for the rest of our university careers, we carefully avoided each other. Anyway, after that the passion was all gone. And yes, I did *have* a university career; of sorts. I scraped through my exams., oddly aided by the fact that I didn't give a toss, spilling out information I could only have picked up through osmosis, because it certainly wasn't by design. At the end of my three years I got a Third, and *that* set the tone for my shuffle-step into Local Government and my subsequent half-hearted attempts to *climb the career ladder*. Few rungs missing there, dearie.

The rest, as you can imagine, was a little less clear cut.

* * *

It was the morning following Ginny's incarceration that I understood I had betrayed her. I woke up in the limitless emptiness of my single bed to the realisation. It was Ginny young and unclothed in the echo of our favourite position, curled into each other, that I had trampled all over. Guilty as hell. Simon Donaghue, still seventeen, staked out in his grubby day-after bed, guilty as hell. That's such an accurate expression. Hell not as in quaint mole-hills of bubbling sulphur and goatish gnomes wielding pitch-forks against a thunderous sky, but as in interminable prickling tedium, inescapable restless impotency. I felt guilty before I even fully appreciated why I should. Lying in my own space, and with my arm stretched across the space that should have been Ginny's, I should have been able to convince myself that I'd done the best for her. I couldn't. I was Judas. I'd stood and watched – though it wasn't evident how I'd gained. Where were my silver pieces to jingle? I was that dark star Stalin. I was at heart a Kim Philby, betraying my country, betraying Ginny, my continent of treasures, my new found land, my *terra firma*. Now there was nowhere I could put myself. The romantic squalor of my room, our room, had overnight taken on a mean look, was simply dreary. Without her, I was a stupid child, a spare part. I could no longer remember why I'd allowed her to be taken from me. As for Dr. Fell's suggestion that I could go and see her at any time I wanted, it seemed a lost Eden of an idea, a right I had forfeited, a gold ring slipped from a finger and lost down a drain. Dr. Fell had not seen, as I had, Ginny's face when she dismissed me: *you bastard; you complete bastard.*

Have you ever seen Meryl Streep and Goldie Hawn in *Death Becomes Her*, which is possibly the most dire film ever to come out of

Hollywood? It's a one joke movie, almost totally reliant on special effects, and when we watched it we couldn't really even appreciate those, since we had it out on video and our t.v.'s a little twelve-inch. Only *Henry* laughed when Meryl Streep's head fell off and rolled down a flight of steps. Streep and Hawn are two rich bitches who stumble across an elixir that gives them immortality, but fails to stabilise their molecular structure – I'm slightly hazy on the exact science behind it – so that their bodies become more and more fragile as the story unfolds: endless life but not youth. Though they keep their looks – I really *am* unclear on the science behind this part – they become literal crumblies. At first they're simply elastic. Meryl Streep twists her head round like a stubborn piece of toffee, for one thing. Towards the end, though, bits of them start to fall off; an arm coming away at the shoulder socket, the aforementioned head rolling down the stairs to lie furiously complaining at the bottom; as who wouldn't? Alex found all this diverting. I yawned through it; yet now, trying to find some way of pinning down how the boy in that morning-after bed felt, I'm surprised to find it relevant. Without Ginny I really thought I might fall apart, as if she'd been some kind of superglue, as if, now that I had no centre, the separate parts of me might just as well drift off as stay put. I rattled around in that bed, the thoughts rattled around in my head, my bones seemed to be rattling themselves looser by degrees in my body, working themselves away from my musculature as if eventually I'd simply fly apart into different corners.

In a distant way, lying in that bed I toyed with the idea of taking Jules' way out. I might have been making desultory decisions concerning the future of, for example, one of my mother's goldfish for all the real connection I felt. Outside a bell started to chime from one of the nearby towers and I even had a part of my mind spare to consider which tower it must be, judging from the volume and direction of the noise. I lay, sometimes sweating, sometimes cooling to a chill, cataloguing to myself all the many routes that led, finally, to Jules' destination. At the very end of my list came the method that Jules himself had chosen. Dreamily I found myself yet again before the cream door speckled with so many drawing-pin holes it looked as if it had advanced woodworm, the line of light at its edge almost silver by contrast with the shadowy mushroom shades of the walls. No-one had bothered to turn on the landing light. Why would Jules have bothered? The door gave at a push and I walked through into the mild disorder of Jules' room. The bedside lamp was on and the shabbiness of the room softened and blurred into something better under its influence. As I walked towards the bed I dropped the book I'd been holding onto the arm-chair where it slid to one edge of the sunken seat. The carpet held an oriental pattern and its reds, ivories and blacks fell into dozens of shades dependent on the wear of different patches. My feet followed the path the pattern made over to the bed. The curve of Jules' back was to me and his knees were drawn slightly towards his torso so that his shape released the faint suggestion of an Iron Age burial. The shadow of a helmet, a spear, a pot might lie in the dip of the mattress between the cup of his body and the wall. There was a kind of grace in the falling curve of his shoulder blade, rib-cage, pelvis, muffled though they were by the layers of clothes and the dressing-gown. Upon the jumper he'd screwed up to use as a pillow were several flicks of his blonde hair, spread out into separate strands: the effect of old static. They asked to be laid back neatly against his head.

On the bedside table I found the pill-bottles. Sleeping pills or painkillers I couldn't have guessed. The names on them meant nothing to me. I tipped whatever he'd left me onto the palm of my hand and shared the glass of squash almost buried by all the old tissues beneath the lamp. Then I lay myself down beside him on the bed. I had to echo his shape to find enough room.

I remember sitting up in bed to get rid of *that* picture.

If I followed Jules I'd find him waiting for me.

The railway station at Oxford had a small cafe, the longest wall of which used to be papered with a spectacularly naff blown-up photographic reproduction of a forest in summer. This I remember in detail because I stared at it for three-quarters of an hour on the Thursday afternoon of the last week of term. It was a European forest – beeches? birches? alder? – in which the trees had grown close, but in which, nevertheless, sudden glades let in long shafts of sunlight. You felt it was late summer. The leaves were too dark for spring and

187

the warmth had a heavy quality. You could imagine the circles of midges, dodging mindlessly where the pools of sunlight gathered. There would certainly have been birdsong, a whole invisible chorus of it. I'd chosen a seat in the centre of the café where I could be far enough away from the wall to fool my eye into at least considering the view as genuine, and I sat slouched with my feet up on my rucksack, carefully, because my records were in it, and my hands round my station cup of coffee, taking the smallest sips I could, to justify the length of my stay. Ridiculously I yearned to step away from myself and through the forest, not to find some Grimms' tale fantasy but to be soothed by the very blandness of the image. It would have been all right by me if the forest had *covered* Oxford, England, why not the whole of Europe?- magically erasing all those messy cities and the complicated people in them. I could have done with a thousand miles of the scene in front of me, even if it had repeated its hundred yards of view – glade, shade, bending branch; glade, shade, bending branch; glade – seventeen thousand six hundred times.

An average British station it was, flimsy, twentieth century, giving an uneasy sense of nothing *gelling* properly; long and low, I seem to remember, with a couple of platforms, and always a flotsam of students, foreign language students off up to London for the day, undergraduates going home for the weekend, coming back after it, travelling to a match. On that Thursday afternoon I was acutely conscious that I should not have been a part of it at all. I was supposed to have remained resident in college 'till the Friday. In fact, I'd been planning to stay as long as possible, until the middle of the next week; not in order to *join in* all the end of term fun and games – sherry parties thrown by tutors, bashes where fifty piled into a ten-by-ten undergraduate room – but to avoid home and the people in it. There was the very practical objection that my mother had to be faced. Not only had she paid my fine, she'd had to send me my rail-fare home. In many ways that was the least of it. What I was putting off was sitting through bacon and eggs with my mother's expression of uncomprehending *disappointment* hanging across the table. I was the first person in my family ever to go to university: *ever.* My mother had waved me off with the same smile on her face that mothers wore as they waved their sons off to war – before, that is, the war with the trenches wiped that smile off mothers' faces for ever. She'd trumpeted my achievements even to check-out girls and now: *what would your father have said, Simon?* And even then, she didn't know the half of it.

It was my room that, in the end, ejected me. I evolved a superstitious belief that the guilt that incapacitated me lived in it. It wasn't so much that a hundred moments I'd had with Ginny sprung into my mind as the dozens of objects she'd touched prompted them, or that the room's specific smell was undeniably a fusion of the dozen odours of two bodies. It was the bed. I could get up and walk to our airing cupboard now, and tell you immediately which pillow cases and which sheet were on that bed then. They were faded enough then, and now they hardly hold their threads together. The pillow case had been my grandmothers when she lived on her own and it's in her taste; a sixties' design of big and little circles in blue. I'm the only one who can read its code. I remember the grey that those blue circles became before full light, and the lighter grey they showed in the green reflection of the curtains after daylight came. I remember the circles' sheered shape as they stretched away from my amphibian eye when I woke up, whenever I woke up. I remember how they looked remarkably like the thought bubbles that came out of comic characters' heads, as if my secret guilty thoughts were dribbling out all night as I slept. I put up with them for a week after Ginny went. Then I thought that if I had to lay down in that stale bed with my arm inadequately covering Ginny's side, if I had to lie in the dark listening to the scuffle of activity from other rooms, if I had to stare at those elongated circles *once more*, I'd start screaming.

Really I sneaked away. I simply woke up and decided to go regardless – although I had done the bare sufficiency of tidying up. I'd attended all the tutorials I should have and gone through the dreadfulness of Prelims.; and after spending the bulk of that Thursday packing, I'd even left the room relatively tidy. I hadn't handed in my key, but I told myself I'd send it, along with some explanation that would no doubt come to me as I sat on the train. I also told myself that it would be easier to face my mother if I turned up on the doorstep unannounced. And I hoped to God that I would leave Ginny behind me in that room, that she'd stay there, a wraith

189

filling the kettle, playing Patience with her scruffy pack, undressing, kicking off her shoes or, god knows, crouching beneath my desk.

I remember when my father died that the first few days, before the funeral, were not too bad. No doubt the Valium the doctor gave us helped, but it was more than that. I even had a hectic gaiety; because I fully believed that, once the funeral was over, he'd come back. The wild illogicality of this belief did nothing to lessen it, neither did the arrangements that were so evidently going on around me: the atypical shopping in the fridge waiting for the relatives, the 'phone calls I overheard to funeral directors and florists, the weird calm that had descended over all my father's belongings, even the coats still hanging in the hallway. I had just decided that we'd drive back from the service and let ourselves into a house that was no longer empty as we had left it, that my father would be in the kitchen sterilising his wine-making equipment or having a fag in the armchair nearest the television. When he wasn't I was devastated.

The reaction that stole over me as I sat in the station cafe was a parallel one. All the days I'd been on my own I'd dwelt – yes, guiltily and with maudlin regret – on *how it had been*. Now, staring into the facsimile of a forest glade, I saw very sharply how it was now. For the first time I tried to visualise Ginny's surroundings at that second. The hospital where she was incarcerated was at most three miles from where I sat. Ginny had not ceased to exist just because she'd walked, or been marched, out of my story. She was, really was, an entirely separate person who was sleeping, dreaming, talking, crying somewhere else.

I left the cafe and wandered onto the nearest platform, stunned by the obviousness of it all. Stunned enough not to realise for a while that I'd not yet bought my ticket. I was just turning to retrace my steps, a train was pulling in at the opposite platform, my glance was haphazardly trawling across the milling assortment of individuals poised to board it when my eyes snagged on the most familiar figure in the world. Almost immediately she was hidden by the body of the train, which drew to a smooth halt and obscured the entire platform behind it. It was Ginny I had seen. I didn't shout, or throw my rucksack to the ground and race towards the passage connecting platforms. It was as if I'd stopped thinking altogether. I stood still, my rucksack uncomfortably hanging from one shoulder, as all the energy drained out of me and I stared into the carriage nearest the spot on the platform where she'd been standing. There she was, one of the first to a seat, unbuttoning her black coat, half hidden behind the other passengers' unhurried movements. There was the short-cropped red hair, the skinny stretch of arm as she leaned up to wedge her coat on the luggage racks above, the wide mouth. It was Ginny, but as she might have appeared in a dream. Everything was very slightly wrong. She was an inch shorter. Her movements were too quick, too uneasy. She was wearing a black top, fair enough, but tight trousers in a fuchsia pink. The wide mouth was unrelaxed, lacked mobility; and it wasn't quite wide enough. She had hidden her eyes behind the kind of dark glasses a child would think flash. She sat down by the window, and looked over towards me.

The rails a few yards in front of me began to sing. Down the line came another train, travelling in the opposite direction to that stationary on the other platform. As it came into the station it slowed enough that several of those waiting near me picked up their luggage and moved optimistically forwards. They were disappointed. It slid straight through, enigmatically empty. Through its flicking windows I watched the dream Ginny and I thought, though she showed it by no change of expression, that she'd seen me. Each window gave me a minutely altered image of her, as she folded her arms, tilted her head, moved back a little. Then, when the through train had disappeared, her train gave one jolt and moved off unevenly. She did not turn her head to see the last of me.

Well, I remember I was oddly calm. I pulled the rucksack more tightly onto my back, turned and jostled my way against the flow, back through the ticket hall, dodging the taxis manoeuvring in the forecourt, cutting a ragged route across the wasteland that did for a car-park. I remember noticing that for once it wasn't raining. My pace was steady and dogged, an unwinding pace that retraced the steps I'd taken only an hour before. Back up Park End Street, characterless and choked with traffic. Thinking of Ginny treading the same pavement, coming back to me from her parents' house, looking forward to seeing me. Along New Road and by Nuffield College with its pen-nib tower, re-viewing the first time – the real first time – we'd made love, taking out the madness I'd put into Ginny's eyes, rewriting the blood on the sheet. Past the prison, the town hall and its turrets, trying to retrieve all the things she'd said to me I'd not listened to because they were *mad*, weren't they? Not being able to remember anything she'd said to me. Up Queen Street and past all the shops Ginny and I had been in that first day, reading the mass of the record she'd bought me then against my back now in the rucksack, as if I were a Geiger-counter and it were irradiated. Skirting the edge of the shopping precinct and skirting the sensation of – difficult to make the name come – *Madeleine*. Trying to push out of my head the feel of her stomach against mine, such hard and tight sensations, and not succeeding; feeling even now the involuntary answer in the pit of my stomach. Dodging buses across Carfax. Down the High Street but not back to the college (never wanting to go back), speeding up past the Examination Schools where I'd so recently had my lucky escape with Prelims. Averting my gaze from Magdalen College and the ghost of the skip in front of it; trusting that Dr. Fell wasn't glancing out from behind those net curtains. Slowing down over Magdalen Bridge to catch an echo of Ginny and me kissing half way across, using that picture to erase the later image of our silent selves hand in freezing hand on our way to Ginny's college and her nun's cell of a room. Then finally heading out of the city along a route unfamiliar to me, a route with no echoes.

After all, it wasn't even a three mile walk; more like two. I wasn't a hundred per cent sure where the hospital was, though I knew the general direction, and I had to ask in a newsagents-cum-off-licence as I bought cigarettes and a couple of bottles – lemonade, wine; couldn't stretch to gin. There was a florists next to the newsagents, so I spent most of the rest of my money, that is, my rail fare, on a giant and ostentatious bunch of flowers which came out looking as if it belonged on a coffin.

By the time I'd started on the last leg of the journey it was growing dark. A solid avenue of fifty foot trees lined a wide road that curved gently upwards between semi-detached houses of such similarity to each other that I began to believe they'd spin out indefinitely. The temperature was dropping but fortunately mine seemed to be rising. I could feel a fine sweat over most of me, especially on my upper lip and eyebrows, where it cooled in the air. Light-headed, I knew my common-sense was evaporating with the sweat and that anything at all might happen. The yellow Cortina coming too fast down the road might contain Jules, waving and tooting his horn like Toad. The old bloke mulching his flowerbeds in the next front garden could twist round and turn out to be my dad: *what about your mum, Simon? you are looking after your mum for me, aren't you, Simon?* And under it all my mind was working faster than an electric mixer on top speed, but with the same circularity. I couldn't seem to grasp Ginny as a real person; she'd become an idea. That damn song my mother used to put on the hi-fi – who *was* it by? – churned round and round and round; and what was worse, I only knew the chorus: *is that all there is? is that all?*

It was easier walking there than arriving there.

The semis finally gave way to the kind of high wall that you'd expect to find running alongside deep rural lanes. I skirted it, sandwiched between its soft stone and the traffic – fractious rushhour traffic. I noted a couple of side entrances to the hospital campus, gaps that showed beyond a jumble of buildings with the unmistakeable utilitarianism of the public institution, and it would have been easy to step through one of these without attracting attention. Yet I felt somehow that I had to do this thing *properly*, since I didn't seem to have done anything else *properly*. So I had to follow protocol and find the main entrance. From the glimpses I gained through the back entrances it was evident that it was all disconcertingly open-plan. I mean, weren't there dangerous people in there?

The trouble with the plan I'd formulated was that I hadn't and it didn't exist. The front entrance declared itself with N.H.S. signs and boards listing directions and a buzz of traffic in and out and gatehouse architecture. The lack of real lockable gates bothered me. The bus-stop thirty yards away on the pavement bothered me. The dozen or so people waiting there were cold and bored with nothing to look at but the cars turning into the hospital; and me, the tramp with the big bunch of flowers clutched to his chest. I couldn't shake the feeling that they could read me like a hoarding, that I had the dazed look of the survivor. I imagined they thought I belonged in the hospital. I smoked a cigarette just outside the boundary and wondered what the hell to do.

It reminded me of what University had meant to me. It had been an end, the end, not a means to an end. I'd unquestioningly assumed that all *I* had to do was *get* there and that, somehow or other in some vague and undefined adult sort of way, the rest of my life would stretch away from me, organised and effortless. All I'd have to do was follow a clearly signposted route. God, what a shock it was to discover you had to do it *all* yourself, that it was more a case of Hansel and Gretel in the woods, trying to follow their breadcrumb trail after the birds had been at it. Now, here I was, frozen with indecision, stuck between the intention and the outcome. I made the cigarette last, half-pretending to be waiting with the others for the next bus, actually staring across the dark pool of the lawn at the main body of the hospital a couple of hundred yards from me. The place looked more like Lord Thing's country seat than a mental hospital; cupola, clocktower, pillars, parkland – some quaint Victorian idea of disguising the turmoil within, no doubt.

Three buses had come and gone and a steady flow of nurses, visitors, unknowns had straggled past before I budged. The simple mechanics of walking the shortest route to the lit doorway of the building, under the largest spreading chestnut and over the lawn, or even the longest route, by the hospital's internal roadway and through a small carpark, were impossible. Then again, so was the idea of turning round and walking back to the station (no money, anyway) or college. I was the nearest to Ginny I'd been since she'd been frogmarched past me and the Christmas tree. This was the last ditch. If I moved further away from Ginny again without even having laid eyes on her, I might as well admit I'd had it.

Night had almost completely fallen by the time I hauled the rucksack back on, shambled back along by the perimeter wall and hovered while two cleaners came out of the swing doors of one of the hospital blocks that loomed up just inside the grounds. Then I slid in the open gateway they'd used to leave.

* * *

There's a particular tree in the grounds of that hospital that I believe I'd be able to find even now. It had a remarkable growth on its trunk about three feet off the ground and bark as subtly wrinkled as an elephant's backside. Its roots had broken up out of the ground to form a series of low benches. Nothing much grew under it, not even the die-hard weeds that seem to be able to survive winters. It was part of a row of trees that lined one complete edge of the hospital's grounds, roughly ten yards parallel with the perimeter wall and divided from it by a track that only groundsmen can have used.

I slept beneath it. Rather, I dozed fitfully with my head resting on the rucksack, paced to keep warm, drank, smoked. I even think I sang to myself. Why not? Nobody was around to hear what a godawful voice I had. Here it never got entirely dark because of a street lamp among the houses built the other side of the wall and I could see my hand holding the cigarette when I sat and smoked, my Doc. Martens scuffing up dead leaves as I walked. I cried, embarrassing myself. I dreamt.

The first time I dreamt not with the terror that visited me in my own warm bed, but with a strange and long-lost poignancy; as if my surroundings were punishment enough. There was a kind of mercy in the images, though they left me as lost as ever.

I was walking in an ancient windowless tomb of gigantic dimensions past the toes of statues whose jaws I could only just see. I was ant to their giraffe. The statues were the effigies of Pharoahs or Caesars, seated and static, dead. It was a lifeless place with spores of grief carried on the air. Every stone held the story of one individual long dead: all that was left of them. I found my father's stone and sat down by it and cried myself dry. That was it. When I woke up I felt I'd walked a mile, there was such a sense of time having passed, though I knew it hadn't: the unchanging sky told me it hadn't.

I knew I'd got off lightly with that one and decided I'd not allow myself to slide into anything worse by not allowing myself to sleep. I'd sit it out. So I straddled one of the tree's roots and leant against a stretch of bark that had two or three sharpish protuberances, crossed my arms and stared up at the roofs of the houses beyond the hospital perimeter.

Before too long my crossed arms had crept into a rigid self-hug that did little to preserve the pockets of warmth my profuse sweating produced. I played with all the stories of exposure I'd ever heard – the boy in the year below me at school who'd had to wear slippers all the time for an entire term after an Easter camping trip – but couldn't make myself care very much. Gradually the feeling came to me that different parts of my mind were dancing off in different directions; like couples in a country dance, they'd skip behind each other quite happily in a neat circle, then without warning spin off into independent corners. Music came and went, and somehow connected up with a fizz in various muscles, a buzz in my ears.

Any kind of pleasantness in the sensations leaked away as a little more every minute I focussed more attentively on the chimney stack and t.v. aerial on the nearest roof. The street lamp and the chimney stack together conspired to cast a deep irregular shadow slantwise across the roof tiles. Increasingly I could pick out greater and lesser densities in the black of the shadow. With the first flutter of panic came the realisation that *something was crouching beneath the stack*.

It was real. By this I wouldn't dream of suggesting that at that sick moment I threw all rational belief over my shoulder like so much salt, instantly embracing the flitting image of every little dancing devil; but I do mean that I can think of it while I'm walking along the pier or playing with the computer or sitting over egg and bacon in a Greasy Spoon and it's a real memory. I saw what I saw, and I don't need dubious lighting and a ghoulish soundtrack to recreate the substance in that shadow. It's lodged as a memory, not a memory of a mistake.

What had been flat black gathered in itself a mass. I was an animal responding to the animate: it didn't have to move for me to *know* it was there. The darkness shifted round, its densest part fluid so that I strained my eyes to see any kind of distinct shape. The curve of a haunch dissolved into the worming of a tail dissolved into the rigidity of a hunched shoulder. I was convinced that the very tips of a prehistoric wing had flicked up out of the shadow and in front of the aerial, a millisecond of trespass that had me thinking in a sweaty panic, *that's not fair*. What had started as a stiffly crouching gargoyle of a thing was turning into some creature who could writhe and sink and bloat, flooding me with disgust. It was the same deep disgust as when for the first time you find the maggot in the peapod, realise the universe you've been trying to construct from the titbits the grown-ups throw you has been based on false premises, that the fluffy lambykins tell maybe not even half the story, and that there's more to come and maybe worse: disgust mixed with outrage at the betrayal of it all.

The darkness feeding the creature and shifting behind it had depth that was impossible, stretched back well into the chimney where it had no right to be. None of the nice adjectives had any claim on it, *velvety* or *silky* or *furry*, unless by *fur* you'd mean the mould that grows on abandoned tea dregs or the fuzz you were shocked to catch sight of creeping round the edges of the adults' swimsuits, that time at the lido. It was a sticky, cloying, bad-breath dark and all the worse because I could pour into it not just the undefined horrors of the five year old but also the refined terrors of the half-way adult. I thought it had crawled from a medieval hell to take me home.

I *knew* I was still awake, even though I began to realise I was lying flat on my back in a confined space which I had reached by climbing all the way down through the Tower of Babel on hundreds of metal-rung ladders at frantic speed. The creature on the roof had followed me down, gaining on me all the time, and now it was all around me. In some perfectly logical way it was the walls of the hole where I was laid, it was in every stone; it was a possession so total I couldn't even hope to crawl away through the cracks of mortar. It had made me an oubliette of such claustrophobic proportions that I could raise my arms only a couple of inches. Sideways there was yellowing wallpaper so close it flaked off over the pyjamas I was wearing. This I knew, though the darkness was complete. I knew I'd be on my own for eternity. But the most intense horror came with the understanding that the oubliette had not been sealed, which would at least had given me a predictable kind of suffocation. Half way along my body a shaft opened up in the ceiling, while behind my head a slit to nothing spanned the wall. Eventually the creature, in whatever form it chose to present itself, would seep its rancidity through these crevices and closer yet. Even if I could somehow have turned – though I was too big to turn – in the thick air, even if I

197

could have crawled to the bottom of the shaft, I hadn't a chance of even a chance of escape. I had found myself in the dungeon. I was at the very centre of the tower. Below were the lonely indeterminate spaces, disused wells, blocked off tube tunnels, dried up sewers, and below them only the blind earth itself. Above were so many miles of rooms that even to reach one where the memory of light and love faintly glowed would take more years than I had. As for the sunlit halls themselves, they seemed too magnificent ever to have existed at all and the faint impression of them the mind could draw just a cruelty to sharpen loss. And the most terrible fear that the stones contained was the possibility that there never had been any sunlight anyway: god was dead and the very idea of light a fantasy created out of insanity.

That was the worst.

When I woke up finally to a light that could pass for daylight, I didn't just feel like The Wreck of the Hesperus. I felt like shit. I'd developed an interesting cough with which I tried to remind myself of Keats rather than Steptoe. The glands in my neck had swollen dramatically and I suffered from not having a mirror to check the damage. Despite the jumpers I'd unpacked from my rucksack to pile on in layers, cold and damp had stiffened all my joints like rigor mortis, while the top layer of clothing was covered with moisture I supposed was dew. I felt like Frankenstein on the run from the mob. Rock bottom.

Here was the contradiction. I could almost not have cared what happened to me: so I might as well stay around and see what did. I'd go and find Ginny: just as I was. And I'd go now, before some early shift groundsman found me and threw me out and put a security alert out on me so I couldn't get back in.

As I say, *I'd* seen 'One Flew Over The Cuckoo's Nest'. I'd seen the poor sod who'd had the electric shock treatment jerking and twitching. While I finished off the lemonade and had that morning cigarette – the one that out of all the cigarettes of the day gives the most vehemence to your *I really must give up* – and listened to the muffled noises of the hospital cranking into daytime gear – reversing cars, odd slams and clanks, even a distant laugh – I had the sudden conviction that now, *at this very moment*, robotic orderlies were dragging Ginny screaming down a corridor as white as a space-ship towards Room 101 and the bed with the straps. *The atmosphere's abattoir and side doors give horrific glimpses of hosed walls and windows too high for exit and suggestive electrical apparatus. If you could see through the walls Ginny tries to clutch you'd see ranks of cots filled with pale straight-jackets and the ghastly faces of zombies. I may be the only one who can stop Ginny joining them, waving my knowledge of Madeleine's existence like Sir Galahad's sword (I've forgotten about her parents). I may, of course, be too late. What about lobotomies? Ginny drooling in a wheelchair.*

You can't run with a rucksack, but I tried. There was a compost heap, or at least a large mound of withered prunings, at the end of the avenue of trees. As I jogged by it, I threw the bunch of flowers onto it. Buying them in the first place seemed stupid.

Eventually and by a series of errors I found the right women's ward. Inside, the place looked just like any old hospital. The images of lobotomised zombies fizzled out in cold water normality – kind-of normality. The only oddity I'd come across so far had been a waltzing inmate. He was being led by a nurse who out of necessity had to shuffle along in three-step with him to get him from A to B. On the other hand, it might have been like visiting the Soviet Union. Perhaps what I was seeing was the equivalent of the model communal farm and the model communal factory. Perhaps if I got lost and opened the wrong door I'd stumble on the State Asylum after all.

Ignorant of hospital-visiting etiquette, I walked straight by the nurse on the reception desk. She called me back. The sort of young woman my mother would have loved me to bring home she was, bright and clean and practical, but I knew I'd forgive her if she'd only let me past. She had a name-tag on her overall: Sasha Price. My mother would even have liked the name. But if Sasha thought *I* was the opposite of what *her* mother would have chosen for *her*, she was far too sweet and suitable to say so. I was trying hard not to look desperate, I was trying not to sweat; but I was sweating, freely. I struggled with the sensation that my head was trying to float away from my body. I doubted that I'd got all the bits of leaf out of my hair. Dear Sasha: maybe the rucksack gave me a last-chance look or maybe she was so used to weirdness I was nothing much. It was not, apparently, quite yet visiting time, but......visitors were good for patients. A relative? I was a friend? Virginia's parents had been every day, but it was a bit early for them now. If I wanted to catch them, I'd have to hang on for a while. Did I know her parents? No? It would probably be useful for them to talk to me. They were trying to work out what happened.... That door at the end.

Another corridor and another door, the quick resonance of the moment before I'd pushed open Jules' door, a second resonance of steps leading me towards the room where Ginny crouched beneath my desk – both hastily pushed from my mind, but slowing my feet nevertheless. As I got closer I could hear a sinister low-key mumbling punctuated by a sharp, repeated slapping sound, coming from behind the door. I already felt repelled by the image that rose before me of Ginny's warm skin shrouded in the white hospital gown, her face almost transparent upon the thin white pillows and the institutional coverlet diminishing the unique outline of her body, shrinking it into a dead weight to be fed drugs, or rolled over. I couldn't shake the dread that she'd already have that cadaverous look my father had slowly acquired. God is dead.

I walked through the door to find myself very obviously in a day room. It was extremely warm. It reminded me of the common room in the youth hostel that I'd stayed in on a fifth year trip to Wales. You know the kind of furniture; utilitarian and cheap but with a stab at style. Last year's colours, last *decade's* colours. Assortment of armchairs. Table with a scrabble set, and monopoly; a pack or two of cards. A bookcase with *Reader's Digests* and thrillers and stories about vets or animals adopted from the wild. Attempts at cheer: flowery curtains and framed prints. Definitely institutional, but not irredeemable. In one corner stood a monolithic drinks machine. The voice I'd heard came from a television set that nobody seemed to be watching, though an obese middle-aged woman napped close to it. There were only four people in the room, all wearing what had to be their own clothes: the napping woman, a girl not much older than myself with bleached hair and a grey face who was roaming around the room as I came in, biting her nails; a heavy-set woman of indeterminate age slumped across an armchair; Ginny.

Ginny lounged in a chair she'd angled to face the big picture window. In one hand she held a cigarette and a cup of tomato soup, in the other a woman's magazine. I was surprised by the cigarette, and more surprised by the magazine, which I could see lay open on a cookery spread. When I came in, anyway, she wasn't looking at the magazine, but at the skinny straw-haired girl, as if they'd been talking. All those awake looked up at me as I came in, indicating that event was an animal rarely sighted here, but with expressions that could hardly have been more different. The slumped figure swivelled in my direction and fixed attention on me as you might on a light switch or someone else's empty cup. The young girl pacing between the armchairs lit up like a firework and threw me a voracious hello. Ginny could not help the first moment's recognition, the quick surprise, but then resolutely turned in her chair away from me, took a disgustingly long drag on the cigarette, and stared blankly down at the recipe spread.

I chose the route that kept me as far from the others as possible and walked self-consciously towards Ginny, then eased the rucksack onto a chair, feeling foolish for having convinced myself that she might be thrilled to see me, might be angry to see me, might be upset to see me, but would at least *see* me.

"Hello, cowboy. Are you Virginia's bloke?" The straw-haired girl had a local accent, an Archer's burr. Her skin-hugging black leather trousers revealed legs as pitifully thin as a deprived child's. Ostentatiously *new*, the leather creaked as she came too close, and I couldn't help her reminding me of straw man and tin man rolled into one. "I'm Dinah. I'm a mate of Virginia's, you know. She's a good cow, your girl. You've got to stick together, haven't you? Haven't you? In this kind of dump you have. What's in that rucksack? Got anything good in it? Anything you want to offload? I've got money, you know. I can give you money. What's your line? You interested in getting me something in?" Staccato as the yapping of a dog. I added Toto to my composite.

"I-"

"Keep your voice down. Do you want to get us into trouble? Look, doesn't matter if you've not got anything on you," – though it looked as if it did – "Bring it in tomorrow, all right? I'm *dying* in here, you know? They don't care. They-"

"Excuse me."

I sat cautiously in the nearest chair to Ginny. Disconcertingly Dinah began to pace again, *creak, creak,* then took to inspecting the drinks machine closely. With the tiny reservoir of hope I'd been tending leaching away, I leaned towards Ginny's cold shoulder, her averted face.

"Hello," I said, and paused. "It's not too bad here, is it?" Not a tremble came from Ginny. I waited.

"I'm a really good friend of hers," said Dinah, suddenly at my shoulder, nodding at Ginny, who could have been in the room on her own for all that she registered of either of us, "I've been looking after her for you. You ask her. Yeah, you ask her. I've been in here two weeks, you know. I'm in de-tox. They don't care, you know, *they don't care.* They don't." She kept on with sulky vehemence, as if I'd contradicted her. "You can't tell me they do, because they don't. I don't suppose you've got a spare fag, have you?" – wheedling – "You've got a kind face, you know that? Look, you could get me some stuff, couldn't you? You must know...."

I kept looking at Ginny, at the clear outline of her cheek and jaw, the thin hands with their neat nails, lying now against the magazine photo of a Christmas cake, the ostensibly relaxed posture of her body, actually as tense as a cat's. Every part of her I had touched. Now I couldn't even get close enough for my breath to reach her, defrost her a little.

"It could be worse, couldn't it? It's, uh, just like a, uh, normal" – I couldn't say the word 'hospital' – "place, isn't it?"

I'd thought I'd be able to tell her I'd seen Madeleine. I found instead that, as each minute passed, it grew more impossible. I'd have had to admit too openly to the truth that I'd only believed in Madeleine at all since that moment on the station platform. I needed the truth to be obscured. After all, you can't claim to be one of the faithful if it takes a miracle to convince you. Faith has got to be blind to deserve the name. And I'll admit that I never told anybody, anybody at all, that I'd seen Madeleine boarding that train.

"Isn't there anywhere more private than this?" My voice came out breathless and unfamiliar, but I couldn't get it to sound weighted with all the meanings I *somehow* – how? I didn't know that language – had to convey. If anything it came across as peevish, little boy. At least I could search her face; the section she presented to me, that is. It was extremely pale, but not a hair had been shaved, no shadow of an electrode burn could I trace. She seemed: intact.

I said to Ginny, "I couldn't come and see you before," then couldn't explain why.

Dinah said to me, "You look bloody awful."

I said to Dinah, "Look, I'm trying to talk to this woman."

She said to me, "It dun't look like she wants to talk to you though, does it? And you know what?" – biting her nails viciously – "I don't fucking blame her."

I thought I saw the faintest flicker of a smile on Ginny's face. I tried again: "I just wanted to see if you were all right." She moved not at all, but the blood edged up her cheek and the quality of her breathing altered so that I realised that somehow or other even *that* wasn't the right thing to say. God only knows *what* the right thing to say was.

I sat for ten minutes or so, waiting for a miracle, sunk in the ridiculousness of it all, helplessness keeping me in my chair as surely as a hand on my chest. As the minutes passed, the room ceased to remind me of the Welsh Youth Hostel. I began to think that, after all, I'd stumbled into a kind of hell-hole limbo. It would have been easy to start breathing in rhythm with the sleeping woman by the wall, or to start pacing and nail-biting with *Dinah*. At one point I turned to find *her* uncharacteristically still, but only because she was attempting silently to unzip the side-pockets of my rucksack. At another the sharp slapping sound I'd heard as I approached the room was explained. We all leapt – even the sleeping inmate rocked in her sleep – as the heavy-set woman slumped in her chair started to moan, and then quite deliberately slapped herself around the head four times, hard.

"What the hell's she doing?" I hissed to Ginny, "Why's she doing that? Shall I get the nurse?"

Ginny turned the page of her magazine. Dinah laughed nervously, and launched on another monologue. The sleeping inmate subsided further into her chair.

I gave it another five minutes, until Dinah came and sat on my lap. Then I left.

I only had six days. My college room was only open to me for that length of time, then it had to be home, and judgement day. It was the length of time I gave myself. If Ginny hadn't cracked by the time I was kicked out of college, well, she probably never would. I refused to think beyond. I couldn't consider such desolation. That was how I managed to keep hold of the resolution so oddly formed beneath the tree in the hospital grounds: blind hope and faith; and the absence of any idea of how to live my life without Virginia. So I lived each day in the present; but with the giant face of the clock looming above me, its ornate hands scooping round, its intricate mechanism cranking up ready for the chime.

On the second day Ginny was in the day room again, as she was on the third. On the third day I even had her to myself, though it made a fat lot of difference. On the fourth day she'd adopted the tactic of evasion and locked herself in the bathroom for the duration of my visit – and presumably beyond, since she had no way of telling when I left.

I'm pretty sure it was on the fourth day too that, waiting three-quarters of an hour outside the bathroom door, I misjudged the timing. I was leaving, in fact I was within spitting distance of the double-doors that would lead me out of the ward to the saner world beyond. Another thirty seconds would have done it.

I knew them the minute I saw them, though I'd given them no more than five minutes' thought in my entire life. He had the wiriness, the erect posture. She had the wide mouth, the red hair, or would have had, had it not paled over the years to the colour of sand. They looked anxious, alert, sharp as knives. I could easily imagine Ginny walking between them and looking like the blend of them both. Their tasteful, understated clothing told me they had money, well, at least more money than my mother did. I thought of banks, of accountancy firms, of solicitors', saw that their natural habitat was the plush-carpet hotel for Sunday lunch, the golf club, the commuter train.

Even then, I could have slid by them without challenge (how would they have known me? Unless, of course, Ginny had told them about the hair) – but there we all were before the reception desk and there was Sasha who knew my name and some of my business, who looked up now from whatever she was writing and saw me leaving and them arriving and called out, "Well, Virginia's a lucky girl today, isn't she? A whole stream of visitors."

I watched mesmerised as the couple directed all their foxy intelligence in my direction. The last straw I was clutching, that Ginny had still not told them about me, slipped from my fingers. Sasha, so blithely unaware, *being helpful*, bobbed up to add, "You know, if you three want a bit of privacy to have a chat there's an office free just on your left there. Nobody'll need it for half an hour. Virginia seems very well today, don't you think?"

Ginny's father nodded and smiled at her, cleared his throat and spoke to me with slow deliberation, "Simon, is it?" It could have been the voice of Jehovah. I nodded dumbly. "Let's just...." and he motioned towards the empty office. Ginny's mother seemed entirely rigid, as if speech, at that moment, would have choked her.

In the empty office, they stood between me and the door; perhaps by chance. We did not find chairs. We stood beside a set of shelves on which medical books and pamphlets were stacked. Finally the mother spoke.

"You fool," she said, to me.

"Well now, Helen," her husband objected.

"What exactly do you think you have done to our daughter?" she continued, "How *could* you incarcerate her in this place with these *people*? Are you aware that even the psychiatrist's assessment is that she is, I quote, 'exhausted and overwrought' but by no means mentally ill? What is she doing in this place?"

What could I say?

"You can't deny you were instrumental in all this. I've talked to the psychiatrist. I've talked to the G.P.. I've talked to Virginia.

Everything seems to lead back to you. What leaves me entirely baffled is why? Why did you do this? *There's nothing wrong with the girl.*"

I struggled to formulate some kind of a defence; or perhaps diversion, "Can she, um, go home then, if they don't think she's ill? If it's all a mistake?"

"Your mistake," she came back at me, razor sharp, ignoring my question, "Your mistake."

The father's gaze was steadily taking in my dishevelled state – I could tell it; even his breeding couldn't disguise his incredulousness that here, here, looking like The Green Man, was the great sex symbol who'd bowled Virginia over and knocked out all her common sense.

"If it had been up to you she'd have been stuck in here for twenty-eight days," went on the mother, "For observation. Even if that means observing someone who's completely sane."

"But didn't you, didn't you agree to it? I mean," I hurried on confusedly, "Uh, didn't one of the doctors ring you up or-" I was trying to remember who'd told me this, trying to get the story straight. I knew somebody at some point had told me something to that effect. I remembered it. Didn't I?

"The college doctor rang us up and presented us with a *fait accompli*. And anyway, which daughter do you think we assumed she was talking about? The one with the psychiatric record as long as your arm or the, oh, *brilliant* little girl who'd worked so hard and done so well for herself and always coped so well? And it's not always been a picnic, you know." An unconscious gesture: she brushed the lapel of her tailored jacket just about in the spot where on my donkey jacket a smear of mud had dried white. And went on. "Do you have any insight? Do you know what I'm talking about? We heard nothing till after the damage had been done. Until *you'd* done the damage. We came immediately, of course. We just dropped everything and ran. And I'd ignored all the things the doctor had said on the phone that didn't quite make sense – she even gave us the name, your daughter Virginia, I'm afraid your daughter Virginia.... but we just assumed it was Madeleine being naughty-" She must have thought she could read scepticism in my face – not so, not so – because she grew twice as urgent, "Don't you dare try and shift the blame, my boy. It could have been, it could so easily have been Madeleine. Sometimes she'll call herself Virginia. Not that she means any harm – she didn't mean any harm by it, did she, Jonathon? It's really a sort of hero-worship. You could even take it as a, well, almost as *flattery*, if you wanted to. Isn't that so, Jonathon? And it wasn't until we got here, till we walked onto this ward – can you imagine that? Do you have any thread of intelligence? It was dreadful enough that we thought we'd see Maddy, but we saw *Virginia*."

"It's a terrible business; a terrible business," her husband interjected.

She patted his hand, and he caught hers in his. Propping each other up.

"Her tutor," she shrugged, "A nice enough woman, but totally deluded about Virginia. And Virginia's doctor – totally deluded. The only person who's not is Virginia. Why were they all so determined not to believe her? They all thought she'd *made up* her sister. Why would she make up a sister?" The look she gave challenged me to own up. I couldn't think where to begin.

"All over Christmas," she went on, more to her husband, "We thought we wouldn't have either of the girls over Christmas."

The use of a past tense registered and parallel came the generous reaction – *thank Jesus, they're letting her out* – with the ignoble – *she'll leave before I can reach her. If only they'd.....*

She'd watched me like a specimen of something nasty throughout. *She'd* measured me up, bar-charted me, graphed me, bloody *x-rayed* me. So it was seeing the give-away lightening of my expression, I think, that made her turn the full weight of her distress onto me, "You don't know what you've done, do you? Do you?"

It was too much. I looked sideways at the medical books.

There was a grief-stricken elation in her voice now, as if she were thrilled to have discovered me even worse than feared. "You really haven't the first idea, have you? I can't think you'd have the temerity to show your face here if you did. It's neither here nor there whether she's in here for twenty-eight days or two. Whether she's in here for a couple of hours or five minutes. Can't you grasp that? We're talking about something that can't be undone. We're not talking about a *mistake*, we're talking about a disaster. Virginia had done so well for herself. We were so *pleased* for her. And you see, her life's changed now. I can't see how she'll extricate herself from this. Everyone in the girl's *college* knows where she is."

"It goes on her medical record; permanently," Ginny's father added, with defeat.

"And even then, how could she finish her degree in her condition?"

"This has been the worst year of our lives," her father said in a strange, vague voice, and then, "Didn't you....?" like one emerging briefly from a nightmare, experiencing the brief comfort of a novel thought, "It was you who saw Madeleine, wasn't it? Virginia said a friend had seen Madeleine..."

I nodded warily.

"There's been no word, you know," he said sadly, "Not a word. She's nineteen, you see; they think of her as an adult. The police don't think of her as a missing person because she went of her own free will."

"Free will," echoed his wife, oddly.

They were so bleak, I felt they were dragging me down with them. That was it- I had the sensation of drowning with them.

"It's ironic, isn't it, Jonathon," she went on musingly, "One girl needed help they couldn't give her," – she turned to me, momentarily forgetting how she hated me in her need to explain, "We could never find a, a *place* for her, you know. And the other girl's *splendid* and they lock her away."

They fell silent. I was at a loss. It was a situation with no precedent.

"I'm really sorry," I said, and meant it, with all my heart.

They both looked at me, he with enormous exhaustion, she drily, with anger spent, hatred refined to its pure state.

"I just don't think that's enough," she said finally.

On the fifth day I couldn't find Ginny at all, though the nurse – not Sasha – told me she'd seen her not five minutes before. I waited for as long as I could bear in the day room, with little hope and Dinah for company. I left at a low ebb. By the time I'd rung my mother to ask her to send – first class – money for the coach fare home (coach rather than train equals cheaper equals more diplomatic), I was at my lowest.

The next day was the last at my disposal. The day after that I had to go home. Short of sleeping rough – I thought about it – I had no means of staying. I had precious little cash. As it was I'd been living off college food and withdrawing from alcohol. I had no money to do anything (*oh, we made our own fun in the old days*) and, even knowing it was ghoulish, I'd taken to playing Patience with the cards Ginny had left by default on my desk, playing it obsessively as a useless compliment to her, and playing the most difficult version of the game purposely to use up time.

It was standing in my room holding Ginny's pack of cards that the impulse came to me. I'd not bothered to unpack much and the place looked bare, resentful that I'd turned up again to litter it. I'd just straightened up from picking a dropped card off the floor at the end of the bed and my guard must have been down because I looked square in the mirror I'd been avoiding for days. And there he was. *What, still here, Simon?* This was the boy Ginny had *fancied*? I'd forgotten to wash my hair for so long I couldn't remember how long and I certainly hadn't bothered to comb it. I was sick to death of looking in this mirror and seeing the same boy. I loathed him. I would have been glad to vomit him away. I remembered Ginny standing behind me on that first day and scraping all the hair back from my face, offering to cut my hair.

The afternoon was closing in, but if I hurried I'd still have time. So I pocketed the very last of my spare cash and tramped into town. Of necessity I had to go to the most down-market barber's I could find, down-market as in twenty year old photos of *gents' styles* in the window, as in cracked lino, spotted mirrors and pucker courtesy – 'sir' this and 'sir' that. Yes: the proprietor even called me sir. I was amazed that he agreed to lay a finger on my hair, let alone *handle* it with the gusto he did. I asked for a crop.

"Short," I said, "Short-short."

"Number three, sir?"

I had no idea what he was talking about. "Number two," I said fearlessly.

I half expected him to offer me my hair in a take-home bag, it had been part of me for so long. When Alex had her childhood plait cut off a while ago the hairdresser gave it to her. Sometimes you come across it unexpectedly, as you idly pick a book off her desk to find it underneath, or rummage in one of her drawers to borrow staples; a faintly obscene golden tail, like that of a fat golden pig.

My hair fell to the floor in clumps. As the barber twittered on about sport or current events or films on the telly, I watched the clumps form an unwholesome version of a fairy ring round the base of my chair, the kind of ring drop-out fairies might use, fairies who'd hang around the nettles and nightshade when they should have been tucked up under the red-spotted toadstool.

I thought I'd feel it like the loss of a limb, the death of youth, the end of an epic etc. etc.. I didn't. It was just hair, for god's sake. I had the uncanny sensation of growing lighter by the second, and afterwards I couldn't recognise myself. Suddenly I'd aged several years. I looked at the same time both bizarre and ridiculously exposed, then again unbelievably ordinary: a bloke. And when I passed Beverley McKenzie and Stephanie Zielinski in the college lane, when I nearly brushed shoulders with them, *they didn't recognise me.*

On the last day, I tracked Ginny down in the hospital grounds. She was way across a sloped lawn, smoking a cigarette, wrapped up in a warm winter coat her parents must have bought her and staring intently at the lower branches of a monkey puzzle tree – survivor of the garden's former glory. A magpie had come to rest by the trunk. Even from my distance I could see its black and white, vivid as a flag on a pole. I trekked across the lawn, feeling my shoes soaking up water from the spongey grass, wondering how close to her I'd be able to get before she realised who I was and turned on her heels with that terrible blank look that wiped me off the face of the earth. My heart leapt as she glanced over at me and quickly away and *didn't recognise me.* For a second I recognised the curious spontaneous wish to be the somebody else she thought I was – a gardener? another inmate? – so that I could hold out my hand of rescue to her without the disadvantage of being the bastard who'd shoved her over the cliff

210

in the first place. A swift, intense ache of a wish. As I covered the last twenty yards, I looked back and saw that I had left a distinct trail of footprints right across the lawn.

"Oh, you've frightened it off," she said to me, and then stopped incredulously as her eyes settled on my face.

We stood there, spinning on that moment. We could have fallen off in any direction. Thank god; Ginny laughed.

"I'm sorry," she said, "You just look funny." It was strange laughter, and she couldn't stop, although she hugged herself, then put her hand over her mouth, then turned away, then turned back. I wasn't sure how to react, and then Ginny laughed at my vacant expression. Finally she stopped, and looked instantly exhausted, and grim. Another spinning moment. I laid myself completely open.

"I love you, Ginny." I hated each and every soapy actor who'd ever stolen those words to sell them on the black market. I wanted them to sound expensive, as unique as a Fabergé egg. "I do love you."

She sighed and shook her head, but still looked at me. I daren't move an inch. I thought of the rapid flick of black and white as the magpie had launched itself expertly up against the grey sky, and imagined Ginny evaporating with the same speed.

"What are you going to do, Simon?" she said distantly.

"*Me?*"

She took a packet of cigarettes out of her pocket and lit one. It was only then I could see how jittery she was. "This is temporary." She indicated the fag in her hand. "I've worked out how long I can get away with it. The foetus doesn't start developing until it's two or three weeks old so it won't be breathing my smoke. Did you know that, Simon?" Cold. "Actually I'm being over-generous with myself on that one. My three weeks is up. This-" She regarded the cigarette clinically. "This is the last one." Without warning she threw the packet at me. *Go and kill yourself with those.* Automatically I caught the packet, and stood holding it while the significance of what she'd said sunk slowly through the layers of my solipsistic skin; the skin I'd thought to save by sticking Ginny in this place.

"I'm going to keep it, Simon." She tilted her face, as she'd done in the photographs I'd taken. The slightest challenge.

211

Some new-developed instinct told me not to show my shock. I nodded slowly, and she went on, gently kicking the base of the tree-trunk with the toe of her shoe: "You can't move me on that decision. I've had days and days to think it through. And it seems to me that there's got to be one good thing that comes out of this farce."

I nodded silently again, keeping my expression still with will-power I hadn't known I possessed, while inside I was thinking with wild indignation, *the condom, the damn condom, I could sue them: was it me? Am I really that inept? My god, a child, how can I be a father, I can't do this, can I? Can I? Somebody tell me.*

"I don't care what you think about it," she said stiffly, looking everywhere else except at me, "And really it's not that important what you decide to do with yourself." The words grew tighter and tighter, as if control was proving difficult, "Although I think some money would be nice. When you're working, I mean. But we can do all that through solicitors."

"Solicitors?" I shook my head, aghast.

"It's better to keep things clear-cut," she said so tightly I almost didn't catch the words.

"Is that how you want it?" I tried to sweep my hair back from my face in a desperate gesture and found air between my fingers.

She half turned so I couldn't see her face, though I could still see the smoke she was blowing out mixing with her condensing breath. That, and the cut of her coat – nice, suited her, cost a bob or two – put her beyond me and into a *Casablanca* realm of sexual sophistication and courageous tragedy. She was Bacall to somebody's Bogart, though god knows what that made me; the organ grinder's monkey.

Yet when, after an interminable pause, she tilted her head so she could look back over her shoulder at me, you wouldn't have thought she was looking at the organ grinder's monkey. There was just that unmistakeable hint of light, the flash of quartz in a pebble, that allowed me to see depth in her regard of me and, please Jesus, for me. At last she replied, with a question. "What do you think?" Low, tremulous, almost indistinguishable.

I felt I'd reached the eye of the tornado. I had the slimmest chance of sliding to safety. An inch either way and I'd be sucked back into the spiralling wind with the rest of the debris. I meant to tell her the whole story from start to finish, but when I tried, different words came out. "Help me," I muttered.

"Oh, come here," she said, caving in. The distance seemed a mile, and then tentatively we had our arms round each other. I closed my eyes and thought of nothing. At some point I realised she was crying, then that she'd stopped.

Eventually she spoke.

"One thing, Simon," she said thickly, "Don't ever call me *Ginny* again. I hate it. My name's Virginia." I nodded my head against hers, no longer capable of surprise.

After another long while she said, "Why couldn't you just believe me?"

"I don't know," I whispered miserably.

"You could just have believed me."

"I know."

We walked a little way so that we were more hidden from the rows of windows that gave onto the lawn, our bodies instinctively adopting that jigsaw-fit of hip against hip.

"When do you get out of here?" I made myself ask.

"Tomorrow," she said soberly, and neither of us needed pointing out the closeness of our call. Two parallel futures, and we'd just stepped over from one to the other.

"How the hell will we manage?" I said, awestruck, thinking *nowhere to live, no money, can't even look after ourselves.*

"You mean-" She lifted her chin; and this time I could identify the shade of danger in the almost imperceptible flare of that nostril, "with the child?"

Child: what a serious word, a world-changing word. "Yeah," I said, "the child."

"I don't suppose we will." She shrugged. "I expect we'll make a pig's ear of it, just like the last generation."

"But I mean, do you know anything about *babies*?"

"No."

"We'll turn into our parents."

"No, we won't." And she gave me the first good, honest to god smile.

We got married.

I sit here on the beach with my back against the concrete of the promenade, the hundred rounded pebbles of our very pebbly shore supporting me like an orthopaedic couch. The concrete's hot as a radiator. Even through the sunglasses I've stolen from Virginia's bag the sea's glitter dazzles; and if I shut my eyes the background noises become instant seaside soundtrack – children's voices, waves, seagulls. Two of those children's voices belong to me. In a matter of minutes – ten, if I'm lucky – they'll carry their owners across the stretch of beach between us until each syllable becomes louder than understandable. I may have freezing water dribbled from a bucket onto my leg. Then a small damp bottom may lower itself onto my groin, or an older hand begin to pile pebbles to bury my legs.

In between summers your body completely forgets the sheer animal pleasure of a hot beach and how intense it is. Each year it's a remembered revelation, connecting you back and back to times when *you* were bought ice-creams rather than buying them yourself. Even the tar's familiar. I used to think those little sudden puddles of tar you'd find as you turned stones, looking for shells to finish off your castle, were natural as starfish.

And here they come, Alex lugging Henry like a sack of potatoes.

"Where's Mummy?" I ask.

"Over there down by the waves. She's met that woman you don't like."

"I like everybody," I tell her, as she unceremoniously dumps Henry on my lap. It's not too difficult to spot Virginia among the other bodies, even anonymous as half-nude flesh tends to be, since she's always the whitest woman on the beach. Tanning hardly comes into it. She doesn't. In May she coats herself with Total Sunblock Factor Five Hundred and reapplies it throughout the summer every five minutes. The sun's rays never get their chance to frazzle her red-head's' skin. The swimsuit that shows her at her best I'm proud of having chosen: black, sculpted, *Next*.

"Oh, *her*," I say, picking out the well-meaning, incorrigibly bland figure at Virginia's side, "She's all right, I suppose." It's somebody Virginia met at some evening class or other, somebody who occasionally *pops round* for a cup of tea.

"Oh *father*," Alex drawls with mock exasperation. Recently her exasperation with me is more real.

"What? What did I say?"

"Do you know what you called her the last time she came round?"

"No, but don't tell me." I really can't remember. Just as well.

"Tee hee," says Alex, scooping pebbles over my ankles so my toes stick up, obscenely, like fat sea slugs washed ashore. I think about the sand fleas that will be crawling over my skin. "You called her *Mrs. Colon*."

"*Did* I? Why would I do that? You've made it all up. You're just trying to get me into trouble."

"You did," she contradicted, "Because you heard her tell Mum about how good colonic irrigation was."

"Oh. Well. Yes, okay. I might have done. I admit it. Now will you stop tormenting your poor old dad?"

"Poor old Daddy," she cries suddenly, and throws herself at me.

"Oh, Alex," I grouch, "Get off. If you really want to show me how contrite you are, get some money out of my jacket pocket and go and buy me a cup of coffee from the café."

"Oh, all right." She extricates herself and dances off, trying to make 'cup of coffee from the café' into a tongue-twister; but it's too easy.

"Well, Henry," I say to his plump little face, "She's a one, isn't she? Don't you think?" He stares at me nonchalantly. I stick his hat back on his head. He pulls it off.

Virginia's loose held shoulders and the angle of her head convey to me even at this distance the slight boredom she's feeling. Her body's particularly expressive; and I know every nuance. She's my Virginia, still the same Virginia. But *that*, of course, is a stupid thing to say.

Anybody who's dragged a relationship back from the brink will know how grindingly difficult it is, what a haul. It took Virginia years to trust me again, and even now it's a more cautious, lawyer-like trust than it might be, could have been. At the finish, the moment of safety – if it ever comes – you've both been altered by the process; sobered up. The good old bad old days are dead and buried never to be exhumed. There you are, terribly grown up, masters of compromise and tolerance; you think. Then again, the very effort of it all binds you together. Here we are, survivors.

We have more to bind us than most.

It must have been at least two years ago now that I bought that copy of the *Big Issue*, paid my – what? Fifty pence was it then? – shoved it in my backpack with the old receipts and, probably, last week's copy. I might never have opened it, but I needed something to read in the bath, I remember. So that's where I came across her again. It felt as indecent as a grave-opening. Virginia and I had never been able to say her name, though sometimes we'd manage an oblique reference. I cannot speak for Virginia, but for myself, I'd come to think of her as long dead. The skeleton in the cupboard dressing itself in the clothes on the hangers and dancing out into the bedroom.

The pages of the magazine had crinkled dramatically in the steam and water creeped up the lower edges where I'd rested them on my ribcage. Sound carries in our house very well from the kitchen below to the bathroom above, probably through the pipes, and downstairs I could hear the reassuring mumble of the radio. I had a notion Virginia was finishing off some work on the kitchen table, but perhaps she'd wandered off and left the radio talking to itself. It must have been before Virginia fell for Henry (that weird expression; as if the weight of the pregnancy tipped the woman's balance and toppled her off her feet). Alex was supposedly tucked up, but I could hear the surreptitious pulling out of drawers and padding about. All was well in my garden. Objects and subjects were all where they should be. Then I came to the *Missing: can you help?* feature near the back of the magazine. It's evidence of my sense of her as dead, too, that I read it at all. I didn't think of that page as in any way related to anyone I'd ever known. I started to read it as others do, unwholesomely inquisitive.

Beneath the headline, which was in bright red, came a brief on The National Missing Persons Helpline and beneath that a row of four photographs, three of men and one of a young woman: and there she was. I didn't realise at first. The photograph was small, in black and white, and had been taken without those shades on. It was in fact the first time I'd seen her eyes. It was the eyes, you see, that really set her aside from Virginia. That must have been the reason, maybe the sole reason, for those Debbie Harry specs. The eyes hadn't Ginny's shape or her warmth, though the face cracked in a wide grin. The smile sat so unsuitably on that page I was arrested by it, but even then all that ran through my head were the normal transitory thoughts, love-to-be-titillated-by-it thoughts; *god, her family! looks happy enough there, how can people just... selfish really, can any of these people still be alive?* It wasn't until I moved on to the description beneath the photo that I realised the young woman with the throwaway smile was Madeleine.

Madeleine Patricia Oxley, it ran, has been missing from her home in West Sussex since October 1979. She was unemployed at the time and was feeling under pressure. Madeleine was seen in Oxford later that Autumn, but since then there has been no news of her.

Madeleine's family would dearly love to get in touch with her and find out how she is. They think she may be in London and have visited various hostels. Her mother wants her to know that they all love her and just want to know that she's all right. She also has some family news for her.

Madeleine will now be 32 years old. She is 5' 9" tall, with a fair complexion and blue eyes and has red hair which at the time of her disappearance she wore short. She was last seen wearing a mid-calf black winter coat.

Have you seen Madeleine? If you have any information about her well-being or whereabouts, now or at any time since she went missing, please get in contact with the helpline. All calls are treated with the strictest confidence.

So the world shifts. I remember listening to the water tank refilling and the background radio, the illicit shufflings in Alex's bedroom and understanding with horrible suddenness the fragility of that most precious equilibrium. To her parents Maddy might be a poor sick girl, but to me she was nothing less than the first messenger of the forces of disintegration and chaos, hoof marks on the frosty roof; a wrecker. Perhaps she had died years ago, filthy and hypothermic under some dismal railway bridge; or perhaps she was waiting for some random moment, dictated only by her anarchic whimsy, to walk back in and rip up the peace that Ginny and I had found. The 'family news' the text mentioned? Well, that must be Alex. As if I would let Madeleine within a thousand miles of Alex, as if I would let her touch one red hair. My impulse was to run to the front door, dripping and naked, to draw the extra bolt. Not the English way, of course. What I actually did was remain exactly as I was, slowly freezing as the heat left the water by gradual degrees. How naive of me to imagine that Madeleine's parents would have abandoned her memory as I had tried to do. How many such adverts had they placed, how many times over the intervening years had they trawled the hostels, searched the mainline stations, stepping over the sleeping bags of all the flotsam people in their decent leather shoes? Did Virginia know? Had it been her idea? Had she gone with them?

My wife the lawyer. Virginia hadn't the heart to return to college after that desolate Christmas. Her pride wouldn't even consider tolerating the over-careful looks she'd get, the gaping distance that had opened up between her and her contemporaries – people that, because of me, she'd only cultivated half-heartedly in the first place. "I will not be," she stated, "the college lunatic. The juicy bit of

219

gossip. I won't have the sideways glances." She was enervated. She was pregnant. We married and my college gave us a flat, the top half of a terraced house. Alex came: perfect. Later, in Brighton, Virginia went back to university and studied law. Just as well that one of us earns. The prizes I scooped were not glittering; more the sort of thing you pick up from the school raffle really, boxes of Milk Tray and bottles of Liebfraumilch. When Henry came along – and didn't that give us a shock – it was I that went part time. Why not? The kind of work I do – local authority – is bread and butter stuff; I'm not that bothered. I don't need conversations about traffic calming measures and refuse collections to survive.

Later on, who knows? I might irritate Virginia's parents and cheer up my mother by making something of myself. On hot summer nights I sometimes feel the merest stirrings of a creature I thought had died long ago: ambition. I've done my time, paid my dues. As my old pal Elvis Costello said: *Don't bury me cos I'm not dead yet.*

So leave me here on the beach. Give me a soundtrack of, oh, world music as we like to call it, something African, massed drumming and trills, or something Latin, something with a bit of life. Smash all the 'seventies discs, all that up-your-arse nihilism. Give me the fat little boy on my middle and the skinny girl buying the coffee. Give me the battered bag by my side, with its shoved-in picnic, its bad-for-them crisps and slapped-together sandwiches and – hallelujah – its bottle a darn sight more decent than *Liebfraumilch*, which we'll open soon, now, and drink from plastic beakers. Give me the woman in the black swimsuit down by the waves.

Virginia puts on the tortoiseshell sunglasses she's had dangling from her hand and I notice they're mine. She must have sneaked them out of my jacket. With a quick smile she manages to disengage herself from Mrs Colon and turns away from the sea. The swing of her shoulders and the half smile lingering are as familiar to me as light and dark. I know she's looking at me from behind the glasses. With the tortuous movements the pebbles force on her she begins the long walk up the beach towards me.

ABOUT THE AUTHOR

The author lives in Brighton.

Printed in the United Kingdom
by Lightning Source UK Ltd.
111224UKS00001B/175-267